VIRGINIA ANN

A Cryptic Death

A Pooka Women's Club Mystery

Contents

1	Sister Dymphna	1
2	Biddy	8
3	Sheila	14
4	Megan	22
5	Ruby	33
6	Sister Dymphna	41
7	Biddy	48
8	Sheila	55
9	Megan	62
10	Sheila	67
11	Megan	74
12	Biddy	83
13	Sister Dymphna	89
14	Sheila	98
15	Megan	104
16	Biddy	111
17	Sheila	125
18	Sister Dymphna	133
19	Megan	142
20	Biddy	150
21	Sheila	156
22	Biddy	161
23	Megan	170
24	Biddy	178

25 Sheila   184
26 Sister Dymphna   193
27 Sheila   204
28 Sister Dymphna   213
29 Biddy   221
30 Sister Dymphna   229
31 Sheila   244
32 Sister Dymphna   254
33 Sheila   268
34 Megan   275
35 Sister Dymphna   281
36 Biddy   288
37 Megan   294
38 Preview of Book 3: THE THIEF OF TRAMINETTE 302
About the Author   315
Also by Virginia Ann   316

1

Sister Dymphna

The school looks like Alcatraz.

"Sister Dymphna," Sister Mary Bernice peers at me as if I might be the reason we need those 'caution: contents hot' labels on takeout coffee. "How could you forget to lock the doors?"

I try to recede into the folds of my habit, confusion coursing through me.

She frowns. "Look what you've caused to happen."

I pull my eyes from Sister Mary Bernice's purplish face and study the crayon drawings covering the walls of the long grammar school corridor. From an objective point of view, the drawings are remarkably well done—not that this point is relevant at the moment—but they make the hallway look like a prison wing complete with narrow bars from the floor to the ceiling. Behind the bars are lifelike renderings of students in their plaid uniforms with balls chained to their legs. It's hard to believe crayon can achieve this.

"Yeah," Tommy O'Shaughnessy says.

I look down at the young boy standing next to me, his red

hair flopping over his freckled face as he nods vigorously.

"I'm practically the victim here. If you hadn't left the doors unlocked, I wouldn't have done this. You got me into trouble."

Tommy O'Shaughnessy may be a good artist, but he is not one of our brighter students.

Sister Mary Bernice's frown deepens and transfers from my direction to the boy. "The VICTIM?"

Tommy flinches, and even though I know this isn't very Christian of me, I'm grateful for the reprieve from her attention.

"You are certainly not a victim," Sister Mary Bernice says to him. "Myself and Sacred Heart of the Woods are the victims. And I'm confident your mother will feel the same way when we call her now and tell her what you've done."

Tommy's face goes white. "Aww, Sister, is that entirely necessary? Maybe we could work something out. Off the books, you know?"

"I think I'll stick with the path of righteousness." She takes his arm and follows the red arrow pointing to the room labeled hell, previously known as her office. His protests echo as they move down the deserted tiled hall and pass through the freshly drawn gates on either side of the office's entrance.

The thing is that I'm positive that I locked the school doors. I distinctly remember doing my usual routine. I waited for all the teachers to leave yesterday, then walked from room to room to make sure the classrooms were empty and the lights off, and then I went out the main door, pulling it shut behind me. AND I LOCKED IT! I know I locked it.

That Tommy O'Shaughnessy found the door unlocked last night to do this makes no sense. I head down the dark hall, in the opposite direction of Sister Mary Bernice's fluorescent lit office, and open the janitor's closet. At least it happened on a Friday, leaving me the whole weekend to clean it up.

Tommy's shrill voice carries towards me as he continues to present the case for his innocence. I flinch when I hear him telling his mom on the speakerphone that he had not broken in. That the door was unlocked.

It wasn't. I know it wasn't. And yet, when Sister Mary Bernice and I had reviewed the security camera footage, Tommy O'Shaughnessy wasn't lying. The door was unlocked when he tugged on it.

I remove the large yellow mopping contraption from the closet and pull the lever that wrings water from the mop. Then, I mop the walls. It doesn't take more than five minutes of vigorous rubbing to see that this will not get the crayon off. Maybe I'd be better off just repainting the walls. I shove the mop back into the bucket of soap, sit down on top of the contraption, put my head between my hands, and try not to cry.

"Baking soda."

Like the voice of God, these words come from above. I look up and see Sister Mary Bernice looking down.

"Mix a little baking soda with water and it will get the crayon off."

I wish she had more words of wisdom. Apparently, I could really use them now.

"Where's Tommy?" I ask.

"Waiting out front for his mother to pick him up."

"Don't you want to wait with him?"

"It's you I'm more worried about." She sits down beside me and the space is so tight part of her habit dips into the water bucket. She shrugs, wrings it out and pulls it onto her lap.

"You've been forgetting a lot of things lately."

This is putting it mildly. The reason I came to live in the convent is because I forgot who I was. Sadly, this isn't some sort of spiritual revelation. I literally forgot who I was. Over a year ago, Sister Mary Bernice found me unconscious, with a huge gash on my head, lying on the side of the road. Doctors thought the amnesia would pass. With time, my memory would come back. It didn't. So I gave up on it and moved on with my life, becoming a novitiate—a nun in training. Thus, in defense of Sister Mary Bernice and everyone else, I can understand why they don't believe me when I tell them my memory is fine.

"I swear I locked the door. I know I did."

She inclines her head as if considering this. "Let's say you did. But then there were the taper candles you forgot to snuff after vespers—"

"I did snuff them."

"And there was the car you left running in the garage."

"Who leaves a car running? Why would I do something like that?"

"Sister." Mary Bernice looks at me. Not that different from how she had looked at Tommy O'Shaughnessy. "The only two people who have keys to that car, the church, and this school, are you and myself. Do you think I'm setting you up?"

I hadn't thought of that. But I immediately dismiss it. Sister Mary Bernice would not play a prank on me or anyone else. She has no sense of humor. I know I sound crazy even considering this. But I am certain that I am not responsible for the above failures. Still, I keep my mouth shut.

"You've been through a great deal of trauma. Even though your accident was over a year ago, maybe your brain hasn't healed."

Flashes of bright lights, tires squealing, and money floating through the air hit my brain like a truck. But that's all I can remember.

"Maybe you're memory is getting worse. I think we should go see Dr. Inniskillen."

"No." My voice is sharp and I regret that immediately. However, I've seen the doctor many times. It isn't helping. "I'll do better. I'll write things down."

Her forehead creases into a frown. "Is there something you aren't telling me? Something seems to worry you."

Other than all these unexplained occurrences? Other than no one believes me when I say I'm not doing these things?

"Everything is fine, Sister." I smile at her. "I just haven't been sleeping well lately."

"Any reason why?"

"No Sister."

"Well, I suppose lack of sleep would take a toll on anyone."

Although her words are dismissive, the crease in her forehead is not.

The sound of a car door slamming and shouting drifts through the walls. At first, I think it is one of my flashbacks, but then I realize it is not.

"That must be Mrs. O'Shaughnessy," Sister Mary Bernice says. She puts a hand on the mop and uses it to pull herself up. "We can finish speaking about this later."

Truthfully, I never want to discuss this again. I just want it all to stop. I watch her figure recede and then look at the drawings on the wall. I tell myself she is right. I am the common denominator in all these happenings. My forgetfulness explains everything. I forgot to lock the door to the school. And I forgot to snuff the candles when I locked the church. And the car…well, perhaps my mind is still well and truly broken.

I take a deep breath and tell myself that the only thing wrong is my forgetfulness. That my mind will heal with time. I incline my head and study Tommy's artwork. It really is quite intricate. In fact, if you look ever so closely behind the children, you can see Sister Mary Bernice depicted as the jail warden. With horns.

But, as I stare more closely at the mural, I see something else. And once I see it, I can't unsee it. What looks like a swirl of dark clouds above the scene is actually a hidden message. The lines forming gusts of wind are really calligraphy and the message goes all the way down the hallway in big, scrawly font.

SISTER DYMPHNA IS A MURDERER.

There is no way I'm responsible for writing that. And there is no way a grade-school boy is either.

The front door booms. Tommy O'Shaughnessy races into the hallway. "Sister Dymphna, I'm sorry Satan tempted me to take advantage of your forgetfulness. I will find the path of compassion going forward!" he says to me, clearly repeating the words Sister Mary Bernice told him to say.

Then his eyes follow my eyes, and he sees it too. His face goes white. "I didn't write that." His eyes are like saucers. "I swear I didn't write that."

"Did you see anyone else here last night?" I whisper.

He shakes his head and backs down the hall, his eyes never leaving mine. Then he runs out the door and into the sunlight as if he's afraid of me.

I jump up, grab a box of baking soda from the janitor's

closet, dump the whole thing in the mop bucket and scrub the words furiously, drenching myself in the process. Tommy O'Shaughnessy is a handful, but he is not cruel. I know he did not write this. Nor did I in some mental fog. Someone else did. The same someone who unlocked the school doors, who relit the tapers, and who started the car in the garage. Someone smart enough to avoid the security cameras. Someone vicious enough to want to make me look crazy. But who? And, even more importantly…is what they wrote about me true?

2

Biddy

Biddy drives through town at a snail's pace with Ruby in the passenger seat. They are following a stream of cars that have turned off the stone bridge and now snake in the same direction as her house. Pooka's traffic is quickly becoming on par with Boston. Speaking of which…she turns her attention back to the voice emanating through her car's speakers.

"Megan," she says to her daughter, "I'm not coming back to Boston, and that's that."

"It's been over a year since Dad has died and you keep saying later! We should honor his birthday."

Biddy never said she'd go to Boston later. She said she'd never go to Boston again. But it's like Biddy is the only person Megan knows. Biddy thinks Megan needs a puppy. Or a best friend. Anyone beside Biddy.

"I know you're still angry with him," Megan says.

"You are still angry with him," Ruby whispers from the passenger seat.

Biddy frowns at her. She certainly doesn't need her best friend to chime in on this, too.

"But we should do something as a memorial," Megan continues. "Despite what he did to you, he's still my dad."

What Megan's father did to her was to cheat on Biddy with a former friend of hers. And this was after Biddy had given up her hopes and dreams for a career to take care of him both in the heyday of his career and then through his long illness.

"That's a nice thought," Biddy says with as much patience as she can muster. "He is still your dad and you should give him a memorial. You have my blessing. But I will not attend. In fact, why don't you call Serena Von Staadt and invite her? Apparently, she looks so much like me, your dearly deceased father couldn't tell the difference."

Biddy ferociously punches the disconnect button on her steering wheel. She misses being able to slam a phone down.

"That wasn't very nice," Ruby says, nodding at the button.

"Megan needs to move on," Biddy says.

"So do you. Did you know that the opposite of love isn't hate? It's indifference."

"Did you hear that on Oprah?"

Ruby shakes her head. "Elie Wiesel."

Once again, Biddy is impressed with Ruby's eclectic approach to reading—her favorite book series is still Nancy Drew. But regardless, Elie Wiesel may have had a point. She looks out the car window at a town that also needs to move on. Her car creeps past a dilapidated farmhouse that, just last year, had been a shiny white home to a family of five. Now, it sits empty. Its next-door neighbor is in similar disrepair and has a bright orange eviction notice pasted on the door. Spray painted across the entire front of its chipping white clapboard frame are the words: *Thank you Pooka Women's Club*. Biddy is quite confident they aren't sincere in their thanks. But the

Women's Club had nothing to do with any of these houses or the troubles of the people in them. Still, this hasn't stopped the whole town from blaming the Women's Club for their current woes.

"You should share your moving on advice with the rest of the town," Biddy says.

Ruby's cheerful round face crumples. "We did the right thing."

"Of course we did," Biddy says, secretly wondering if this is true.

She sighs and refocuses her attention on the bumper ahead of her so she doesn't have to see the multitude of other doors with similar orange eviction notices. In her heart of hearts, she knows Ruby is correct. She and the Women's Club had done the right thing. They had stopped a major illegal operation. That the ancillary damage to this was the loss of a major source of income for the town is not their fault. But the people in Pooka can't see that. They only see their farms are now failing. All except one, that is. The one she is now approaching.

Her car creeps up to the source of the traffic jam—her family farm, now owned by her niece. This would be the one and only business in town doing well. Too well. And it certainly isn't helping to improve relations with the Women's Club, given that Biddy, the Club President, has family ties to it. Little does the town know that Biddy agrees with them. It is now an ostentatious eyesore.

Standing at the foot of the long drive to the farmhouse is a garish two story tall inflatable farmer and wife. Above the drive is an arched sign welcoming the visitors to Corny Acres Farm, which…as her co-Women's Club member, Sheila, likes to comment…carries a kernel of truth. The former working farm, lovingly cared for by Biddy's father, and his father before that, is now besotted with trampled corn mazes in the summer and pine tree scavenger hunts in the winter. Farm animals can be fed for the small fee of $5 per packet of grain. Horseback rides through the fields will cost $60 an hour. A restaurant serving "fresh baked goods" which are actually freshly baked at a production factory near Indianapolis, provides breakfast, lunch and dinner. A retreat/wellness center with rooms so exorbitantly priced as to be unmentionable and a reception facility for weddings round out the offerings. The farm also holds weekly events ranging from hoe-down harvests (despite Pooka never hosting a hoe-down in its entire existence little less at harvest time when everyone is working), to wine and dine with a pig Wednesdays (an actual pig, not a pig roast), to 'Friday Furr-iends Forever' (a woman and dog retreat). The result of all this nonsense? The most financially successful farm not only in the town but in the top five of the nation.

Ahead of Biddy, numerous cars screech to a halt, blocking the flow of traffic. Drivers fling open their doors and leap out to wait patiently in a ridiculously long line to take their photos beside the unsightly display.

"I still can't believe Maude did all this," Ruby giggles. "I just love the name."

"Only you could love that name." Biddy blares her horn as the blond driver of the car in front of her stops driving, puts her car in park, and jumps out, clad in a brand new looking flannel shirt and cowboy boots that no one in this town would be caught dead wearing. Biddy throws her hands up in the air. "How can you even call this mess a farm? It's an insult to farms."

On this point, she agrees with the rest of the town. "And

let's be honest, Maude had nothing to do with this."

Ruby frowns at her. "You should be grateful to Sheila for taking Maude under her wing and teaching her marketing. She has created the only thing thriving in this town."

"She created an absolute disgrace to a dignified and historical occupation," Biddy mutters while waiting for the woman with her selfie stick to finish taking her picture with the inflatable farmers. The only soothing balm being that her father…the man who once threw her out of this same home… would roll over in his grave if he could see the family farm now.

Finally, the blond returns to her car with what Biddy considers an insincere wave of apology. The car makes its turn into the farm entrance, and Biddy can see the open road beyond. She breathes a sigh of relief and punches her foot on the gas pedal.

"Biddy! Stop!" Ruby shrieks.

Biddy slams on the brakes as a flash of black moves in front of her. She looks to her right and sees she just narrowly missed a collision with a nun running towards the field beyond the road.

"Jesus." Biddy glances at her shaking hands, still gripping the wheel, the knuckles white. The nun hadn't even paused, despite the near miss.

"Was that Sister Mary Bernice?" Ruby asks.

Biddy shakes her head. "Sister Mary Bernice is eighty. She can't run like that. It has to be that novitiate she took in."

The two stare at the figure now becoming smaller in the distance. Biddy wonders what she is running from.

"I think she's running towards the pooka," Ruby says.

The pooka are two rocks sitting on either side of the road at the entrance to town. One looks slightly like a rabbit, or maybe a goat. The other is definitely a bear. Or maybe a dragon. Both have slashes of yellow near the top that look remarkably like eyes. Folklore has it that pooka are shapeshifters who like to have a bit of fun but also have good hearts that protect the town and its people.

"Do you think she needs help?" Ruby asks. "Is she going to them to ask for their protection?"

Biddy shrugs and gently taps the gas so as not to collide with other potential running nuns. "If she does, I hope the pooka can provide it. I've learned my lesson. Don't get involved in town problems. The Women's Club needs to focus on rebuilding trust, not looking for more trouble."

3

Sheila

Confidence, Sheila tells herself, looking in her bedroom mirror. Have confidence. You are ready for this.

At least she knows she nailed the outfit. She spent hours picking it out. She's learned a few things from her time with Biddy Bramley, and one is how to power dress... with a few age-appropriate tweaks, of course. So today, she dons her new Shanel tweed skirt suit bought at Hookyourman.com, one of her favorite shopping sites for her gentlemen's companion business. They have everything you could ever need for a bargain. For example, this outfit looks just like a real Chanel but is literally a tenth the price and better fitted. For makeup, she goes all in on the red lip and is certain she's done Coco... and Biddy... proud. As Sheila always says, if you dress the part, you can play the part. She stares at her reflection. She has dressed the part.

"Now, you can play the part," she whispers. Then she grabs her keys and heads out the door.

Biddy's house looks like a fairy tale home as she drives up. Nestled in a blanket of fallen multi-colored leaves, the stone house stands proud beside a little stream, where it has been rooted for centuries. When Sheila first saw it, she thought its owner would be one of those perfectly manicured old-money people who are born, live, and die, all in the same beautiful place. The ones who spend more time lifting their eyebrows than their fingers. But over the last year, she's come to know Biddy better, and Biddy is not one of those people. It turns out she is a self-made woman. In fact, the two of them are a lot alike in that way, even if Biddy refuses to admit to it.

Sheila strides up the walkway toward the door, trying to settle the butterflies in her stomach. She hasn't wanted something this badly in years. And she's surprised how much she cares about these women's approval.

Through the picture window to her left, she can see the rest of the Women's Club has already arrived and sits around the massive stone fireplace. They are an unusual group. Amelia is in a folding chair with her eyes closed and wearing her trademark baby-food-stained sweater with carrot puree in her hair. Ruby bustles about with trays and trays of little cakes and cookies as if this were a party of twenty and those twenty hadn't eaten a meal in a decade. And Megan, Biddy's spoiled daughter, stares out at this vignette through the computer screen set on the coffee table. Sheila isn't really sure why she is still part of this club, since she doesn't live in Pooka. But somehow these women who Sheila never would have met without her mandatory service hours (the result of a ridiculous law and conviction, of course) have become family. In fact, they are the first female friends she's ever had.

She rings the doorbell, and within seconds, hears Biddy's confident footsteps tapping on the other side. Sheila breathes in. Biddy swings the door open and her eyes grow wide.

"Look," Sheila says. "We're twins!" She knew she nailed the outfit.

Biddy's forehead creases. "We most certainly are not."

"Yes, we are." Sheila holds her blue and green tweed-clad arm against Biddy's. "It's the same suit."

"You need to go home and change." Biddy makes to close the door, which is rather shocking to Sheila. If it were her, she'd be flattered that a younger, more beautiful woman selected the same clothing.

But Ruby's hand shoots out to stop the door from completely closing. "What's going on here?"

Ruby appears at Biddy's side as the door reopens, still holding one of her trays. "Oh look," she giggles. "You're twins!"

Ruby opens the door wider and Sheila heads past a glaring Biddy into the living room. This isn't exactly the way Sheila hoped to start today. She'd hoped to impress Biddy. However, it's also not the first time Biddy has tried to close a door in her face either.

"Hello," Sheila says to Amelia and Megan.

Megan squints through the computer screen at her and laughs. "You have the same—"

"That's enough!" Biddy picks up her gavel, bends down, and taps it on the coffee table. "Welcome to our first annual year-end board meeting. A year ago, I officially filed all our necessary paperwork to become a 501(c). Under this designation, we are required to hold annual board meetings to elect directors and approve budgets. This meeting today will fulfill that obligation. Let's start with club updates. Amelia, do you want to review the minutes from the last meeting?"

Amelia, the club's secretary, pulls a stack of papers out of her handbag, wipes a smear of banana off the top one, and looks down at her notes. "At our last meeting, we discussed doing a project to help the free food pantry."

"Yes, that was a great idea!" Biddy says.

"Biddy," Ruby tugs at her sleeve until her best friend looks at her. Ruby is the Vice President. "I called the pantry, and they refused our help."

"Oh." Biddy looks momentarily flummoxed.

In truth, the club has pitched many charity projects and no one in the town wants anything to do with them, even when they are donating money. The townspeople are still a little bitter that the club shut down Pooka's major revenue stream on their last project. That the revenue stream was illegal doesn't seem to matter to them. Sheila has learned that people only seem to care about the legality of revenue streams when it applies to single women, minding their own business, and doing what they need to do to support themselves, like herself.

Biddy shakes her head. "Well, let's move on to our finance report from the Treasurer."

This is Sheila. She clears her throat. "We agreed to annual dues of $20, so everyone hand it over."

Biddy rolls her eyes as everyone reaches into her wallet and passes Sheila the money. Megan Venmo's it. Amelia's face turns red as she passes Sheila $8 and then opens up her change purse and begins counting quarters. Sheila hands her back the $8.

"I've got you," she whispers.

This is the perk of owning a successful business. Sheila's job is surprisingly recession—and anger—resistant. Amelia's blush deepens, but she takes back the money and nods gratefully.

Sheila takes the rest of the money, adds hers and enough to cover Amelia, puts it in an envelope, and passes it to Biddy. "We have $100."

"Wonderful," Biddy says, but she doesn't look like she means it. "In the future, perhaps it might be better if you mail out a statement and then people can mail you back the dues."

This doesn't seem like a better method at all. Sheila can tell you that rule number one in business is that a customer doesn't leave your workplace without paying in cash on the spot. On the front-end of delivery, in fact. But she keeps this thought to herself.

"Next up, is membership. Ruby—any updates?"

Besides being Vice President, Ruby is also in charge of new member recruitment. Now, she shakes her head.

"No new members."

Biddy's forehead creases. "What about the ones who signed up at the launch of Eileen's exhibit in the museum?"

"They all quit when the co-op failed and their farms went under. I'm barely staying afloat myself," Ruby says.

Ruby runs the local pub and if that is hurting, the town has truly hit rock bottom.

"Well." Biddy gathers herself together and appears taller. "That's okay. Moving into our second year, as the President, it's my mission to make sure the club stays relevant and healthy—"

"Wait a minute," Sheila says. "Aren't we supposed to have an election?"

Biddy looks shocked.

"Well, yes," Biddy says. "But do we really need one?"

Shelia frowns. "According to Roger's Rules of Order, I

thought we were supposed to have one."

"It's Robert's Rules of Order and no, that doesn't dictate leadership terms. Our bylaws do."

"Well, whatever. I thought there was supposed to be an election."

"She's right," Megan says helpfully, although she looks like she's fighting back laughter.

"You are right." Biddy always looks to be in pain when she utters these words. "I'm jumping the gun a little, but I thought we'd all just keep our current positions since we don't have new members vying for leadership roles."

"Oh goody," Ruby claps her hands. "I love being Vice President. I'm number two again."

Sheila's heart is racing. She takes a deep breath. "I'm running for President."

Everyone freezes. Four pairs of wide eyes stare at her. Sheila reminds herself that she is ready for this. She needs to project confidence.

"YOU want to run for President?" Biddy says. "That's ridiculous. I'm the one who created this club and bring years of experience serving on boards. You aren't qualified to be president. This is your first club. And you have a criminal record."

"That hasn't stopped other politicians," Ruby points out. "In fact, it's quite the trendy thing these days."

"I think it's a great idea." This unexpected announcement comes from Megan, of all people. "That'll free up some of your time, Mom, and you can come back to Boston to help me with Dad's memorial."

"I'm not going to Boston and I'm certainly not attending a memorial for your father."

Apparently, Biddy still hasn't gotten over learning that the man cheated on her. Sheila doesn't want to say anything to anger her further, but in her experience, it happens more often than one would imagine.

"I think it's a good idea," Amelia says quietly. "I'm always telling my children that they should take turns and try new things. I think that should apply to us adults, too."

"Thank you, Amelia," Sheila says.

She doesn't like to brag, but she's pretty good at math, and thus far, if you include her own vote, along with Amelia's, and Megan's, it looks like she's got three in her camp and only two for Biddy. Ruby, of course, would never vote against her best friend. She was hoping for unanimity and Biddy's blessing, but she's got to take what she can get.

"Then it's settled," she says. "All for me being president?"

"Aye." Megan's, Amelia's, and her own hands shoot up.

"Nay," says Biddy.

Ruby says nothing and looks at her hands folded in her lap.

"I'll just mark you as abstaining," Amelia whispers to her.

Ruby looks back gratefully.

Sheila looks around the group and can hardly believe it. She did it. These women trust her enough to be president. She blushes as they all clap. Biddy rolls her eyes, but Sheila knows she can win her over. She will spend the year proving she learned so much from Biddy.

"As my first act as president, I'd like to propose that we reinstate Ruby as Vice President since she's done the job so competently."

"Really?" Ruby's eyes light up.

"I second the motion," Amelia says. Even Biddy agrees to this. And in no time at all, Ruby is Vice President once again.

"I'd actually like to try my hand at Treasurer," Amelia says. "I'd love to learn more about finance."

"Good for you," Sheila says. "I'll give you all the help you need." They vote and she is in.

Sheila looks at Biddy. "With Amelia taking my place as treasurer, that makes you Secretary."

"You've got to be kidding," she mutters. "I should at least be President Emeritus."

"If Emeritus is Latin for Chief Note-Taker, then you're good to go!" Sheila says cheerfully.

Biddy frowns and is about to speak but Megan interrupts.

"I'll do it," she says. "I'll be Secretary and Mom can be President Emeritus."

Sheila shrugs. At least Megan finally has a job, and Biddy is looking slightly mollified.

The room falls silent, and everyone looks at Sheila. She looks back at them and realizes something upsetting. Sheila hasn't really thought much about what she should do after winning. What will be their mission this year? Sheila suddenly misses the drama and near death incidents of last year. It's going to be hard to live up to Biddy's year without something to do. The doorbell chimes cut off her dilemma. She looks out the bay window.

"Is that a bloody nun?" Ruby asks.

Sheila's lips pull up in a smile. This, she thinks, will do just fine.

4

Megan

Megan has forgotten how amusing these meetings are. She wouldn't want to tell anyone, but she secretly looks forward to them.

To say that things aren't going well in Boston is an understatement. She had quit her job at Harvard after her former fiancé had an affair with her Department Chair's wife. She'd been so confident that she'd find a great new position all on her own—not using her father's pull this time. But few other universities had openings, and the ones who did all hired people with more experience than her. So she works as an adjunct professor at a Boston area Community College where her salary of $2,000 per class with no benefits can't even make ends meet. None of her previous colleagues are speaking to her since her fall from grace. It's as if they think failure is contagious. Sadly, this lot of women in the Pooka Women's Club are the closest things she has to friends these days, not that they think of her that way.

It's also partly why she wants to hold a memorial for her father on his birthday. She misses him with all her heart, but she also hopes that reconnecting with his university friends may help her find a new position. Her mother had been so wrong to encourage her to strike out on her own instead of following in her father's footsteps. She should have just kept her job at Harvard and been thankful to have it, no matter how she got it. No matter, that everyone called her a nepobaby.

"Who's at the door?" she now asks through her Zoom screen. The way her mother has set the computer on the coffee table means all she can see is the middle of people's bodies. "Are we getting a new member?"

Someone laughs. She thinks it is Ruby. Sure enough, Ruby's face fills the screen. Completely. All Megan can see is a closeup of her nose.

"You've been gone too long. Everyone hates us!"

Megan knows how she feels.

"It's probably just the Amazon delivery guy."

Still, everyone runs towards the foyer and now Megan can only see their behinds as they stand in the doorway peeking around the corner. As she stares at this undesirable visage, she thinks Sheila's skirt really is a bit too short, even for her. But Megan's learned a lot about these women throughout the year. Everyone has her own approach to dressing for battle. With Sheila, her skirts get shorter. She was well prepared for her coup today.

"Is that a bloody nun?" someone—Megan thinks it's Ruby—asks.

"Bloody as in covered with blood or bloody as in you're surprised to see a nun?" Megan asks. These days, neither answer would surprise her.

But no one hears her. The club doesn't notice her presence, which is also nothing new.

There is a shuffling at the door as the crowd of behinds tries to push past each other to get into the foyer.

"Can you move aside?" Megan shouts. "I can't see!"

Again, no one responds, but now the mass of bodies is being pushed back into the living room.

"Get these women a chair," Sheila commands.

Two sets of torsos and thighs move off screen and return bearing folding chairs. Someone thankfully sets these up right in front of the computer. Then a body is shoved into one and another body takes a seat in the other.

"My God, it really is a bloody nun," Megan says.

As in a nun covered in blood. The other new arrival is an older nun who appears a little angry. Both are in old-fashioned habits and Megan is just beginning to ponder the feminist implications of this practice—a subject interesting to her as a Women's Studies professor—when she gets a close-up of the younger nun from the nose up.

"It's not blood," the bloody nun says. "It's just paint."

"I don't care what it is," the other nun says. "It was shot at you through your bedroom window. You could have been killed."

The younger nun sits back in her seat. "I'm sure it was just a prank."

"And I'm sure there is something you aren't telling me. God sees all, Sister. I know this isn't the first time you've been threatened."

The bloody nun looks like she'd rather take her chances with her paint gun-wielding attacker than the voice of God sitting beside her, and Megan can understand that inclination.

Megan's mother returns to the room and bends over to hand the young nun a cup of tea. The nun takes it gratefully.

"We need your help," the old nun says to Biddy.

"Removing the paint stains?" her mother asks.

"No!" The older nun frowns. "Finding out who and why someone is trying to kill her."

"No one is trying to kill me," the other nun says. "I think they are just trying to scare me."

"Absolutely not," Biddy says. "Our club is supposed to be a women's club. This is not what women's clubs do. We should never have gotten involved in that last affair. This—" Biddy gestures at the paint-covered nun—"is a matter for the police."

"No police," the young nun says, her tea cup shaking in her hand.

Her reaction surprises Megan. It's almost as if the nun is afraid to be on the cops' radar.

"The police haven't been very helpful," the older nun says.

"The police are never helpful," Sheila says.

Sheila comes into view and stands next to Biddy. Megan now has a perfect view of both their backsides—clad in matching green and navy tweed, but at very different lengths.

"I was just voted in as president," Sheila continues, "and our club would be happy to consider your case." She offers her hand to the older nun. "My name is Sheila Ryan... President Sheila Ryan."

The old nun's eyes travel up and down Sheila's figure. Then she shrugs. "The Lord works in mysterious ways." She puts her hand in Sheila's. "Thank you for helping us. My name is Sister Mary Bernice. I'm Mother Superior at Sacred Heart of the Woods."

The image of the two shaking hands is an unusual one. Megan wishes she had a camera. Actually, maybe there is a way to take a screenshot of this.

"And this," continues the old nun, "is Sister Dymphna, a novitiate."

"Your mother named you Dymphna?" Sheila asks her.

"No. Nuns take on new names. I chose it for her," Sister Mary Bernice says.

"Were you angry at her?"

"Sheila!" Biddy admonishes, even though Megan is pretty sure they were all thinking it.

"It's a beautiful name," Sister Mary Bernice says, proving that beauty truly is in the eye of the beholder. "Dymphna is the patron saint of those with mental and nervous disorders. I thought it appropriate, given her condition."

This, Megan thinks, just gets more and more interesting.

"Sister Dymphna has amnesia," Sister Mary Bernice continues. "She can't remember who she is or where she's from. That's how I came to name her."

"Really." Sheila sits back down in a chair.

"You poor thing," Ruby says.

"Your family must be so worried," Amelia says.

Sheila studies the young nun. "You know," she says slowly, her forehead creasing, "you seem familiar to me."

"Do I?" The nun looks both hopeful for and afraid of the answer at the same time. Why would that be?

"Maybe from mass at church?" Ruby asks.

Megan suppresses the urge to laugh.

"No. I'm pretty sure that's not it." Sheila tilts her head, trying to get a better look at Sister Dymphna. "From somewhere else. I just can't place it."

The club sits silently as Sheila continues to study her. Finally, she shakes her head. "I can't figure it out. Maybe it will come to me later."

Sister Dymphna relaxes. Again, an odd reaction to someone possibly being able to solve the mystery of her identity.

"Perhaps it would be helpful if you could tell us the whole story of your problems from the beginning," Amelia says.

Sister Dymphna looks annoyed, and Megan can only imagine how many times she's had to tell this story. However, a quick glance from Sister Mary Bernice pushes her into compliance.

"A little over a year ago, I woke up in the hospital. I did not know who I was or why I was there. Sister Mary Bernice told me she had found me lying unconscious on the side of a road near the church and had taken me there. The doctors hoped my memory would come back over time, but it hasn't. After a while, I gave up hoping it would and moved on with my life. I decided to become a nun."

"What put you in the hospital?" Megan asks.

"I don't know." The frustration in Sister Dymphna's voice is apparent. "Most likely a car crash. But I don't remember."

"I checked with the police," Sister Mary Bernice says, "but no one reported a crash. We aren't sure what happened."

"Why were you in Pooka?" Amelia asks. "You must not be from here, or we would all know you."

"Again, I don't know." Sister Dymphna says again and looks down at her folded hands. The knuckles are white. "I don't know where I came from or why I'm here."

"But that's only half the story," Sister Mary Bernice says. "Despite Sister Dymphna's claims to nothing being wrong, there is. I simply can't continue to ignore the strange things that have happened since her arrival. Little things—like doors being unlocked that should have been locked or candles being lit that should have been snuffed. I wrongly attributed these things to Sister Dymphna's memory struggles. But then, one of her students shared this photo with me." Sister Mary Bernice takes out her phone and shows them a screenshot of a painting of swirling clouds with the words *Sister Dymphna is a murderer* written in it.

"Tommy," Sister Dymphna whispers angrily.

"And then today, someone shot her in the face with a paintball through her bedroom window."

"Could it be a kid playing a prank?"

"No." Sister Mary Bernice is firm. "No student of ours would do this."

"Do you think someone died in whatever accident gave her the amnesia?" Amelia asks. "And they are angry enough to want to kill her?"

This, Megan thinks, explains the nun's resistance to reporting the paintball incident to the police. Guilt over harming someone else would keep her from wanting to create further trouble for that person's loved ones. But perhaps there is also a little fear of getting into trouble herself? What if Sister Dymphna caused the accident she was in? What if she is a murderer, intentional or not?

Sister Mary Bernice nods at Amelia's supposition. "That is the question. We've looked throughout the state of Indiana to find car crashes around the time of her injury and have found none where someone goes missing. If someone identified her, why not just report her to the police so Sister Dymphna can take responsibility and accept the consequences of whatever happened? Shooting her with a paintball is not normal. You must agree none of this is normal."

"And you've looked through security cameras?" Sheila asks. "To see who is behind this?"

Sister Mary Bernice nods. "We have. And there's nothing on them. It's as if the person knows exactly where they are."

"Look, I'm very sorry all of this is happening to you," Biddy says to Sister Dymphna. "But this is a terrible idea. The club needs to make peace with the town, not launch a new investigation that could turn up more trouble. We should report this to the police."

"I think Biddy is right," Amelia says quietly. "John lost his job yesterday and the only income we have now is book-keeping work I found online. We can't afford to get involved in anything polarizing again. I can't lose my job because I upset a potential employer."

"I'd hate to not help someone who needs us," Ruby says. "But I'd also hate to cause more problems for anyone else. I don't know what I want to do."

"Well, I know what I want to do and I'm the President." Sheila says. "We are the Pooka Women's Club and we help women in need. We are here to solve this mystery for you."

"This is not what women's clubs do," Biddy mutters.

"This is what OUR women's club does," Sheila says, "and we will sort this out. Much more quickly than the police would. Give us some time to put together our strategy and then we'll be back in touch to interview you."

"I wish you all the Lord's help," Sister Mary Bernice says.

Sheila smiles. "I look forward to working with him. I've heard good things."

Before Megan's mother has time to roll her eyes at this exchange, glass shatters and everyone in the room screams.

Megan stares at her computer screen from her cramped Boston apartment, watching chaos unfold in her mother's living room through their video call. Shards of glass fly everywhere. Something whizzes past the screen.

"What happened?" she shouts at the screen. "Are you okay? Is anyone hurt? Mom?"

The computer flips sideways when someone knocks it. All she can see are the middle sections of bodies as everyone throws themselves on the floor. It's like watching a disaster movie through a keyhole.

"Someone call the police," comes a muffled voice—Amelia, she thinks.

"No," says another voice—Sheila's. "No one move. He may still be out there."

"Who?" Megan demands. "Who may be out there? What happened?"

"Someone shot a bullet through the window," Sheila says, her voice surprisingly calm for someone who just got shot at.

"Another paint gun bullet?" Megan asks. She can hear the hope in her voice.

"No," Sheila says. "A real bullet."

"Mom?" Megan screams. Her heart clenches. She needs to hear her voice. She needs to know she's okay. For all their disagreements, for all the ways Biddy Bramley drives her crazy with her meddling and her stubborn refusal to acknowledge that other people might have valid opinions, she's still Megan's mom. The thought of losing her is unbearable.

"Mom?" she calls again to the screen. "Please tell me you're okay."

She fumbles for her phone and dials 911, giving them the address. The operator assures her that units are already on the way—apparently someone else has already called it in.

"I'm fine, Megan." Her mother's familiar voice, with its persistent undertone of slight annoyance, comes through the speakers. Megan has never been so happy to hear it. "I think they destroyed my living room, though."

"I think Sister Dymphna's been shot," Sister Mary Bernice shrieks.

"That's worse," Biddy says.

Megan watches Biddy crawl towards the center of the room and leans into the computer to see if the nun is okay, but from the angle of the computer screen, it is impossible.

The sirens arrive quickly after that, and Megan sits helplessly as emergency responders flood her mother's living room. She can hear fragments of conversation—an all clear call from a booming voice, then questions about the shooting, discussions about the mysterious nun, speculation about motives.

As the immediate crisis passes and it becomes clear that Sister Dymphna is only grazed, Megan makes a decision.

"I'm coming home," she announces to the room.

Everyone turns toward her computer screen. They all look like they are at a forty-five degree angle until someone rights it.

"Sheila is right. This is a real case," she continues. "And it deserves the full team. I can stay with Mom, and we can work together on this investigation."

She needs to come home, anyway. Her job situation in Boston is precarious at best. Her savings are dried up, and she worries she won't be able to pay rent. The Women's Club mystery might be exactly the distraction she needs from her own problems. Plus, she can help a nun. Maybe she'll put in a good word for her to the man above.

"This is a terrible idea," her mother protests. "Someone could have killed one of us. And you need to be in Boston focusing on your career. We should let the police handle it and stay out of it."

An argument ensues and then a vote is held as emergency workers bustle around them. It's surprisingly close, but Megan is relieved when the Club agrees to take the case. Whatever this mystery is about, whoever Sister Dymphna really is, at least she won't have to face it alone. But then her mother stands up.

"I just can't be a part of this," Biddy says. She has tears in her eyes as she surveys her wrecked living room. "Look at what has already happened. And look what happened last time. Even though we didn't mean to, we hurt a lot of people in this town. And even in this room." She looks toward the computer that houses Megan's face. "My brother is in prison. You're angry with me. My home has now been destroyed. And many of the others here suffered personal losses as well. I can't risk hurting more people if this case takes us down another path of crime in Pooka. I wish you well, but you need to count me out."

And then she leaves the room.

5

Ruby

Why can't everyone just get along? It's a question Ruby asks herself all the time. She stands in Biddy's living room staring at the broken window and shards of glass scattered across the floor. It feels representative of the Women's Club—beautiful as a whole but a little shattered at the moment.

After the police left, Amelia, the bags under her eyes looking even heavier than usual, hurried out to start her second job. The woman works herself to the bone, trying to keep her family afloat since John's farm failed. Ruby's heart aches watching her friend struggle. Megan logged off the Zoom call to buy tickets to come home, her face pale with worry through the computer screen. Sheila went to the hospital with Sister Dymphna. And Biddy—she took one look around her destroyed living room—at the hole in her beautiful bay window where someone had fired a bullet meant for a nun, and stormed off through the kitchen door vowing not to return.

This left Ruby to convince Sister Mary Bernice to let the emergency medical team examine her more carefully to make sure she was okay. And that was when they discovered her ankle had been severely twisted. The paramedics whisked her off, too.

Now, with everyone departed, Ruby surveys the damage and gets to work. This, at least, she is good at.

Ruby sweeps up the smaller pieces of glass. The repetitive action calms her nerves, which jangled from the moment that bullet crashed through the window. She keeps thinking about how close they'd all come to being seriously hurt—or worse. What if the shooter had aimed more carefully? What if there had been more than one bullet?

She moves on to straightening the furniture that was knocked askew during the chaos. Biddy's beautiful antique chairs overturned as everyone dove for cover, and one of them now sports a small chip in its mahogany finish. Ruby runs her finger over the damage, knowing that Biddy will notice it immediately when she returns. Her friend has an eye for imperfection, both in furniture and in people.

The coffee table where Biddy had set up Megan's laptop is now pushed against the far wall, its surface scattered with papers and an overturned tea cup. Ruby rights the cup and begins gathering the scattered documents—meeting agendas, club bylaws, financial reports. All the careful organization that Biddy brings to everything she touches, now in disarray.

When she finishes cleaning, Ruby stands in the center of the room and surveys her work. The space looks normal again, almost peaceful, if you ignore the gaping hole in the window and the way the afternoon light streams through it in sharp, geometric patterns that weren't there before. She'll need to call someone about boarding that until it can get fixed.

But first, she needs to find Biddy.

Ruby heads out of the house and down the gravel road toward the main street. The day's events weigh so heavily, she can't appreciate the crisp fall weather and the leaves that are bursting with color. The maples are gold at their edges, and the oaks are a deep russet. It's always been her favorite time of year—that brief, perfect moment between summer's heat and winter's harshness when everything feels possible again. So why does this autumn feel so very different?

She crosses the small two-lane road, pausing to let Mrs. Henderson drive by in her ancient Buick. The woman waves, and Ruby waves back, grateful for this small moment of normalcy. Mrs. Henderson must not know about the shooting yet, which means Ruby has maybe an hour before the whole town is buzzing with rumors and speculation.

Ruby heads into the cornfield beyond the road, following a path that's worn smooth by decades of feet—first by Biddy as a lonely child, then by Ruby when she started joining her friend on these expeditions, and now by both of them as middle-aged women still seeking solace in the same places they'd found comfort as girls.

The corn is nearly ready for harvest, the stalks tall and rustling in the breeze, heavy with ears that will soon feed livestock through the winter. Ruby remembers when this field belonged to the Morrison family, before they lost their farm to debt. Now it belongs to some corporation downstate, and the corn will be shipped away to feed cattle they'll never see in places they'll never visit.

That only a cornfield separates Biddy's new house from the pooka guarding the entrance to the town is rather fitting. Ruby knows her friend spent much of her childhood hiding out with those rocks, spinning stories about ancient Irish spirits and magical transformations. Back then, Biddy had been a dreamy child with wild hair and a wilder imagination, nothing like the composed, elegant woman she's become. But Ruby has found that most people stay exactly the same in their core, no matter how much their surfaces change.

So it is no surprise she finds Biddy, now a little older than the girl of her memories and hopefully a little wiser, sitting with her back against a tree facing the towering pooka rocks. What is a surprise is that there is a goat laying right next to her, as calm and content as if it belongs there. Many goats run wild through this town, the result of a misguided attempt to achieve a natural means of lawn clipping for Pooka. Mostly, the goats want nothing to do with the people and just wander wild now.

Ruby walks through the cluster of trees separating the cornfield from the rocks, her feet crunching softly on fallen leaves. She falls to the ground beside Biddy with a small oomph. It's a good thing she carries extra padding on her figure to cushion such a blow, but getting down is the easy part.

"How are we going to get back up?" she asks Biddy. There is a reason you don't see people their age sitting on the floor.

Biddy shrugs. "I'm not entirely sure. Maybe I just won't ever get up again."

Oh boy. Ruby fights the urge to shake her friend. She nods at the goat. "Did the pooka rock finally shape-change for you?"

"Don't be silly," Biddy says, even though Ruby is confident it is Biddy being silly right now. "It's just a goat. Stupid thing was standing on one of the rocks and when I shooed him off, he came to sit by me."

Biddy's eyes flash yellow as she glares at the goat, who seems completely nonplussed by her anger. Both Biddy and her daughter, Megan, have this hint of yellow in their eyes, especially when they're upset. It's almost as if they are pooka themselves—yellow-eyed creatures of transformation and mischief. But no, that's just a myth, Ruby knows.

She watches as the goat takes a bite of grass and chews contentedly, completely unimpressed by Biddy's mood. Biddy's mood doesn't impress Ruby either, but she does feel bad about the real reason for it. And that reason, Ruby is sure, has nothing to do with a broken window.

"It's not your fault Declan is in jail, Biddy."

Declan is Biddy's brother, and right when they were reconciling after years of estrangement, Biddy had played a role in his arrest. The guilt has been eating at her ever since, though she tries to hide it behind her usual composed facade.

"I didn't say that it was." Biddy's response comes too quickly, too sharp.

"Maybe you didn't have to."

"The whole town is suffering. My brother is in prison. Maude has money but everyone hates her even more for it. And Megan... well, Megan can't get a job to save her life. I know she blames me, and I can understand why. I told her to stand on her own two feet. To follow her dreams rather than what her father chose for her."

Ruby feels her heart ache for her friend. Biddy has always carried the weight of the world on her shoulders, always felt responsible for fixing everything and everyone around her. It's both her greatest strength and her greatest weakness.

"None of this is your fault, Biddy." Ruby looks beyond the huge rocks at the road to Pooka in the distance. "They all chose their own paths and they all have to accept the consequences."

"The club just fired me as President."

Ruby looks at her friend. "I don't think that's what happened. I think you've inspired Sheila so much that she wants to follow in your footsteps."

Biddy sniffs. "Well, the last thing I need is another person to blame me for her choices."

The words might not show it, but Ruby can see she's mollified by this interpretation of events.

"You need to get out of this funk. People look up to you, and if you've given up on everything and everyone, so will they. The town doesn't blame you for everything. You are just an easy way of avoiding blaming themselves. Besides, did you hear they are considering overthrowing Arthur Dillon as mayor?"

"Really?" For the first time, Biddy sounds genuinely cheered.

"Really."

"Well, I guess there is a bright side to everything." Then Biddy's smile fades. "Sister Dymphna was shot."

"Well, maybe not to that."

Ruby bumps her friend with her shoulder, the way she's been doing since they were teenagers, sharing secrets and dreams. "Problems don't go away just because you choose not to get involved. Sheila's right. This may not be what normal women's clubs do, but it is what our women's club does best. We help women in need no matter what the consequences."

Biddy strokes the goat absently. The animal seems to have a calming effect on her. "This isn't what I thought it would look like. The Women's Club. I thought we'd be planting gardens.

Planning lectures."

Ruby giggles. "Really? You thought Sheila and Megan would be planting gardens? With each other?"

Biddy smiles. "Well, maybe the membership also looked a little different in my head."

Ruby forces her to meet her eyes. "Biddy, you founded this club. And that fact alone is enough to guarantee the club wouldn't be planting flowers and hosting fashion shows. I know what lies underneath that Chanel suit, and it's a toughness that would make those society ladies blush. Let Sheila take the lead on this. She learned from the best. And why don't you focus on building bridges again with the town? If that's what's making you sad, then fix it."

Biddy considers this, her fingers still moving through the goat's coarse hair. "That nun really doesn't want our help."

Ruby giggles. "She's having nun of it!"

Biddy laughs. "The situation is nun-sensical."

"It's a con-nun-drum."

"So we help her, anyway."

"Because that is what we do."

"It is."

Biddy rolls to one side, gets on her hands and knees, and then pushes up with her hands until her knees straighten and she can stand. She then takes pity on Ruby, extends her hands to her, and leans back to lever her up. Ruby gives a sharp tug with her hands at the end to prevent Biddy from over-levering herself right back onto the ground.

"That used to be easier," Ruby says, dusting her behind off and trying to ignore the way her knees protest the movement.

"Everything used to be easier."

"That is not at all true. Remember the time we painted the

town red?"

Biddy laughs. "That took an awful lot of paint."

"It was a whole lot less fun than it sounded."

"How were we to know they weren't being literal when we heard that phrase? We were only nine."

"It is a stupid saying." Ruby shakes her head. "They deserved those red houses."

The two best friends stroll back through the field toward Biddy's house, the goat trailing behind them like a new strange, four-legged member of their group. The afternoon light slants lower, and Ruby knows that soon the whole town will buzz with news of the shooting. Tomorrow, there will be questions to answer and plans to make. But for now, she's content to walk beside her oldest friend, watching the way the golden light turns the cornfield into something magical, something worthy of the ancient Irish stories that gave their town its name.

6

Sister Dymphna

Someone just tried to kill me. This goes to show that not only is it true that you can't escape your past, but apparently, it even holds true if you can't remember it. The hospital released me since the bullet only grazed my arm. But I was lying when I told them I felt fine. I still feel physically nauseous for so many reasons. One, I almost died. Two, I hate to think that I was a bad person before becoming Sister Dymphna, but I'm afraid I can deny it no longer. Someone hates me enough to kill me. Three, my presence is putting good people in danger. The bullet that grazed my temple this afternoon could have easily found its mark in Sister Mary Bernice, or in any of those women who were trying to help me. And, four, the thing that makes me feel sickest of all, is that I know what I must now do. I pull the suitcase out of my wardrobe and unzip it on the bed.

The thought of leaving breaks my heart, but I've come to love Sister Mary Bernice. She is all I have in this world. I'm terrified of dying, but I'm even more terrified of being responsible for her death.

I put my one outfit from my past life in my suitcase. The clothes feel foreign in my hands—jeans that are softer than anything the convent provides, a cashmere sweater in deep blue that must have cost more than Sister Mary Bernice spends on groceries in a month, leather boots that fit my feet like they were custom made. These things belonged to someone with money, someone who cared about appearances. Someone who is clearly nothing like the person I've created over this past year. Not only do I no longer want to know who she is, I've come to hate her recently. She is responsible for me having to leave a life that I love.

The rest of the convent is quiet. Sister Mary Bernice didn't even appear when I returned from the hospital, and I don't blame her. If I were in her position, I wouldn't want to see me either. I've brought nothing but trouble to this place that gave me sanctuary.

I hesitate as my fingers brush my spare habit, the rough cotton rubbing on my skin. My habit has become like a favorite sweater over these months—I feel safe and protected in it, like I'm wearing armor against a world that seems determined to hurt me. But I have no right to it anymore, if I ever did. But still.

I fish in my pocket for a $100 bill, smooth out the creases, and leave it on my desk before folding the habit carefully and placing it in my suitcase. I know I'm overpaying, but it's the least I can do for this church that has sheltered me when I had nowhere else to go.

Did I forget to mention that I had $1200 in cash in my pocket when they found me? Crisp bills, mostly hundreds, wrapped in a rubber band like I was a drug dealer or had plans to pay someone off. I can't help but think this isn't something good people carry around. What I didn't carry around was a purse, though. No driver's license. No credit cards. No identification whatsoever. No family photos or business cards or any of the normal stuff that accumulates in wallets. It was like I had deliberately scrubbed myself clean of any identifying information before... before whatever put me in that hospital bed.

What type of person does that? What type of person travels with a roll of cash and no identification?

I zip the suitcase closed with more force than necessary and take a last look around the room that has been my home for over a year. It is sterile, but oddly cozy in its simplicity. There is the desk by the window where I've spent countless hours trying to pray away the nightmares that plague my sleep. The simple wooden cross on the wall that someone gifted Sister Mary Bernice during her novitiate years, its edges worn smooth by decades of handling. The single bed in the center with its thin mattress and rough sheets that somehow became the most comfortable place I'd ever slept. At least that I can remember.

And there, on the nightstand by my head, is the vase of fresh flowers Sister Mary Bernice places there weekly without fail. I think I will miss this the most. This week's arrangement is sunflowers and blue stock.

I'm oddly going to miss her, this stern woman who took in a stranger with amnesia no questions asked, who taught me to find peace in prayer even when I couldn't remember if I'd ever believed in God before. She could have turned me over to social services or the police. She could have washed her hands of the whole messy situation. Instead, she gave me a home and a purpose, asked nothing of me but honesty and effort.

And I repaid her by bringing violence to her doorstep. And trying to convince Tommy O'Shaughnessy to keep secret the writing on the wall. That somehow feels worse.

I close the door behind me and tiptoe down the stairs with my suitcase. The convent is ancient by American standards, built in the 1800s by Irish immigrants who wanted to create a piece of the old country in their new home. The floors have settled over the decades, developing their own language of groans and sighs.

Sister Mary Bernice sleeps in a bedroom on the first floor. Her door is closed as I pass it, and it's probably for the best. I don't think I could face her disappointment in me.

"Sister Dymphna, where do you think you're going?" The voice cuts through the silence. "I hear you creeping past my room."

I freeze in the narrow hallway. This must be what Catholic school is like. I hesitate and then decide to do the right thing. No matter who I was in the past, I can decide who to be in the present. I turn the doorknob and enter her room, bracing myself for whatever lecture awaits me.

She's lying on top of her bedding, still fully dressed in her habit, propped up by a mountain of pillows. The room is sparse like mine, but there are small personal touches—a rosary with worn wooden beads on her nightstand, a photo of what must be her parents or siblings from decades ago, a stack of well-thumbed theological texts. Her face is pale—too pale—and her hair, normally hidden beneath her wimple, is loose around her shoulders, gray streaked with white and thinner than I expected. But these details I don't notice until later, because it's her right leg, heavily bound in medical tape and elevated on additional pillows, that draws my attention.

"You've been shot," I cry.

"Oh, calm down," she says, waving her hand as if this were nothing of consequence. "I haven't been shot. I twisted my ankle while avoiding being shot. It's difficult to duck at my age, you know."

I'm not entirely sure that this is better. Her leg is swelling around the bandage and I can see a purplish-blue bruise deepening along her shin that is nowhere near her ankle.

She shifts against the pillows and winces. "And where do you think you're going?" Her eyes are peering past me at my suitcase in the hall. Then they focus back on me.

"I don't know yet." This scares me and is something I should figure out. "But far away from here. I'm sorry for the damage I've done. I never intended to hurt you... or anyone else."

"Hurt me?" She frowns. "You didn't hurt me. Someone else hurt me."

"Because of me."

"You don't think I have my own enemies?"

Without thinking, I laugh.

"Mmm. You should speak with some of my past students."

This I don't doubt. But I do doubt any of her former pupils would point a gun in her direction, no matter how strict her teaching methods might have been.

"Now, what is hurting me," she continues, "is that you want to leave me in my time of need." She gestures down at her injured leg. "How am I supposed to serve this community if I can't walk?"

My eyes widen. This is admittedly a problem, but I don't want it to be my problem. I need to put as much distance as I can between the two of us, for her own safety. The person who shot at me today might come back, might decide that anyone helping me is a legitimate target. I can't live with that on my conscience.

"I'll call the Women's Club. Who is that woman you like? Biddy? I'm sure she'll help you."

"Not Sheila?" She raises her eyebrows with what might be amusement. "She made it pretty clear… repeatedly… that she is president."

I say nothing. There's something about Sheila that makes me feel uncomfortable, though I can't put my finger on why.

"Well," Sister Mary Bernice waves her hand again as if erasing the entire discussion, "I don't want the Women's Club's help."

This is something we have in common.

"I want you. You are the one I trained on how to run this church and provide moral guidance and support."

"Sister, someone is trying to kill me. I'd be putting you in danger. This parish in danger." My eyes drift to the cross above her head. "And I don't think I'm in the position to be providing moral guidance to anyone."

"Modesty is not a good look on you," she says. "I think you are in the perfect position to provide moral guidance. I've watched you strive very hard to be a good person over these months. And I need you. Are you really going to deprive an old nun of the healthcare and support she needs? After all I've done for you? I mean, I was almost shot because of you."

As I look into her doe eyes, I'm pretty sure that this is what manipulation feels like. But she's right, of course. She took me in when I had nowhere else to go, asked no questions when I appeared on a hospital bed with amnesia and a roll of unexplained cash. She's fed me, clothed me, given me purpose when I felt utterly lost. And now she's injured because of me, unable to care for herself or her parish.

"Why would you still want to help me?" I ask. Because I know this request for help isn't to help her, but to help me.

"Because we're sisters," she says, as if this were the most obvious thing in the world. "We call each other that every day as a reminder."

I look at this woman, lying in this bed because of me, choosing to be my sister, even though I might be everything she stands against. Then, without another word, I turn around, pick up the handle to my suitcase, and wheel it back towards the staircase.

"What do you want for dinner?" I shout as I climb the stairs.

"Shepherd's pie," is the immediate answer. "For the Lord is my shepherd, and there is nothing I shall want."

This is laying it on a bit too thick, but I smile as I put my suitcase back in my bedroom and look at the vase of sunflowers and cream roses. Perhaps I can cut Sister Mary Bernice a vase of her own flowers before dinner.

And then I head back down the stairs, trying not to let it bother me that I could have sworn the floral arrangement was sunflowers and blue stock the last time I was in the room—not sunflowers and cream roses.

7

Biddy

The next day, Biddy gets in her car, fights the traffic and congestion around the farm, and finally drives over the bridge toward the prison housing her brother. On both sides of her car, fields with six-foot-high cornstalks wave in the wind. The stalks are a golden color and will soon grace entrances to homes and create intricate corn mazes for children. Time marches on, ready or not.

Biddy has not seen her brother, Declan, since that fateful day last year when he turned himself in to help save Megan's life. She is indebted to him in a way she doesn't know how to repay. Visiting him is a terrible idea. She should let sleeping dogs lie, just like she told Ruby and the rest of the club. The only problem is that, as Ruby pointed out, the dogs aren't really sleeping. The trouble is continuing to fester where they lie. She needs to make amends to her town, and that begins with her brother.

She pulls off the highway and into the town of Albion. Like Pooka, it is a town under financial stress, but that is where the similarities end. While the townspeople of Pooka stayed on and still maintain their gardens and homes as best they can, the citizens of Albion have fled, leaving behind crumbling factories and row houses for the vagrants who moved in. Once the hub of operations for Lucifol, a burgeoning chemical cleaning solution company, the plant closed its doors. Now, the only business in the town is the prison. And the only real residents are the guards and the recently released inmates with nowhere else to go.

Biddy drives carefully down the main road, passes some prostitutes on the street who carry none of Sheila's flare—or determination—and focuses on avoiding shards of glass from broken bottles. Sheila is lucky that she wasn't born in a place like this. This would be too much for anyone to overcome. Biddy suddenly wonders where Sheila is from. She'll have to ask. She pulls into a parking area surrounded by high fences topped with razor wire and walks to the front desk to announce that she is here to see Declan.

Twenty minutes later, she finds herself seated on a metal chair bolted to the floor. Her brother sits across the table from her. She braces herself, waiting for him to lambast her for destroying his life. For putting him here. Instead, his eyes light up.

"Biddy! You came!"

Declan wears the traditional orange prisoner jumpsuit, but the rest of him is not at all what she expected. He's put on enough weight to look healthy. His familiar squinty blue eyes are bright and shining. And his large frame is relaxed and open.

She leans in to whisper for privacy. "Are you on drugs?"

"What?" He throws his head back and laughs. "No, Biddy, I'm not on drugs. I got sleep! Uninterrupted sleep."

He leans back in. "Do you have any idea how wonderful it is not to have to run the farm? I don't worry about money, or the weather, or animals dying, or other animals eating the crops. I don't worry about demand trends, or supply trends, or international trade relations. I just wake up, someone feeds me, someone else mandates that I go outside and get fresh air, and then I go to bed. I wouldn't want to be here forever. But, boy, it sure is a nice break from things. I think this is what heaven must be like."

Biddy looks around the room filled with rusting tables and chairs and surrounded by chipping cinderblock walls with wired windows. If this is what heaven is like, she will start a garden club if she gets there, no matter what Ruby says.

"How's the farm doing?" Declan asks, his eyes still dancing.

This is exactly the question Biddy was hoping to avoid. When he was arrested, Declan gifted the family farm to his niece Maude. Biddy fears that hearing that all his hard work has turned into the equivalent of a theme park might upset him.

"It's financially sound," she hedges. This, at least, is true.

Declan laughs again. "Oh, Babs, you should see your face. I know Maude turned it into a rich people's resort. The boys from the other farms come to visit me once a week and tease me incessantly. Some even snuck onto the property to take pictures. I particularly like the giant farmer. I think he looks a little like me."

"Declan, I'm so sorry." Biddy feels like her whole adult life is a string of events that let her family down. "I didn't mean for her to make a mockery of our family farm. I should have said something to her."

"Mockery?" Declan's eyes widen. "Goodness, Biddy! She's

made more of a success of it than any of the rest of us. I say good for her."

Biddy feels like she's entered the twilight zone.

"You're not mad? Aren't your friends furious?"

"Aww." He shrugs. "They're just jealous. Whose idea was it, anyway? Maude could never have dreamed this up."

Biddy thinks of Sheila. Even Biddy has to admit that what she lacks in class, she makes up for in street smarts. But Shelia is not why she is here.

"I've come to apologize."

"For what?" Declan looks genuinely confused.

"For putting you in here. Although you seem oddly at peace with this."

"Biddy." Declan shakes his head and takes her hands. "You had nothing to do with it. I was the one who went along with that whole affair. I knew it was wrong, and I did it anyway. My actions probably harmed others. This—" He waves his arms to gesture at the room. "—Is my doing."

"No, it's my doing."

His expression is one of shock. Then annoyance. "You don't control everything, you know. God, you've been full of yourself since you were a kid."

Biddy feels blood fill her face, a sure side effect of anger in the Irish population. "I'm not full of myself. I helped put you in here. The Women's Club uncovered the crime."

"Yes, but I did the crime. My fault. Not yours."

"Well." Biddy shrugs and sits back in her chair. "I wish the rest of the town felt the same. They hate me."

"You are easy to hate." Declan smiles and then leans toward her. "Look, you need to stop looking backwards and blaming yourself for the past. Move on, Biddy. If you want forgiveness, help fix the mess that remains."

"That's what Ruby said."

"She was always the brighter of you two. Although that really isn't saying much."

"Says the man in prison to a free civilian."

"You got me there." He shrugs. "Anyway, I'm sick of thinking about the past. It's all people do in here. Tell me about the Women's Club's next crusade."

Biddy can't believe that this is it. That the apology has been issued and the forgiveness granted. That she spent so much time worrying about feelings that weren't even felt. She takes a breath and thinks of Ruby. Of moving forward.

"We are trying to help an amnesic nun who someone is trying to kill."

"Seriously?"

"Seriously."

Declan smiles. "You really know how to pick them. But look at you all, doing God's work. Even the hooker?"

"She's the new president."

"This makes me almost miss being back in Pooka."

Even Biddy has to admit it's a little funny.

Declan shifts in his seat. "In all seriousness, though, there was always something a little off at that convent."

"Declan, it's a convent." Biddy shakes her head. "What on earth are you talking about? Clearly, this has something to do with the nun's past. She just can't remember anything about it."

Declan leans in and Biddy sees that his reddish hair is regaining some of its thickness. "I'm not so sure about that. Remember the stories the kids told at Halloween? They could hear screams coming from the windows of the convent in the middle of the night. And then, the next day, there'd be wheel tracks leading to the crypt. I bet someone in the church is trying to kill her."

"You're nuts!" Biddy smacks his hand. "Are you suggesting Sister Mary Bernice is torturing the novices?"

Declan shrugs. "She sure tortured me in grade school."

"You've been in here too long."

"I'm being serious!" Declan says. "Something was going on in that convent and maybe your nun stumbled into it. This story reminds me of the factory here in Albion. Remember Lucifol? Supposedly, it's cursed. All the chemicals they produced there had cancerous side effects and then the place burned to the ground. Now, ghosts of former workers haunt the factory. No one can escape the past. I'm telling you… look at the convent."

Biddy thinks this is all silly. She doesn't believe in ghost stories. But she believes in fixing past wrongs. And she owes Declan. If this story piques his interest, then she'll indulge him. "Fine," she says. "Just for you. I'll look at the convent."

"But be careful and whatever you do, don't go there at night."

"You missed your calling writing horror movies."

"Maybe I'll give it a try. I'm certainly not going back to farming." Declan takes her hands. "It really is good to see you, Biddy. Will you visit again?"

"Until you hang up a sign on your cell forbidding girls to enter." The days when they locked each other out of their rooms at the old farmhouse seem so long ago.

"Then I'll see you soon. And don't forget to tour the crypt. I can't wait to hear what you find. This is like reading a good mystery."

"I'll find nothing. It'll be something from that nun's past."

"There's my old sister. She's never wrong until she is."

Biddy leaves the prison with a lighter heart and more ghost stories than she wanted. She climbs in her car and starts it. Ruby was right, as is usually the case for a woman who thinks with her heart instead of her head. Visiting Declan has brought her closure. As she drives down the graffiti-lined street toward the highway, her attention returns to the new case and the ghost stories the kids used to tell around a fire outside the church with the locked crypt. Her brother is just being silly, she tells herself.

8

Sheila

It's been a week since the last Women's Club meeting—the one where Sheila was elected, a nun was shot, and Biddy stormed out, threatening to drop out of the club. This meeting has to go better than that, Sheila assures herself. It'd be really hard for it to go worse.

Thankfully, when she arrives at Biddy's house, she looks through the newly paned bay window and sees all the women there, sitting in their usual chairs with Biddy bustling about as if she owns the place-which Sheila admits she does. Sheila had been a little worried that Biddy wouldn't be home, little less let them continue to meet at her house. Her presence is a step in the right direction. Now the group needs to take a few more.

She rings the doorbell, storms past Biddy when she answers—not even waiting for her to insult Sheila's black pantsuit that in Sheila's world is called a cat suit,—and stands in the middle of the living room.

"We can do better!' Sheila shouts. "There will be no more fighting. No more turning on each other. No more being chickens. We stick together and we help other people. Because that's the right thing to do. And that's who we are."

She looks at the circle of women around her. Biddy and Ruby are on the couch next to the massive stone fireplace. Amelia and Megan, who is newly arrived from Boston, sit across from them. The coffee table is overflowing with little cakes and pastries Ruby made for the meeting. Sheila quickly realizes that Ruby doesn't need to do better. She is always perfect. But the rest of them could try a little harder.

"When I joined this club," she says. "I didn't want to be here. Not because it bothers me to do volunteer work, but because I didn't believe that the people who run charity organizations are as selfless as they try to appear to be. But you were. And that's why I wanted to be president. Because I was proud to lead you. And now I'm not. How can you even consider not helping a nun in need? Because you are worried about your own popularity? What about my popularity? Do you really think hanging out with a bunch of nuns is doing much for my business? Well, it's not. But I still want to help Sister Dymphna."

Client bookings have been down 30% in just two days. Some clients are troubled that Sheila may go to confession, which she wouldn't, of course. Others are simply afraid that she— and her business—are now on God's radar. That's fair, she guesses.

"Anyway, I'm reconsidering being President. I have no intention of taking up gardening projects." Sheila sits down in the nearest folding chair with a thunk.

"You will do no such thing," Biddy says, standing up. She dusts off the leg of her black pantsuit, as if a speck of dust would ever deign to fall on it. She is wearing a scarf knotted around her neck, not too dissimilar to Sheila's. It is uncanny, Sheila thinks, that Biddy is starting to dress like her.

"While I had my doubts about you," Biddy says, looking at Sheila. "I've changed my mind. I think you are exactly what the club needs right now."

She looks like she is choking as she says this last bit, but still. This is not what Sheila expected to hear.

"I agree with you," Biddy continues. "This is who we are. We help people. Especially women in need. Anyone who thinks they can shoot a visitor in my house and get away with it has another thing coming."

She sits down and takes a small cake.

"Biddy is right," Amelia says quietly. "I was being unchristian, and there is no excuse. Of course, we'll help Sister Dymphna. It is the right thing to do. Just let me know what you need."

Sheila takes in Amelia's gaunt appearance, which barely looks capable of supporting the size of the bags under her eyes. Even the piece of spinach in her hair looks limp today. Sheila can't help but give her a pass on not wanting to add more work to her plate.

Megan shrugs. "I voted yes the first time around. Don't look at me, you heathens."

This leaves Ruby. Sheila looks at Biddy's best friend who is wearing her Jessica Fletcher Murder She Wrote sweatshirt and the woman smiles back, her eyes dancing with excitement. Shelia can't help but think this seemingly unassuming woman is the force behind Biddy's change of heart. But the who, how's, and why's don't matter. What matters is the team is back together.

Sheila smiles and stands back up. "Alrighty then. Time is

of the essence. The attacks are escalating from attempts to scare Sister Dymphna, to actually trying to kill her. We should form investigative groups. The focus will be on figuring out who Sister Dymphna is and what she did in her past to upset someone."

"Actually," Biddy looks almost bashful as she speaks up. "I think we should also investigate the church in case it is the cause of the death attempts. It has been brought to my attention that there may have been prior crimes at the convent years ago. Way before my time."

Sheila takes in Biddy's wrinkles and thinks this must be a very, very, long time ago.

"There were rumors of screams in the night and wheel tracks towards the crypt. I'm sure it's nothing, but I promised someone we'd look into it."

"Oooh, I remember those stories." Ruby clasps her hands. "As kids, we loved them. One Halloween, we hid a boom box in the bushes near the crypt with a tape of us screaming. Remember that, Biddy? Susie Dunlopy wet herself."

Biddy laughs and Sheila really wishes she could have known these two when they were younger.

"As I said, I'm sure it's nothing." Biddy recovers her typical controlled persona. "Just a ghost story kids told each other."

"I don't think it's nothing."

This, surprisingly, comes from Megan. Megan is nothing but surprises these days.

"Many historical discoveries start with embellished stories and other local folklore. While the facts become larger than reality over time, they can carry a hint of truth regarding the origin. I'd love to look into this."

Okay Professor, Sheila thinks. It sounds like a real dead

end to her and she wants nothing to do with it. But if Megan wants to close out this line of inquiry, then have at it.

"Can I join you?" Amelia says to Megan.

"Don't you have enough going on with your jobs and the kids?" Sheila asks. "We don't mind if you step back a little from this investigation because of extenuating circumstances." The others nod in support.

"No," Amelia says. "I want to take part. This is important to me. I'll make the time."

"Okay then." Sheila is a little worried that the time will come from her sleep, but also believes in letting women make their own decisions. "You and Megan will head up the investigation of the convent and its history."

"That means," Sheila says, looking at Ruby and Biddy, "we will look into Sister Dymphna and her past."

"Where do we start?" Ruby asks. "She could be from anywhere."

"We start by searching her room," Sheila says. "No one can just walk away from their past scot free. It's been my experience that everyone holds on to a piece. In fact, when I took her home from the hospital, I saw she had a $1000 pair of boots in her closet."

Amelia's eyes flutter open. "Someone makes $1000 boots?"

"Were they real?" Biddy asks. "You can't trust anything these days."

For no apparent reason, Biddy eyes Sheila's Pheragamo purple stilettos, ph intended.

Ruby frowns. "We can't just search her room. That's an invasion of her privacy."

Sheila shrugs. "Not really." She's thought this through. "I'm sure the order owns the convent. Since Sister Mary Bernice is the Mother Superior, she can legally grant access to any part of it."

It almost scares Sheila how much she has learned about search laws over the last decade, but she's glad to see it finally come in handy.

"It's a good idea," Biddy says. "Speaking of the past, does Sister Dymphna still look familiar to you?"

"She does." Sheila has wracked her brain and, for the life of her, she can't remember where she might have seen the woman.

"Could she be from your own past?" Biddy asks.

"Oh, no." Sheila laughs. "There's no way." Sheila prefers not to think about her childhood, but Sister Dymphna oozes wealth and privilege. That was not her childhood experience.

"Where are you from anyway?" Biddy asks.

Sheila doesn't like where this discussion is going. This is supposed to be about Sister Dymphna, not herself.

"Albion," she says cautiously.

Biddy's face relaxes into a new expression. Pity. And Sheila hates it.

"As I said," Sheila repeats firmly, "she wouldn't have crossed paths with me in my past."

"Probably not," Biddy agrees. "But it's always best to leave no stone unturned. So, why don't you and Ruby search her room and let us know what you find? I'll see if I can find an overlap with your life."

Sheila does not enjoy having her life under a microscope, especially when Biddy is holding it. However, Biddy can dig all she wants. Although Sheila prefers not to think about the past, she has nothing to hide. And if it will put Biddy's questions to rest about Sister Dymphna somehow knowing her in Albion, then let her have it.

"Fine," Sheila says. "We all have our marching orders. Meeting—"

"Wait!" Biddy jumps up and does something unexpected. She reaches into her handbag, which is resting against the skirt of the couch, and pulls out a hammer. No, Sheila realizes, it's not a hammer. It's her gavel. Her precious gavel. She hands it to Sheila. "What with the gunfire and all the shattered glass last week, I didn't have the chance to follow the proper formalities of passing the gavel to the newly elected leader. May your presidency be filled with many successes!"

Sheila smiles and takes it as everyone claps. Megan even takes their picture. She is touched. She knows how much Biddy likes her gavel. This must be what it feels like to have a mentor. She flips it around in her hands to get used to its heft and then bangs it against the coffee table. Biddy flinches and Megan cringes. Next time she'll have to remember to use the coaster, Sheila realizes.

"Meeting adjourned."

9

Megan

"Cousin!" Maude shrieks. "You're home!"

Megan lets Maude into the kitchen through her mother's side door, smiling at the relative she somehow acquired last year. Her mother had insisted on hosting a family welcome home dinner on her first night back in Pooka. Now that it is here, Megan admits it's a great idea. The kitchen smells of sherry beef—her favorite. The scratched, yellowed cabinets are inviting rather than worn in the dancing candlelight. The beamed ceiling is ancient, the table scarred, and every inch already feels happier than anything she remembers in Boston.

Maude thrusts a bottle of Corny Acres Sparkling Apple Wine into her hands. Megan pours three glasses without flinching at the label, which feels like personal growth. She hands one to Maude and one to her mother, who is stirring the stew like she's conducting an orchestra.

They clink.

Megan braces herself for a sad syrupy excuse of a wine, but her taste buds tingle. "This is… actually good."

"It better be," Maude says. "I wanted to mix apple juice with cheap wine and slap our label on it. Sheila insisted on using a real winery. Cost a fortune."

Thank God for Sheila, Megan thinks. She might even take a bottle back to Boston. "How much?"

"Eighty dollars."

Never mind.

A second shriek cuts through the kitchen, this one not from Maude.

Maude gasps. Megan jumps. She grabs a frying pan.

"What is that?" Megan shouts.

"The goat," her mother says calmly.

The sound comes again—part hyena, part existential crisis.

"Is it dying?" Megan lowers the pan.

"No. It's aggravated." Her mother tastes the stew. "It wants dinner."

She sets the spoon down and heads to the refrigerator, where she pulls out a salad. She dresses it and heads for the door.

"You're feeding it a salad?" Megan asks. "With vinaigrette?"

"I like quiet," her mother replies. "And this achieves that goal. Oh—I almost forgot the bread roll." She pauses and reaches across the counter to pick one up. "I'm coming, Charles," she shouts to the goat.

Megan freezes. "You named it after Dad?"

Maude peers through the curtain. "He's adorable."

"Thank you, Maude." She turns to face Megan. "And yes, I named him after your father. He has a tendency to follow me around demanding things. It seemed à propos."

She opens up the door, and the goat wags its little stump of a tail like he's a dog. Biddy pats the goat, sets the salad down, and comes back inside.

"This is insanity," Megan says. "You're going to get rabies."

"Only if he hurts me. On that note, he's better than your father. He hasn't. Dinner's ready!"

Megan wants to push this issue. It is rude…disrespectful… to name an irritating goat after her father. But she doesn't want to start a fight. Not in front of Maude. She takes a breath and pushes it out of her mind.

They sit. Candlelight flickers. And Megan has to appreciate that her mother can make anything look elegant. Maude looks… less so. She's dressed head to toe in rhinestones and logos—a look that Megan would deprecatingly describe as new money. But the plate beneath Megan's meal stops her judgment short—white, faint green glaze, delicate hand-painted scrolls shaped like looping b's.

"I designed it for your mother," Maude says proudly.

"It's beautiful," Megan says. And it is. This is the thing about family. Just when you are confident they are all nuts, they prove themselves to be savants.

Conversation turns…as it always seems to when you don't want it to…to jobs. The farm and pottery, which are making hundreds of thousands of dollars annually. Megan's new teaching job, which is not.

Maude frowns "You should have Sheila look at your resume. She's a genius."

Megan's face burns. Sheila is a hooker, not a genius. Megan is the genius. Megan is the one with a doctorate.

"Sheila already does enough," Biddy says quickly. "I'm surprised she still has her other job, what with helping you make the farm and pottery such a success."

"Oh I don't pay her," Maude says cheerfully. "She volunteers."

Biddy nearly drops her fork.

Then Maude offers Megan a job butter-churning at the farm and Megan is sure she is slowly dying a little more each day and drains her wine.

"Speaking of Sheila," Biddy says, entirely too casually, "did you know she's from Albion?"

Megan narrows her eyes. "Mom."

"She told me," Maude says. "Her dad ran out on them when the factory shut down. Her mom got sick. Sheila supported them."

Megan looks down at her plate. She suddenly feels terrible. And not for herself.

"She was the smartest kid in her high school," Maude adds. "Dropped out to help her mom. Almost had a scholarship to Princeton."

Megan swallows and looks at her mother.

"Which is why," Megan says carefully, making a mental note to be less judgmental, "you should not poke around in Sheila's past. She deserves privacy."

Biddy sighs. "I'm asking because of the case."

"Of course you are."

"I am," her mother protests. "Sheila thinks she recognizes Sister Dymphna. I'm trying to figure out from where."

Megan doesn't believe this is the drive of her mother's curiosity one little bit, but she finishes the last of her sherry beef and pushes back her chair to go get seconds. "I don't think this case has anything to do with Sheila or Sister Dymphna. I think it's someone in the church who's out to get her."

"No way." Biddy waves her hand as if she can erase the suggestion. "You're wasting your time. Those are silly ghost stories."

"Stories have to come from somewhere." Megan turns to Maude. "Since you are a book of knowledge these days, are there any rumors about Sacred Heart of the Woods?"

"Oh yes," Maude says eagerly. "There's a vampire cult draining nuns' blood and hiding the bodies in the crypt."

Biddy laughs.

The goat shrieks.

Maude smiles.

"Ha ha," Megan says. "Laugh all you want, but I'm going to prove you wrong."

Biddy heads to the fridge. "It's time for Charles' dessert."

Megan sets her refilled plate back on the table, sits down, and takes a long sip of apple wine. Her family has completely lost it. And yet, she somehow is happiest here.

Now, she just has to figure out what has started all those rumors about the church and its crypt. Despite what her mother says, she is confident something is hidden there. Mothers aren't right about everything.

10

Sheila

Early the next morning, Sheila and Ruby let themselves into the convent. It feels odd to be sneaking around a convent, but with Sister Mary Bernice on bed rest and Sister Dymphna out on an errand, this seems the perfect time to snoop around. Sheila had asked Sister Mary Bernice for permission to search the rooms yesterday. That was the important part, she tells herself. Now, it's just trespassing with consent.

The old brick convent sighs around them as they step inside. The walls—once white, now a sort of exhausted gray—bear the weight of a hundred years of restraint. Dark wood trim lines the hallway, unsoftened by art, plants, or joy of any kind.

It is the least festive place Sheila has ever been, and that includes a rather unfortunate motel on the highway. But ambiance isn't the point. This search is her first official act as president, and she intends to do it properly.

"You look like you belong here," Ruby whispers, nodding approvingly at Sheila's ankle-length black pleated skirt.

Sheila laughs. "You don't need to whisper. We have permission to be here. And you are probably the first and last person who would ever tell me I fit in at a convent."

Still, she's glad that Ruby noticed the effort she is putting into her new role. She'd bought the skirt specifically for today. She doesn't want to offend her new clients. Sheila learned long ago that if you dressed the part, people relax. That said, it truly is a shame to hide her legs.

She gestures toward the stairs. "Sister Mary Bernice said Sister Dymphna's room is on the second floor."

The stairs threaten to buckle as they climb and Sheila can't help but wonder why any young, attractive woman would be drawn to this lifestyle. Sheila has done her research. The number of nuns in the US has fallen over 75% in the last sixty years. So what drove Sister Dymphna to this profession? Was she running to God, as she claims? Or was she running away from something else?

When they reach the second floor, Sheila pushes open a door on the right, revealing a bedroom as spare as the rest of the house, but somehow warmer. Sunlight spills through a street-facing window. A small desk sits beneath it. On the bedside table, a vase of sunflowers and cream roses tries valiantly to cheer the place up.

"There isn't much to search," Ruby says, scanning the room. "There's barely anything in here."

Sheila's heart plummets, and she feels a flicker of panic. Failing at your first presidential task is not ideal for inspiring confidence. Still, it doesn't take much to squirrel something away. You just have to know where to look.

"We'll split the search," she says. "You take the desk. I'll take the bed and nightstand."

Ruby carefully opens a desk drawer.

Sheila flips the mattress onto the floor.

Ruby gasps. Her face fills with horror at the mess Sheila made.

"What?" Sheila frowns at her. "I'm investigating."

Ruby cringes but doesn't push back, so Sheila returns her attention to the mattress and checks the seams. People never hide important things in obvious places like desks. They use cracks, folds, forgotten corners. Banks are for amateurs. Sheila trusts mattresses.

Ruby flinches with every tear to the mattress but finishes emptying the desk. "Nothing." she announces. "Just pens, blank paper, and a rosary."

The mattress, too, seems like a dead end, devoid of anything but stuffing. Sheila shakes the sheets, drops them to the floor, and checks between the mattress springs.

"Sheila!" Ruby can't help herself any longer. "We're trying to help her, not traumatize her further."

"I am helping her. A bed can be put back together. Another bullet wound...not so much." Sheila finds nothing and concedes the bed.

Ruby rushes over to fix the linens while Sheila opens the closet. Rows of black habits hang neatly inside. At their feet sits a suitcase.

She opens it.

Inside is a pair of jeans and a plain white T-shirt. Simple enough, she thinks, until she checks the labels.

"Oh," Sheila murmurs.

"What?"

Sheila turns the suitcase so Ruby can see. "These are designer."

Ruby blinks. "Like Levi's?"

"Like Versace."

"Do those cost more than Levi's?"

"A little more." Sheila thinks back to the Vanity Fair she read while getting her curls set. "About three thousand dollars."

"Three thousand dollars?" Ruby's eyes widen. "People pay three thousand dollars for jeans? Have they not heard of Farm and Fleet?"

Judging by the suitcase, Sheila is pretty sure that Farm and Fleet was not on the radar of Sister Dymphna. What she wonders is how the nun heard of Pooka. These clothes speak to a wealth beyond even Biddy's sizable financial portfolio. What would draw someone like that to this farming town? Who was this nun before she arrived here and why did she come here?

"I'll take the nightstand next," Sheila says. "You check the bathroom."

Ruby wanders off. "Do you ever think," she calls, "that maybe she's just a normal person and someone randomly decided to attack her?"

"No."

Sheila opens the drawer and freezes.

Three leather-bound journals sit neatly stacked inside.

Now they are getting somewhere.

Ruby returns holding a toothbrush, toothpaste, deodorant, and a bottle of Lucifol cleaner. "This is all I found."

Sheila flinches. Lucifol. She can't see the stuff without cringing.

"Put that back," she says. "Let's hope these journals are more helpful."

She opens the top one and frowns. It's in Latin. Why can't anything be easy?

"Can you read Latin?" she asks Ruby.

Ruby giggles. "Only the pig version."

Sheila closes the book. "Next time, I'm bringing Megan."

"She probably knows Latin," Ruby agrees.

"Probably," Sheila says. "But I know someone else who definitely reads the language. And that is Sister Mary Bernice." She gathers the journals and heads downstairs, Ruby following behind. Sheila pauses at the closed door to Sister Mary Bernice's room, bracing herself. Nuns have a way of looking straight through you—like they know exactly what you've done and are quietly disappointed. She hates to be judged. But she will not let this woman's opinions interfere with doing what is right for this case.

She knocks. As she waits for a response, she becomes acutely aware that her ankles itch furiously with all the fabric rubbing against them. The things she does for her new role.

"Come in."

Sister Mary Bernice lays propped against her pillows, reading.

Not the Bible.

It's *Murder, She Wrote.*

Ruby beams. "That's my favorite book!"

Sheila sits and tries not to pull at the scratchy skirt.

"How goes your search?" the nun asks.

"Sister Dymphna has minimal belongings," Sheila says. "Extremely expensive clothes. And these." She hands over the journals.

"How expensive?"

"About three thousand dollars."

"My goodness." Sister Mary Bernice lifts her eyebrows delicately—like a religious version of Biddy Bramley.

"A complete waste of good money if you ask me," Sheila

says. "But the journals are likely more important. Can you translate them for us? Sister Dymphna wrote them in Latin."

Sister Mary Bernice hesitates.

This is the problem with women who have morals.

"I don't usually read another sister's private thoughts."

"Well," Sheila says with as much patience as she can muster, "I'd assume that you also don't usually have someone trying to kill those other sisters."

Sister Mary Bernice sighs. "Fair point."

She opens the first journal and begins reading. Slowly at first. Then faster. Eventually she skims, moving from one journal to the next. Ruby drifts to the window. Sheila forces herself to sit still.

At last, the nun closes the final book and rests her hand on the stack.

"Well?" Sheila asks.

"She takes her faith seriously," Sister Mary Bernice says proudly. "Exceptionally so."

"That's lovely," Sheila says. "Anything else?"

"She also has an excellent business mind," the nun adds, glancing at Sheila. "Much like you."

Sheila doesn't know whether to feel flattered or alarmed to be compared to a nun. Either way, she makes a mental note to tell Biddy that Sister Mary Bernice made the comparison. It will probably annoy her. "And her past?"

Sister Mary Bernice's face falls. "Just one cryptic thing."

"Which is…"

"She says she feels guilt. That she senses she did something terribly wrong and needs to make amends."

Sheila sits up. "Does she say why?"

"She can't remember. She just knows she needs to serve

penance."

Sheila groans. Finding the answer in a journal would have been too easy. "Where is she, anyway?"

"I sent her to the pharmacy," Sister Mary Bernice says. "So you'd have time to search."

Ruby stiffens at the window. "That's weird."

Sheila looks up. "Why?"

"Because she's sneaking down the church basement stairs. She seems to be looking around to make sure no one notices."

"Why would she do that?" Sister Mary Bernice says. "The crypt is locked. No one has a key except for me. She knows that."

So why, Sheila wonders, would a nun have any desire to go to a locked crypt? Even more importantly…didn't Megan say that she and Amelia were investigating the crypt today? How could they do that without a key? Sheila suddenly wonders if she's the only person in the club who bothered to ask for permission for her investigation. How the state of Indiana considers her the criminal and none of the rest of its residents is beyond her.

11

Megan

Megan pulls into the church's gravel lot, with Amelia in her passenger seat. She sees Sheila's car already parked there. No matter what you have to say about Sheila, she certainly has a strong work ethic.

Sacred Heart of the Woods rises ahead of Megan in white-washed simplicity, its tall steeple stabbing the blue sky. Stained-glass panes glitter like a cascade of gemstones, catching the morning sun and throwing ribbons of color across the grass. She has spent hours on these grounds in the past year—walking the rows of gravestones, revisiting Eileen's towering marker, feeling strangely steadied by the hush of the place. But today she isn't here to wander. Today, she is going below.

The religious history of Sacred Heart of the Woods runs deep. She spent half the night scrolling through online archives, nursing the last few sips of Maude's surprisingly good apple wine, as she read about the Irish families who hauled their lives into these woods.

The accounts were fragments—diary entries in shaky ink, parish bulletins digitized crookedly, letters from homesick fathers sent back to County Clare. But the story was always the same: a dozen immigrants carving a chapel into the forest, raising it with bare hands and borrowed faith. They brought cracked statues wrapped in burlap, a wooden crucifix that had crossed the Atlantic in a grain crate, and a fierce need to anchor themselves to something familiar.

Over the decades the little church expanded—timber replaced by stone, a steeple added, stained-glass windows commissioned by parish families whose names still dot Pooka's mailboxes. Weddings and baptisms filled its aisles; midnight masses lit its windows like lanterns on the hill.

And then, as the town modernized, came the stories.

Footsteps in the empty choir loft.

Candles that flared to life without a spark.

Irish hymns sung by no human voice.

People whispered that the first parishioners had stayed behind—guarding the church, refusing to surrender the old ways even as Pooka paved and modernized around them.

Megan doesn't believe in hauntings. But she does believe in history that refuses to stay buried. And as she closed her laptop near 2 a.m., she felt a prickling at the back of her neck—anticipation.

She is getting close to something.

"Have you heard the stories about the crypt?" Megan asks Amelia, as they head towards the church.

Amelia brushes a smear of green mush—shaped unmistakably like a toddler's handprint—from her shirt. "The haunted crypt stories? Sure. But doesn't every town have stories like that?"

"Every town has stories like that because they all have a history. Every myth has a fuse. Something lit it."

Amelia shakes her head. "Sometimes stories are just stories. Maybe the priests and nuns were using them to scare kids into better behavior."

This would be terribly disappointing. It's not that Megan is looking for disaster—not exactly. Just something interesting to research and write about.

They reach the narrow concrete stairs leading to a heavy door beneath the church. Moss creeps along its edges, giving the doorway a damp, forgotten look. Megan looks at the lock. It's the oversized type that looks more like it belongs in a Gothic novel than an Indiana church. She pulls out the lock pick set she borrowed from her mother.

Amelia stares at it. "Didn't you get the key from Sister Mary Bernice?"

"She wasn't able to give it to me."

This is the diplomatic way of saying that Sister Mary Bernice refused to give her the key. The elderly nun had said that the crypt always remained locked and therefore, it held no secrets regarding Sister Dymphna. Megan views this differently. She is a firm believer that if someone locks a door, everyone else wants to get inside. There has to be a reason for a door to have a lock. And, thanks to her mother, she has also learned never to let a lock stand between her and what she wants. She inserts the picks like her mother showed her and the mechanism turns with a groan. Megan steps back, pretty proud of herself. The door opens—slowly, grudgingly. A gust of cold rolls out, smelling of mildew, stone, and time. She stares into the black opening.

If priests and nuns did all of this to scare children into righteousness, Megan has to hand it to them. They really threw their backs into it. She takes a step inside, Amelia following. Darkness presses close and it takes Megan's eyes a minute to adjust. Eventually, she makes out shadows and sees that the basement floor plan mirrors the church above. But here rows of squat windows sit high in the walls, each covered by thick black bars that barely allow in any light.

"Bars?" Megan whispers.

"Oh, those went up fifty years ago," Amelia murmurs, peering at them. "Too many teenagers breaking in, hoping to see ghosts."

Amelia finds a switch by running her hands across the damp stone. When she flicks it, a row of low-watt candelabra bulbs sputter awake. Their dim glow barely reaches the corners, where shadows clung stubbornly. The tiled floor is coated in a film of dust so thick it feels like carpet. Columns line both sides, and between each column rests a raised stone crypt—the tops carved with names, dates, and crosses dulled by time.

"This is absolutely fantastic," Megan whispers.

"This is absolutely creepy," Amelia says. "I'm surprised you are so into ghost stories. You usually are so rooted in reality."

"There is nothing more rooted in reality than dead bodies. I just think there are real historic implications by studying them."

"Uh huh." Amelia does not sound like she believes Megan. And if Megan were to be honest, she always loved a good horror movie and there really isn't anything historically accurate about those.

Amelia drifts toward a crypt, brushing dust from its platform. *"Father Tom Flaherty,"* she reads. *"Founder of the Sacred Heart of the Woods School. He taught not only the mind but the heart.* That's a sweet inscription."

Megan walks to another and brushes its inscription clean.

"*Father Bernard Michael Kelleher. Pastor of Sacred Heart of the Woods Parish. A Devoted Servant of God and His People.* That's rather bland."

Amelia reads the next one while Megan's flashlight sweeps the room—and catches on something in the far corner.

A crypt cleaner than the rest.

Suspiciously clean.

Her pulse quickens.

She crosses the room slowly so as not to trip on anything in the dark. This tomb does not need to be dusted. The inscription on the polished stone reads: *Herein lies Father Jedidiah Brown, a committed believer in forgiveness and healing.*

"Jedidiah means 'beloved by God,'" Amelia says softly behind her, making Megan jump and drop the lock pick set.

"Jeez. Make a little noise when you move."

Megan bends down to retrieve the picks, but as she does so, she thinks she sees something. A scrap of paper peeks out from beneath the platform supporting the tomb. Just a corner of it.

She crouches and pulls it free.

"A photo," she murmurs.

It's a family portrait: two blond girls in matching navy coats, their parents posed stiffly behind them. In the background, a large factory looms, its brick façade weathered, its sign faded to nearly nothing. Megan can barely read the remnants of the letters on it—an L, a C, and what might be an O.

She flips the photo over.

The McKellan Girls, 1994.

Before she can further study the photo, footsteps sound on the stairs—rapid, echoing.

Sister Dymphna appears. The nun's expression tightens the

moment she sees the photograph in Megan's hand.

"Sister Dymphna," Megan says, "What are you doing down here?"

More footsteps sound on the stairs and Sheila and Ruby join them, looking a little out of breath. And a little ridiculous. Sheila is wearing an uncharacteristically long skirt. She looks like an Amish hooker.

"We were wondering the same thing," Sheila says. "What are you doing down here, Sister Dymphna?"

Sister Dymphna glances between them. "I thought I saw the door ajar and came to investigate."

"That's odd," Sheila says. "The door looked closed to me."

The nun shrugs, still staring at the photo in Megan's hand. Sheila's eyes follow her line of sight.

"What did you find?" Sheila asks Megan, hurrying towards her—only to catch her toe on something metal embedded in the floor.

"Darn it—ow!" She grabs onto Ruby to steady herself.

Megan moves towards them, checking that Sheila is okay and then bends to see what tripped her. A hinged metal ring juts from the floor. She runs her fingers along its edges, noting the hairline seam around the surrounding tiles.

She lifts the ring.

It resists at first.

Then flips vertically.

Beneath it is a tiny keyhole.

One far too small for the massive key that would be needed to enter the crypt.

"How odd," she whispers.

Sheila, still rubbing her foot, reaches for the photo. "Forget the ring. I want to see the photo."

She pulls the photo from Megan's hand and squints at it in the dim light. "I recognize that place! The factory is Lucifol, in Albion. And these are the McKellans. They owned it." She frowns. "Why is this down here?"

"I don't know," Megan said. "It's far too recent to explain the ghost stories. And the crypt was locked when we arrived. Sister Mary Bernice said she doesn't allow anyone down here."

She glances toward Sister Dymphna.

The nun stands frozen, eyes wide, fingers trembling at her sides.

"Sister?" Megan asks gently. "Are you all right? Do you recognize the photo?"

The nun swallows, her gaze darting toward the barred windows, the crypts, the hidden seam in the floor.

"I… I don't know," she whispers. "I can't remember. But this place—this room—feels familiar."

"Have you been here before?"

"I don't know, but I can't imagine how. As you said, it is locked."

"Then who could have dropped this photo?" Sheila asks.

"Someone else who has their own key," Amelia says.

"Or someone who doesn't need one," Ruby adds. "Megan got in here. If she can manage it, who says someone else can't?"

Megan ignores the barb and crouches once more to study the ring embedded in the floor. She tugs on it again, harder this time. The ring doesn't budge.

"There's definitely something under here," she says, her breath catching with effort. "A hatch. Or a trapdoor. Do you think it could be a passage to someplace else?"

Sheila steps over cautiously.

"Why would a church need a secret room or passage under

a crypt?" Sheila asks.

"Storage?" Amelia guesses.

"Smuggling?" Ruby offers, tone far too hopeful.

"Bodies?" Megan whispers.

"There was a story..." Sister Dymphna murmurs.

Four heads snap toward her.

"What story?" Megan asks.

Sister Dymphna hesitates. "It's silly, but I heard it when I took my first vows. Some of the older sisters from surrounding parishes told me there were rumors of a second burial chamber. Not officially part of the church records. A place Father Brown—Jedidiah Brown—maintained. Privately."

Megan feels her pulse quicken. "A private chamber? For what?"

"For his treasures."

Megan's fingers tighten on the cold ring embedded in the floor. "Did anyone find out what it was?".

"No." Sister Dymphna stares at the ring. "Or if they did, they didn't speak of it."

A sudden clang reverberates from somewhere deep in the church above them—like a metal door slamming shut.

Everyone jumps.

"Please tell me that was just the wind," Ruby says.

"There is no wind down here," Amelia whispers.

Megan waits, heart pounding in her throat, listening for footsteps or movement.

"It's probably Sister Mary Bernice. I knew she wouldn't stay on bedrest for long. We should leave," Sister Dymphna says, voice cracking on the final word.

"But—" Megan begins.

"Now," the nun repeats, firmer this time, already moving

toward the stairs. "She has made it clear that we are not allowed down here."

Sheila doesn't argue. Ruby practically sprints. Amelia keeps glancing over her shoulder.

Megan lingers only one second longer—long enough to sweep her flashlight across the crypts, the bars on the windows, the faint dust disturbed around Father Brown's pristine stone, and the hatch hiding beneath centuries-old tiles.

She can't shake the feeling she is close to a major discovery.

She tucks the McKellan photo into her pocket and follows the others up the stairs.

For someone who thinks she's never been down here before, Sister Dymphna seems to have a rather strong reaction to the space. It's as if something happened here and the memory is fighting its way back.

12

Biddy

True to her word, Biddy stands outside the penitentiary, her second visit with Declan finished. Despite his cheerful optimism, the place still has a way of sitting heavily in her chest with its claustrophobic concrete walls, razor wire lined borders, and the faint metallic smell that seems to cling to everything. She hasn't yet decided whether the guilt gnawing at her is easing or merely learning to behave itself.

But visiting is the least she can do. Rebuilding her broken relationship with her brother is a gift, no matter where it happens. And the two haven't been this close since they were in their teens. At least he was pleased to hear of Megan's mysterious discoveries in the crypt of Sacred Heart of the Woods. He always loved being right.

Beyond the chain-link fence and the cracked asphalt of the parking lot sits the town of Albion. Biddy studies it and thinks of Sheila. Life is full of mysteries and how a young girl could have suffered so many cruelties here and turned into a confident, optimistic woman with an apartment in Pooka is a testament to her—even if the way she achieved this life isn't the safest or most moral. Her path can't help but leave Biddy wanting to learn more. Biddy had not planned on stopping in Albion. She has dinner to make, a daughter to feed, and a goat who has mistaken endurance for an invitation. She is a woman with responsibilities. And yet, she lingers.

Her gaze settles on the factory dominating the center of town, sprawling across so many blocks it appears to have swallowed Albion whole. Its once-red brick is now blackened and pocked, as though the building itself has been diseased. Entire sections have collapsed inward. Lucifol.

During Biddy's childhood, Lucifol had been a triumph, the frame that supported the town. People spoke of the McKellans with a mix of admiration and envy. The papers had dubbed them the Rockefellers of Indiana. Biddy had thought little about them after she left Pooka and moved to Boston, but she just assumed their story ended happily. Success tends to encourage that assumption.

Apparently, it had not.

She checks her watch and notices the library still standing a block away. She has just enough time for a quick browse. She hurriedly climbs into her car, drives out of the prison lot, and pulls it into one of the many vacant spots in front of the library. The drive took less than two minutes. She has more than enough time for a visit. She steps out, hoping her car will still be there when she returns.

The Albion Library rises above the street as though it still believes knowledge matters, even if no one else in the vicinity does. Twenty stone steps lift it out of the present and into a more dignified past. Indiana limestone, a pillared turret, and flanking wings are a monument to a time when no expense was spared and no ambition too large. Biddy has never understood how people allow places like this to be forgotten. The steps are completely devoid of foot traffic despite its open and welcoming doors. She climbs these steps and passes through its doors.

Inside, the air is cool and hushed, exactly as a library should be. A long marble desk stands within the vaulted entrance where a gentleman about her age informs her that the Lucifol factory burned down in 2004. He directs her to a computer containing Albion Ledger editions to learn more.

She takes in the room while the screen loads. Four patrons are asleep at tables, coats pulled close, heads down. The rest of the tables sit empty. Not even students grace libraries these days, since they have computers. Biddy frowns. Benjamin Franklin would be livid.

Her screen fills with information, and she returns her attention to her computer to read.

At first, it is all familiar: fireworks sponsored by Lucifol. Christmas tree lightings also thanks to Lucifol. Births. Deaths. Honor rolls. The rhythm of a small town convinced its future was secure. And then she notices it.

Sheila's name. Again. And again.

By 2001, Maude's story proves correct. Sheila wins a scholarship sponsored by the McKellans and this allows her entrance and funding to an elite private school. The photograph above the article gives her pause. It shows a little girl with sausage curls in a dress too large instead of too skimpy, gripping her certificate like proof that the future looks bright. Beside her stands Edward McKellan, smiling. In the background, two adults look on with unmistakable pride. Sheila's parents.

Biddy feels something shift. She never imagined Sheila's

childhood in any detail. And she certainly had not imagined this.

She flips through the remaining articles. Sheila thrives. Honor roll after honor roll. Winner of the spelling bee. Champion of a math competition. And then comes 2003. The fireworks are canceled. Layoffs are rumored. By Christmas, Lucifol is shedding jobs. Sheila is still on the honor roll, but the school has changed. Now she's back in the public school. Biddy wonders if the McKellans revoked the scholarship.

Biddy's fingers pause above the mouse. She isn't sure if she wants to keep reading. She knows the ending to this story, and it isn't happy. But then she forces herself to click on the link to the January 24, 2004 edition.

The Lucifol factory burns to the ground in the early morning hours. Edward and Constance McKellan die in the fire. Their daughters—Willa and Nina—become orphans. Three days later, police name their primary suspect in the arson.

Biddy stares at the name.

No.

She blinks and looks again, hoping it is just her blurred vision. But it isn't.

The photograph of the suspect is a face she has already seen, smiling proudly behind his daughter.

Carl Ryan.

Sheila's father.

"Well," Biddy says quietly, sliding her chair back. She looks away. Megan was right. This has been a mistake. An unforgivable one. Some doors should remain closed and some information private, even from a woman with excellent intentions. She promises herself she won't mention this knowledge to Sheila—or anyone else.

And yet. She still needs to see how this story unfolds.

She returns her hands to the keyboard.

Carl Ryan runs before he can be arrested. He just disappears. Sheila's mother appears on the prayer list and never leaves it. Cancer. A disease the community says her family deserves. Sheila's name vanishes from the honor roll entirely. Biddy is pretty sure this is because Sheila vanishes from school entirely as well. As Maude said, she quit to provide for her mother. And Biddy knows what job allowed that to happen.

Willa and Nina McKellan inherit a sizable insurance payout, which is just enough to survive the lawsuits that follow. Toxic chemicals have done their damage to employees. They sue. The company goes bankrupt. The factory is never rebuilt.

Biddy exhales slowly.

She searches for the McKellan daughters. Nina left the state, and it looks like she never came back. Willa remains in the family home.

Biddy writes the address down before she can reconsider, packs up her notes, thanks the man at the desk, and returns to her car.

Her drive takes her beyond town limits, through browning fields, to a wooded neighborhood on the edge of a pristine blue lake. She passes between a pair of rusted gates that no longer pretend to offer security. Oaks arch overhead, dappling the sunlight. Houses sit on wooded lots, elegant and empty, their dark windows watching her pass. This neighborhood clearly once housed people who had money. Past tense.

And then there's Willa's house. It stands apart from the others simply because someone still lives in it. It is a beautiful Victorian that has life. Roses and hydrangeas spill over a manicured lawn. A pale blue Chrysler gleams in the driveway.

The lake beyond reflects the late afternoon light. Everything about the place suggests careful preservation.

And even though it is beautiful, it also suggests something else. Loss held too tightly. This is somehow more creepy and sad than the vacancies surrounding it.

Biddy catches the movement of a curtain in an upper window. A watcher. Or perhaps just the wind.

This is quite enough. She snaps her head to bring herself back to her senses. She turns her car around and heads home to Megan, to dinner, and to a goat who has no sense of boundaries. But the unease follows her all the way back to Pooka.

13

Sister Dymphna

I wake up screaming again, my pajamas soaked in sweat, my heart hammering against my ribs. Beside my bed sits this week's arrangement of white chrysanthemums and snapdragons and I stare at it to calm myself. The dreams are the same, only sharper now. Fire. Always fire. The smell of burning chemicals, acrid and choking. Screaming—sometimes my voice, sometimes others. And money. Stacks of it, curling and blackening as it burns.

But when I try to grasp the details, they slip away like the smoke.

I sit up in bed, pressing the heels of my palms into my eyes until I see stars. I used to want to remember who I was. Now I'm becoming more and more confident that I don't want this answer. Did I cause this fire? Are the screams of people I killed? Or am I a victim?

The convent is silent, wrapped in the deep quiet of predawn. Pale light brushes the tops of the oak trees outside my window. Soon, Sister Mary Bernice will wake. Soon, prayers and breakfast and the careful pretense of normalcy will begin.

But nothing feels normal anymore. Not even the *new* normal I was just accepting.

The fragments of memory are getting stronger. Yesterday, while helping Sister Mary Bernice with the church books, the smell of old leather sent a jolt through me. Smoke on my tongue. Sirens in the distance. My hands shook so badly I dropped the ledger, papers scattering.

"Are you alright, Sister?" she asked.

"Of course," I say.

She didn't believe me. One of these days, she's going to send me straight to confession for lying.

I stand and move to the mirror. The woman staring back at me looks hollowed out—dark circles, pallid skin. She looks haunted.

She looks guilty.

What did I do?

The question follows me everywhere now. People don't attempt to kill nuns without a reason. There has to be something in my past—something unforgivable enough to justify it.

My thoughts drift, unbidden, to the crypt. They have been doing that more often lately. I don't remember the first time I noticed it, only that now, whenever I pass the church, my steps are slow. My gaze drifts toward the heavy door beneath the ground level. Toward the cool darkness below. It isn't fear that draws me there—it's something gentler. Familiar. Like standing outside a locked room I once lived in. I hate it feels comforting. Seriously, what is wrong with me? I somehow love crypts?

I shake the thought away and dress in my habit, clinging to routine. But even this betrays me. As I put on my sweater and reach into the pocket, my fingers brush cold metal.

Two keys—one large and one small, both on the same ring.

I'd found them in my jeans pocket when I'd packed my things to leave and had forgotten I'd moved the keyring to my sweater pocket, hoping to discover what they opened. I pull it out slowly. It's old-fashioned and heavy. Ornate teeth are now worn smooth from use. I'd assumed it was from my past life, just like my jeans. But, after yesterday, I know better. I know clearly where their locks are. The crypt.

I shove the keyring back into my pocket as though it might burn me. And this is the worst thing I've learned about myself recently. I am the type of person who wants to hide things from others so that this new life of mine doesn't go away. When I find something off-putting…like writing on a wall that claims I'm a murderer or keys to a crypt I'm not supposed to have…I hide it. I may not know with certainty that I was a bad person before, but I can say with certainty that I am a bad person now.

The only problem is that the rest of the world seems set on discovering this. The Women's Club has been visiting regularly since the shooting. Ruby brings food and chatter. Amelia asks careful questions. Megan studies my amnesia like an academic exercise.

But it's Sheila who unsettles me the most. There's something about her that feels dangerously close to recognition. She watches me with sharp, assessing eyes, and yet when we talk, I feel oddly safe with her.

Yesterday, she'd said yet again, "You really remind me of someone."

The chill had been immediate.

"Have you ever been to Albion?" she asked.

The name slammed into me—red brick, smokestacks, machinery humming—and then vanished, leaving dread behind.

Now, in the quiet morning, I wonder what Sheila suspects. And what I'm hiding.

I force myself to push all this unpleasantness from my thoughts. I am a novitiate and I have things to do. I go downstairs to check on Sister Mary Bernice. I knock lightly on her door and enter when she tells me to. She's already awake, rosary in hand. She is looking better. Her foot is still in a big boot, but her color has returned and her eyes dance with renewed energy.

"Bad dreams?" she asks, studying me.

While she is looking better, apparently I must not be.

"The same ones," I say, not wanting to lie. "Fire."

"Perhaps your mind is protecting you," she says gently.

I can only pray it keeps doing so.

She presses her lips together, and her eyes convey sympathy. "Maybe you should cut back our gardens today? The fresh air might do you good."

This sounds like a little slice of heaven and I smile gratefully.

A knock at the door of the convent interrupts us.

Sister Mary Bernice frowns and checks the clock on her bedside table. It reads 6 am. "Who on earth could that be at this hour?"

I don't know. But I do know, instinctively, that whatever waits on the other side of that door has to do with me. Why can't the world just leave me alone?

The knock comes again, harder this time.

"Well, you best go answer it," she says, pulling herself up taller. "Whoever it is, seems like they have something to say to us."

I have no choice but to do so. I head down the hallway and pull open the door. Sheila stands on the other side, and I can't help but stare. If I thought her black skirt from the other day made her look ridiculous, today I am treated to a real sight. The real Sheila Ryan. And it is something to behold. She is in a skimpy red garment that looks more like a sausage casing than a dress and has paired this with matching sky-high, sparkly red heels. Her hair is in a blonde hair sprayed poof that would do Dolly proud. And over her shoulder is a bag, bulging at the seams. Anyone looking like this before the sun is fully up is a testament to a night fully lived. She doesn't bother with a greeting. Instead, she pushes past me and heads towards Sister Mary Bernice's room.

"We need to talk," she calls over her shoulder. "Now."

She pushes open Sister Mary Bernice's door and heads in. I follow.

"Sheila?" Sister Mary Bernice looks confused as she takes in Sheila's clothing, and I pray that she somehow remains confused. "Did you go to a costume party last night?"

"Someone broke into the church last night," Sheila says, smartly not answering the previous question. "I just checked the video feed before heading home after work."

The words hit like cold water. "What do you mean, checked the video feed?"

"You went to work dressed like that?" Sister Mary Bernice asks.

Again, Sheila ignores Sister Mary Bernice's question. She turns to me. "I installed security cameras after the shooting. Frankly, I do it at all my jobs for safety. I didn't tell anyone because I didn't want to panic you."

She's been watching me? That somehow panics me.

Her mouth tightens as she watches my face. "Oh, get over it. There's no such thing as personal privacy these days. Anyway, the person was inside the church for twenty-three minutes. They went straight to the crypt."

My knees go weak. "What did they do down there?"

Oddly, I notice Sister Mary Bernice looks equally nervous about the answer. Is she worried I am guilty of something as well and is trying to protect me?

"I don't know. I didn't have time to put cameras down there."

Both Sister Mary Bernice and I let out a breath.

"Did you call the police?" I ask.

"They're on their way."

As if summoned by the words, red and blue lights flash faintly through the front windows. The sound of tires crunching gravel follows, then comes the clap of car doors slamming shut.

My stomach drops. This is a convent. It's supposed to be safe. It isn't supposed to be like this.

"I suppose I must give them the key to the crypt," Sister Mary Bernice says. She looks like she's dreading it. Sister Mary Bernice is committed to preserving holy spaces.

"There's no need," Sheila says. "Whoever broke in destroyed the lock. The door is wide open."

"I'll go supervise," I say. I wish I were doing this because I, too, wanted to protect the sanctity of the space. But I'm really doing it to see what they find.

Sister Mary Bernice throws the covers from her body. "I'm coming too."

Sheila and I try to prevent her from standing up, but once Sister Mary Bernice sets her mind on something, there is no changing it. She winces a little every time she steps on her bad foot, but she makes it to the door to the crypt.

The officers are thorough. They dust the crypt door for prints. Photograph the damage to the lock. Measure footprints in the dirt below the steps. One of them—a woman with sharp eyes and a calm voice—asks me to recount the night of the shooting again. Another asks Sister Mary Bernice about keys.

"How many exist?" he asks.

Sister Mary Bernice hesitates. "Two. One kept in the rectory safe. One… misplaced years ago."

My fingers curl in my pocket. Why can't I bring myself to tell Sister Mary Bernice about my key? And how do I even have it?

The officers eventually leave, promising patrols and follow-up. The convent feels different after they're gone—exposed. Desecrated.

Sheila doesn't wait.

She turns, and I brace myself for another round of questioning. But this time, she doesn't face me. She looks at Sister Mary Bernice, who stands leaning against the door to the crypt, peering down into the space.

"Sister Mary Bernice," Sheila says. "I think it's time you told me the truth."

Sister Mary Bernice stiffens, but the odd thing is that she doesn't meet Sheila's eyes. "About what?"

"About the crypt," Sheila says. "And about why someone would break into it. About all the stories. What happened down there? The myths predate Sister Dymphna and I think you know how these stories started."

Silence stretches.

"I saw the look on your face when the police headed down

there," Sheila presses. "You didn't want them there. Why?"

"That's not true," she says too quickly. Now, even I look at her with curiosity. I'd noticed her dread as well. I just assumed she was trying to protect me.

Sheila steps closer. "Why is it always locked? Why are there bars on the windows? And why did someone break into it? Does it have something to do with this?"

She pulls the faded photograph from her coat and holds it up.

I feel the familiarity immediately—the shift in the air, like pressure dropping before a storm. The factory. The family standing in front of it.

"I have never seen that before in my life," Sister Mary Bernice says firmly. I believe her.

Sheila's voice softens, but only slightly. "You do. You just don't want to tell me why."

"That's enough," I say. I may not remember things, but I can feel this has to do with me. Not with Sister Mary Bernice. Not with whatever secrets that crypt holds and that Sister Mary Bernice is keeping.

Sister Mary Bernice looks at me gratefully. For the first time, I feel like she really is my sister. We are in this together.

"No," Sheila says. "That's not enough. Someone broke into a church last night. Someone is trying to hurt Sister Dymphna. You both need to be honest with me. You are hiding things."

I swallow hard.

Sister Mary Bernice shakes her head. "We aren't hiding anything."

She takes the padlock the police gave her and fastens it firmly on the door to the crypt. Seconds later, I hear faint voices…female…coming from behind the door. Sister Mary

Bernice's eyes flick to me and then back to Sheila. Neither of us say anything.

"Do you hear voices coming from inside?" Sheila asks.

Sister Mary Bernice shakes her head. "Don't be silly. The police just searched the whole place. It's empty. It must just be the wind."

The thing is, I heard them too. Women's voices. But I say nothing. I follow Sister Mary Bernice's lead.

Sheila looks from one of us to the other.

"There were voices," Sheila says. "I don't know how and I don't know from where, but there were voices. That's it. I'm moving in with you. I clearly can't trust either of you on your own and I will not have you ruin my presidency by getting yourselves killed."

She turns and tries to stalk back towards the convent, but her sparkly red heels pierce the earth with each step, causing her to yank one foot free of the earth with such force that the other sinks in its stead. Her body, brightly clad in the second skin of red, wobbles back and forth with the effort.

"You have no idea how bad this is going to be for my business," she shouts back at us.

And somehow, despite this ridiculous sight and the notion of Sheila living in a convent, I feel better.

14

Sheila

Sheila stands at her bedroom window in the convent, watching Sister Dymphna cross the grassy field toward the school. The nun gets smaller and smaller until she disappears through the building's heavy wooden door. Now Sheila can rest easy. Teachers and children will surround sister Dymphna until 3:10 when school dismisses. She is safe.

Still Sheila lingers, staring out the window. It's become a habit, this watching. This need to ensure Sister Dymphna's safety. Sheila has been living at the convent for a week now, and this surveillance is part of her routine. Along with helping the church and convent run. Sister Mary Bernice insisted that if she is to live here, she must take part in the rituals and upkeep of their community. Thus, Sheila has learned more about faith and church operations than anyone would have ever imagined.

She is just about to step away from the window when a movement catches her eye. A woman appears on the gravel path leading past the cemetery toward the church. She is older, perhaps in her seventies, with long gray hair that flows loose down her back. Her gait is confident, the stride of someone who knows where she's going. This shouldn't be unusual. Many older women stop at Sacred Heart of the Woods to pray, especially on Wednesday mornings at the children's mass. They like to see the kids.

But something about this woman looks furtive. The woman glances over her shoulder before entering the church, as if to make sure no one is watching. Her hand hesitates on the door handle before pushing it open. It just seems…off. Then again, maybe Sheila has become hypervigilant since someone broke into the church.

Whatever the reason, Sheila hurries down the stairs and out of the convent, her unusually sensible shoes falling easily over the uneven ground. She approaches the church, trying to look casual. She has done a great job disguising herself as a nun. To the woman in the church, she will be just another sister going about her morning devotions.

She eases open the heavy oak door, careful not to let it boom closed—a sound that echoes through the sanctuary like thunder when one isn't careful. She knows this from being late to early morning prayers after a particularly long and profitable night of work. Sister Mary Bernice had not been pleased. Sister Dymphna had found the reason for her tardiness funny.

The scent of incense and old wood envelops her as she slips inside the church door. The building appears empty. Morning light streams through the stained glass windows, painting colored patterns on the stone floor. The altar stands serene and waiting, the tabernacle light flickering its eternal flame. But the woman is nowhere to be seen.

Sheila frowns. She knows she had seen the woman walking

towards the church. Where else could she have gone? Then she hears it—footsteps echoing up the stairs. Was she in the crypt?

The woman emerges from a narrow doorway at the back of the sanctuary. She carries a silver tray of half eaten food—bread, cheese, what looks like cold meats. For a moment, Sheila relaxes slightly. She wasn't in the crypt. She was in the kitchen. Perhaps they serve hors d'oeuvres at the children's mass. Sheila wouldn't know. This is her first school mass today.

But then the woman sets the tray on a side table and moves to the cabinet behind the altar. She produces a key—and this makes Sheila's breath catch, because Sister Mary Bernice was very clear that only she, Sister Dymphna, and Father Doyle have keys to the church and its various spaces. In fact, Sister Mary Bernice refuses to give Sheila keys, and Sheila is practically an honorary nun. Yet, somehow, this woman has a set.

The woman unlocks the cabinet with practiced ease, as if she's done this many times before. The cabinet contains wine, which Sheila now knows priests use in small quantities during the mass. The woman takes out one bottle and sets it deliberately on the altar. Sister Mary Bernice would not be pleased. She had been pretty clear that children's masses did not include wine. Then—and this makes Sheila's heart race—she leaves the cabinet unlocked. Wide open, with all the remaining bottles visible and accessible. Any minute now, 187 first through eighth graders will file into this church for their weekly service. And see the alcohol for the taking.

But the strangest thing is yet to come. The woman reaches into her pocket and pulls out a rosary. Sheila recognizes it immediately with its distinctive blue beads and tarnished silver crucifix. It's Sister Dymphna's rosary.

Just this morning at breakfast, Sister Dymphna was lamenting the loss of it. It had been a gift from Sister Mary Bernice when she became a novitiate. Sister Mary Bernice rolled her eyes and suggested that Sister Dymphna really should see Dr. Enniskillin about her memory. Sister Dymphna was indignant. She insisted that she'd left it on her nightstand, right next to her vase of marigolds. She was certain of it.

The woman places the rosary on the altar next to the wine and arranges it as if it had fallen there accidentally.

Children's voices suddenly erupt outside—high and excited, filled with the barely contained energy of young boys.

The older woman moves swiftly, more swiftly than her age would suggest. She glides toward the opposite side door. In seconds, she's gone, leaving only the echo of the door closing softly in her wake.

The other side door bursts open and three small altar servers tumble in, their black cassocks billowing. The smallest one, a redhead with more freckles than face, spots the wine immediately.

"Wine!" he shrieks with an enthusiasm usually reserved for Christmas morning. "There's wine!"

All three boys take off for the altar.

Sister Dymphna bustles in after the boys, already mid-scold about proper behavior in God's house, when she stops short. Her eyes go wide, darting between the open cabinet with enough wine for a rather healthy party, and the rosary.

"Boys, don't touch—" She grabs the wine bottle from the redhead's greedy hands and hurries to shove it in the cabinet.

"Look, Sister," the redhead says now picking up the cross, "I found your lost rosary!"

Sister Dymphna snatches it from his hands.

Sheila steps out from the shadows.

"I didn't leave this here," Sister Dymphna says when she sees her holding up the rosary. "I'm positive I didn't leave this here. And I locked the wine cabinet after mass. I always do."

"I know. There was a woman," Sheila says urgently. "She set you up. Did you see her leave?"

Sister Dymphna shakes her head, still staring at her rosary as if she can't imagine how it got here.

This is unfortunate. Sheila was hoping Sister Dymphna might have recognized the woman. Sheila moves quickly toward the side door. "Watch the children. Lock that wine cabinet. I'll be back."

She pushes through the door and stares at the parking lot. The space is empty except for the usual detritus—a few fallen leaves, a forgotten soccer ball. The woman has vanished. How is this possible?

Sheila hurries around the corner of the church to see if anyone is in front of the building. She nearly collides with Sister Mary Bernice, who's hobbling along in her medical boot.

"Have you seen an older woman?" Sheila asks breathlessly. "Long gray hair, about seventy, wearing a dark coat?"

Sister Mary Bernice frowns, thinking. "No, I don't know anyone like that. Why? What's wrong?"

"She was in the church. Possibly even in the crypt. She had keys."

Sister Mary Bernice's frown deepens. "That's impossible. Only myself, Sister Dymphna, and Father Doyle have keys. The church is locked tight."

"Do you serve snacks during mass?"

"Of course not!" Sister Mary Bernice looks appalled. "If anything, the children should fast before receiving communion."

"Then why was this woman carrying a tray overloaded with half-eaten food?"

Sister Mary Bernice shrugs, but her eyes dart away from Sheila's. "It was probably a volunteer in our kitchen. You probably scared her, running after her like that."

"Then where was she taking the food?"

"Maybe she just needed food for herself."

"It was a lot of food and she left it behind. Plus, I don't think she was in the kitchen with it. I think she was in the crypt."

"I promise you she wasn't in the crypt." Sister Mary Bernice heads down the side steps to the crypt. She grasps the handle of the door and pulls. It doesn't budge.

"It's locked," she announces, tugging harder, as if the door might change its mind. "You watched me put the padlock on it. It's locked tight, as always."

Sheila just stares at her. She doesn't know how, but something is going on in that crypt. And she knows just who to call to find out what it is.

15

Megan

When Sheila had called and asked Megan to meet her at the church, Megan didn't think the reason was that Sheila was now living in the convent…and apparently dressing the part. Megan eyes her co-Women's Club member, sitting on the church steps clad in a voluminous black habit that makes her look like a Victorian mourner.

"I wanted to fit in like Sister Mary Bernice requested," Sheila says, standing up from the stoop. "And I don't want to hear a word about it. Not one word."

This, Megan thinks, will be a challenge. "So if not to celebrate the new you, why did you ask me to come here?"

"There is something hidden in this crypt."

Megan doesn't even try to hide her glee. "I knew it!"

Sheila frowns. "Don't go getting too excited. I don't think it's ghosts. I think Sister Dymphna hid something down there before she got amnesia. I also think that Sister Mary Bernice knows something about the comings and goings down there. They are both in on it."

Megan doesn't really care what Sheila thinks, she just wants to get another look. Especially at the ring on the floor.

Sheila stands up and leads Megan around the side of the church. Megan tries really hard not to advise her to fold her hands while she walks.

Sheila looks back at her. "Hey, why is your mother suddenly being so nice to me?"

Megan shrugs. She doesn't want to get involved in this, but, in her experience, it is those times when her mother is seemingly at her nicest that she is up to her worst meddling.

Sheila frowns. "It's like she thinks she can fix me. But I don't need fixing."

Megan rests her case. She looks at the woman in front of her, trying her best to look like a nun, yet sparkly red five-inch stilettos peek out from the bottom of her skirt, and she can't help but think Sheila needs a little fixing. Yet, Megan also has to admit that Sheila has done a fine job running the Women's Club.

"Let's just focus on the case," Megan says as they come to a stop in front of the door at the bottom of the steps. She does not want to be involved in whatever her mother is doing with Sheila.

"Fine with me." Sheila pulls out a tiny key. "I took this when I tucked Sister Mary Bernice back in bed."

For the first time, Megan notices that the door to the crypt is now being held shut with a shiny new padlock. It looks like the original locking mechanism broke. Sheila slides the key into the padlock and turns it with a satisfying click. The door swings open easily.

The room is less dank and musty than Megan remembers. She runs her hands along the cold stone wall and flicks on the light switch. Above their heads, black wrought-iron chandeliers flicker to life, throwing orange light across the space. Megan sees many footprints covering the floor. Sheila tells her of the break-in and resulting police search.

Sheila eyes the space thoughtfully. "I'm going to study that tomb where you found the picture. I'm telling you, Sister Dymphna knows something about that."

Megan nods, but her eyes move to the floor. To the spot where Sheila had tripped the other day. "I'm going to start there."

Sheila shrugs, likely thinking her fascination with a tiled floor is unhelpful, but Megan doesn't care. If she finds what she thinks she'll find, she can explain all the mysterious voices.

They work in companionable silence for several minutes. Megan kneels on the cold stone floor, running her fingers along the edges of the tiles around the metal ring. The grout seems different here—not as deep, perhaps disturbed at some point. The ring itself is tarnished with age, but when she tugs on it experimentally, it doesn't budge.

"Megan," Sheila's voice cuts through the quiet, and there's something strange in her tone. "Come look at this."

Megan glances up to see Sheila bent over Father Jedidiah Brown's tomb, her fingers tracing something on the stone surface.

"What is it?"

"Scratches. Deep ones, like someone tried to pry the top off this thing." Sheila's voice echoes in the stone room. "Look at these marks around the edges. Someone was definitely trying to get inside. And not very talented. Really…to leave behind telltale signs like that…not professional."

Megan rises and walks over, leaving the mysterious ring for the moment. Sure enough, there are clear gouge marks in the stone around the tomb's lid, as if someone had used crowbars or other tools to attempt to lift it.

"Why would someone want to get into a priest's tomb?" Megan asks.

Sheila shrugs. "What were you looking at over there?"

They return to the spot where Megan had been kneeling. The metal ring sits flush with the floor, surrounded by tiles that don't quite match the rest of the crypt's flooring.

"I think this is a trapdoor," Megan admits. "The ring is obviously meant to be pulled, but it won't move. And look—" She points to the grout lines. "This tile is newly grouted. The craftsmanship is different."

Sheila kneels beside her and examines the ring more closely. "There's a keyhole," she says, pointing to a tiny opening barely visible in the tarnished metal. "It's a lock."

A lock without a key. Megan pushes back onto her heels. "I'll go see if Sister Mary Bernice has the key."

"No need. She doesn't seem very helpful these days." Sheila reaches into her voluminous black gown and produces a small leather case. A lock-picking case. Megan can't help but think her mother and Sheila are more similar than her mother wants to admit.

Megan watches hopefully as Sheila selects two thin metal tools from her case and inserts them into the tiny keyhole. The silence in the crypt is oppressive, broken only by the soft scraping of metal against metal as Sheila works.

"This is an old lock," Sheila murmurs, her ear close to the mechanism. "Simple but sturdy. Whoever installed this wanted to keep people out, but they didn't expect anyone with my particular skill set."

Megan knows she should put a stop to this. And yet she

says nothing.

After several tense minutes, there's a soft click.

"Got it," Sheila says with satisfaction.

Megan grasps the ring and pulls. This time, it gives way. The stone is heavy, much heavier than she expected, and it takes both of them working together to lift the trapdoor, Sheila tottering in her stilettos.

When they finally prop it open, they're both breathing hard. Shelia fans herself with her habit, allowing Megan a view of much more leg than she wants to see. Megan peers into the opening and sees stone steps disappearing into complete darkness.

"Well," she says, her voice barely above a whisper. "That's not what I was expecting."

"Seriously?" Sheila stares at her, still fanning herself. "What were you expecting? A room filled with jewels? The Holy Grail? Harrison Ford waiting for you with open arms?"

"Don't be ridiculous!" Although she wouldn't be disappointed to find Harrison Ford down there. "I don't know. A storage compartment maybe? Not… this."

The air rising from below is stale and carries a smell that makes Megan's stomach turn. It's not just mustiness—there's something else, something organic and wrong.

"Do you have a flashlight?" Megan asks.

Sheila produces one from another hidden pocket. "Always prepared."

Megan thinks Shelia had better watch out. That habit is proving to be useful. Megan takes the flashlight and shines it down the stairs. The beam doesn't penetrate very far into the darkness below.

"Stay here," she says to Shelia. "Who knows how sturdy

these stairs are? If something happens to me, at least you can get help."

"Alright," Shelia says.

Megan pauses. It was not the response she'd expected. She had been hoping Sheila would insist on accompanying her, but now she is stuck. She looks back down the black hole and then takes her first step. The stairs are narrow and steep and the air grows thicker with each step. The smell gets stronger. Megan has to breathe through her mouth to keep from gagging. Something is wrong. She's been on archeological digs and the smell isn't like this.

"The walls are just dirt," she says, reaching out to touch the earthen sides. "The same people who made the crypt did not build this. Those walls are all stone."

However, the earthen walls swallow the sound of her voice. She hopes Shelia can hear her.

When she reaches the bottom, Megan sweeps the flashlight beam around the small underground chamber. It's cramped and roughly hewn, clearly much older and more primitive than the elaborate crypt above.

And it's not empty.

"Oh God," Megan breathes.

Skeletons line the walls, some still wearing the remnants of what look like dresses and skirts. Their bones are yellowed with age. But it's the way they're positioned that makes Megan's blood run cold—many of them have their mouths open as if they died screaming.

Megan can't move. She's transfixed by the horrific scene before her. These are women. Young women. And there's a fresh carrot lying on the floor.

She screams.

"Megan," Shelia's voice barely pierces this dirt enclosed tomb. "Did you scream?"

Megan turns toward the sound of Sheila's voice and scrambles back up the stairs, desperate to escape the horror below. When she reaches the top of the stairs, her hands are shaking so badly she can barely grip the stone to hoist herself out.

"Bodies. Lots of bodies. We have to call the police," she says.

Shelia's eyes are wide.

Megan shakes her head, trying to clear the image. "I think I counted fourteen. All women."

16

Biddy

Biddy stands in her kitchen and hangs up the phone, ending her call with Amelia. She's feels a little bad having asked her to do additional research when the woman is clearly exhausted from her job and the children. She also wonders how Amelia's marriage is standing up to this financial stress. Nevertheless, Amelia came through just like Biddy knew she would. Mothers are nothing if not superheroes. Biddy looks down at the goat, munching on the salad Biddy has placed at her feet.

"It's Amelia who bends over backwards to help others, and it's you I feed. I'm thinking there is something still very wrong with my loyalties."

Charles doesn't appear bothered by this statement. He looks at her while chewing his lettuce and then turns his attention back to the bowl when he finishes with the mouthful. He has pooped all over the house, chewed at the corner of the carpeting, and his demanding shriek is impossible to ignore around meal times. Yet every time Biddy hears him at her door, she opens it. She wonders if all goats are this obnoxious or only this one. She also wonders why a golden retriever puppy couldn't have followed her home instead.

"Well," she says to Charles, "I best head out to pick up Ruby. Some of us have responsibilities during our days, you know."

Charles screams his dissatisfaction as Biddy picks up his salad bowl and moves him.. and it…outside. She sets the bowl down on the top step of the stoop. "You should try to find something useful to do with yourself while I'm gone. At least trim the grass around the house like you were supposed to do when the town brought all of you here."

She slams the door behind them and locks it, then she heads to her car, leaving the goat to finish his salad by the door. Most likely, when he's done eating, he will run off to have a fling with a girl goat, just like her husband had done. No good deed goes unpunished.

* * *

The drive to Albion with Ruby is both smooth and heartbreaking. Since Biddy is not going to the penitentiary today, the GPS takes her a different route. This one passes through farmland turned wild, with ruined mansions scattered amongst the fields. In its heyday, Albion was the wealthier, more sophisticated sister to Pooka. However, that also means Albion had farther to fall. The mansion-style homes are so large no one wants them. They are difficult to afford and maintain. Weeds coat these crumbling brick buildings that only thirty years ago had been gleaming in their magnificence.

"It almost makes you glad you were never that wealthy," Ruby says. "It makes losing it all that much worse."

Biddy thinks of her old mansion in Boston, now under

contract to be sold. "Sometimes. But sometimes it might be like having a heavy weight removed from your neck."

She drives on until she finds the narrow road that pierces rusting gates and swirls up a hill. The lake to their left sparkles in the clear fall sun. As she drives past the deserted mansions lining the road, she hopes those owners found a new life that brings them joy, just like she has. Clearly, Willa McKellan refuses to make that necessary transition. Biddy pulls in front of her house and slows to a stop.

"Remember," she says to Ruby, "We want to learn if the McKellans have a connection to Pooka and why Amelia found a picture of Willa and her family in the church crypt." She pauses. "And while we're here, maybe we can also learn a little more about Shelia and her family."

"Biddy," Ruby's eyes widen. "That is not why we are here. Our focus is on the photo, not Shelia. Shelia's childhood is not any of our business."

"Shelia doesn't have any family left. It's up to us to care," Biddy says. "And how can we care if we don't understand?"

Ruby groans. "I don't think that is what caring looks like."

Biddy shrugs. "Well, it's how I care."

Ruby shakes her head but opens her car door. Biddy knows she is lucky to have a friend as loyal as her. Even when she disagrees, she'll go along with Biddy. The two climb out of the car and head toward the front door of the Victorian house.

The grounds surrounding the massive mansion are even more impressive close up. Trained roses scale trellises without spilling over their intended marks and nary a weed mars a flower bed. Biddy thinks she should include the name of Willa's landscaper in her list of questions.

She rings the doorbell and a curtain flicks at the window to their left. After another minute, the door opens revealing a young woman dressed more for a day on Martha's Vineyard than a moment alone in a vacant house. She is young—in her thirties, like Sheila—and attractively built with a lean physique and bright blonde hair. In fact, she seems to remind Biddy of Sister Dymphna. Her eyes sparkle blue as she focuses on them.

"Yes?"

Biddy smiles brightly at the young woman.

"My name is Biddy Bramley, and this is Ruby McGibbon. We are members of the Pooka Women's Club and want to sponsor an exhibition of your family and the founding of Lucifol. You've done so much for this region and we want to preserve your legacy." This, Biddy had decided, is the best excuse for questioning the woman. Anyone who holds on this tightly to the past would want it celebrated.

Sure enough, the woman's eyes sparkle even brighter and the door tips open wider.

"I recognize your name!" she says to Biddy. "I saw your episode in 60 Minutes! Oh my goodness, Biddy Bramley is on my doorstep!"

Biddy tries really hard not to be flattered. Still, she hopes Ruby recounts this conversation at the next club meeting so the others can appreciate her fame. She steps into the home with a grin. Ruby shakes her head at the lie but follows.

"What you did for your sister and her pottery is so impressive," Willa continues. "Do you think you can get our story on TV as well?"

"We can certainly try," Biddy says. Ruby appears to struggle to keep her mouth shut. The poor thing was never gifted at fibbing. The truth is, Leslie Stahl probably doesn't even remember Biddy's name.

Willa leads them deeper into the house, and Biddy can't help but marvel at the decor. The walls in the foyer feature hand-painted murals of landscapes in muted colors. The furnishings shine in walnut and speak to frequent polishings and historic roots. In front of them, a white staircase with mahogany railings ascends to the second floor, warmed by a honey-colored seagrass wallpaper on the walls. And beyond that, wide doorways reveal wallpapered rooms in soothing floral patterns.

Willa stops in front of one of these rooms and gestures for the women to enter. "Can I get you anything to drink?"

"I'd love an iced tea," Biddy says.

"Just water," Ruby replies.

Willa leaves, and the two women look at each other.

"I think she's rich," Ruby says.

"She definitely seems to have landed on her feet," Biddy agrees.

She studies the room's smoky pale blue papered walls with painted floral vines creeping up them. She's pretty sure the paper is de Gournay. The theme continues across off the paper and onto the edges of the ceiling, the additional design presumably added by an artist. She walks over to the pair of cream couches in the center of the room and sits on one. Ruby sits beside her.

"Here you go," Willa walks back into the room carrying a silver and mahogany tray with their drinks. She hands the drinks to each of the women and settles into the couch across from them. "So what made you decide to turn your attention to my family's business?"

Ruby's perpetually open face turns to Willa. "Well, we found a pic—"

Biddy lands a kick against Ruby's shin, the pleasant smile on her face never wavering. "We were looking through old pictures and apparently you and your sister went to school with one of our club members."

Now, Ruby kicks her. Biddy's smile doesn't flounder.

"Really?" Willa sips her iced tea. "Who was that?"

"Oh," Biddy waves away Sheila's identity. She does not want to go there yet. "The daughter of someone who worked for your family. Anyway, we thought we'd learn more to see if Lucifol fits for our next sponsorship. The club likes to champion strong local businesses."

"Oh, I think it'd be very fitting." Willa scoots to the edge of the couch to lean into them. "Lucifol was a landmark institution for Albion. We employed about 95% of the town and funded the library, school, and parks. The town grew from a farming community to a small city with a cultural and shopping hub because of our business."

"That kind of success can also lead to enemies," Biddy says. "Did you have anyone who wanted to harm your family or its business?"

"What an odd question," Willa frowns.

"Well, if you remember our Aisling Pottery investigation—" Biddy says.

"Oh." Willa relaxes again. "Of course, you'd be wary of that after finding a killer in your last investigation. To answer your question, my family didn't have many enemies. It's nothing like that." Willa settles back into her seat. "Most of our employees and the town were very grateful to us."

Really? Biddy thinks. This woman clearly lives in a different realm of reality. "What about the lawsuits?"

Willa shrugs this off. "There are always those few employees who complain about having to work so hard and that the factory didn't meet their aesthetics. Some people are just ungrateful. And then, of course, there was the man who set fire to the factory and killed my parents. Carl Ryan." Willa grimaces and sets her iced tea down on a coaster with a thunk.

"Carl Ryan," Ruby says. "Why, he has the same last name as—"

Biddy kicks Ruby again, who looks at her in confusion.

"—as a bunch of people in our town," Biddy says.

Willa shrugs. "It is a common name. I wouldn't read too much into it. He disappeared after the fire and hasn't been seen since. I'm sure he fled the country. Even if your town has relatives, we can't blame them for his actions."

Biddy's heart warms a little to the woman. That was fair of her. Plus, the woman has good decorating taste. "So tell me about the fire itself. What exactly happened?"

"It was devastating." Tears well in Willa's eyes. "The entire factory burned to the ground in the early morning hours. My parents were working late—they often did that. They'd tuck my sister and I into bed for the night and then go back to the office. Anyway, they were trapped in the administrative wing when it collapsed." Willa's voice catches slightly. "Carl had been laid off the week before and witnesses saw him near the factory that night. The police found evidence he'd been drinking and making threats about my family."

"That must have been terrible for both you and his family," Biddy says carefully. "Didn't he have a daughter?"

"Sheila. "

Ruby jumps but says nothing.

"Poor thing," Willa continues. "She was so bright, always

at the top of her class with my sister Nina. We'd given her a scholarship to private school. But after what her father did…" Willa shakes her head. "No one in town would have anything to do with her. She had to leave school, lost all her friends. I heard she had to find a job because her mother couldn't cope."

Biddy feels a chill run through her. A brilliant young woman, suddenly cut off from everything she'd known, blamed for her father's crimes, with no money, no support system, and a sick mother. How hard must it have been to turn to her current career path?

"Tell me about your life after the fire," Biddy continues.

Willa exhales. "It changed drastically. My sister, Nina, and I moved to live with some cousins in Pennsylvania. My father's lawyer managed a bunch of absolutely ridiculous lawsuits against the business, and the business closed because of the settlements. In truth, we should have done much better, but Nina and I were too young to be picking lawyers. When we graduated college, Nina moved to the west coast to start a tech company, and I came back here."

"That must be very lonely," Ruby says kindly.

Willa shrugs. "It is. Our old friends have moved away and want nothing to do with us after all the lies told in the court cases. But I refuse to let our family's legacy die."

This, Biddy knows, is the truth. Biddy likes to know who she is dealing with, and Amelia had been very helpful in that department. Amelia had done thorough research on the McKellans. Willa had been a social climber in college, likely trying to marry back into her rank and way of life. It hadn't worked. While photos show her on the arm of many a handsome and moneyed beau, no proposals ever came her way and no club ever accepted her membership. Her family name was not something others wanted to associate with their own. She got engaged once, but tabloid attention ended it.

"Tell me about your sister and her company," Biddy says. "Is it connected to Lucifol?"

Tears spill down Willa's face. "Do you ever feel like your family is just cursed?"

This is not the answer Biddy expected. She frowns in confusion.

Ruby shakes her head vigorously. "Mine is the best. My dad said we were the luckiest family in the world."

Willa frowns. "Well, mine is definitely not. Nina founded this amazing tech company. Within three years, she had it up for sale and made herself a multi-millionaire many times over. I was an advisor, and we were going to use the funds to repurchase Lucifol and rebuild our family legacy. We were going to put things right here. But then—" Willa pauses and looks at a photo above the fireplace.

Biddy follows her gaze and freezes. It's just as she thought. The photograph shows two young women in their twenties, arms around each other, smiling at the camera. One is clearly Willa, but the other…

The other is unmistakably Sister Dymphna. Older than in the childhood photo from the crypt, but the same face, the same eyes. Nina McKellan.

"—then she disappeared the night the deal closed. No one has seen or heard from her since."

Biddy struggles to keep her expression neutral. "How? Did something cause it?"

"There was an accident." Willa looks back at them. "A car accident with a minivan holding a family. A mother and child died."

"In Albion?" Biddy asks. Biddy would have heard of an accident like this. This would have been all over the news.

"No," Willa shakes her head. "In LA."

Biddy flinches. Then how was Nina found here?

"That must have been terrible," Ruby says.

Thankfully, Biddy realizes, Ruby doesn't seem to have recognized that Nina is Sister Dymphna.

"It was," Willa says. "It brought our family's name back into the spotlight, this time in LA. Nina is not a bad person and I promise you she didn't mean to harm anyone. She just had her own devils. And when she made it in Silicon Valley, it opened a door she shouldn't have walked through. Wild parties, alcohol…"

Willa's voice trails off, leaving Biddy and Ruby to fill in the rest of it. It is hard to reconcile the quiet nun hiding in Pooka with the party girl portrait being painted by Willa, but Biddy believes her. Something terrible is clearly haunting the woman they know as Sister Dymphna.

"Going back to the fire," Biddy says, "you mentioned your dad fired Carl Ryan. Why was your father doing layoffs? Your factory's business seemed to boom?"

"Oh, it was booming," Willa says quickly. She clearly wants to dispel any whiff of failure. "But my father said some employees weren't meeting standards. Carl had been drinking on the job, missing shifts. My dad gave him several warnings, but…"

Something about this doesn't sit right with Biddy. Sheila said her parents had worked in that factory for decades. Why would he suddenly become a terrible employee? And one of many to be fired? Of course, it benefits the company to fire someone for a cause, rather than downsizing. It means the company doesn't have to pay for a severance package.

"Do you think the injured family from Nina's accident could hold a grudge against your sister? Have you ever felt threatened by them?" Biddy asks.

"Oh no," Willa waves her hand as if to erase the thought. "I paid for all the burial expenses of the mother and child who died and offered to cover the other children's tuition and living expenses so that their father can stay home and care for them. I'm positive they aren't the cause of Nina's disappearance. They are very grateful for how I handled it."

This, then, takes him out of the running as threatening Nina's life.

"So what happened to all the money from the sale of Nina's business?"

Willa looks at Biddy as if she has brought up something distasteful. "I don't see how this relates to my family's Lucifol legacy. If you're looking for tabloid fodder—"

"No, no," Biddy says quickly. "I was just wondering if your sister had time to give you the money to rebuild the Albion factory. I apologize for the poorly phrased question."

Willa relaxes again. "Oh, I see. Sorry—I can be a little sensitive since so many people have said so many terrible things. The money went missing with Nina." She waves her hand around the room. "I was a partner in the business. I ran the operations. So I have a bit of money I earned over the years and that's helped rejuvenate the house, but it's not near enough to rebuild the factory and town. I'm afraid I lost our chance of redeeming our legacy with Nina. I'm hoping your story will at least paint us in a better, more fair light. And help me find my sister."

Biddy is becoming more and more sure that Willa is not a

suspect. She clearly wants to return to the best years of her childhood, and Nina's absence has only made that goal a more distant dream. And from the photos scattered around the house, Biddy can see they were close.

"Who else stood to make money off the sale of Nina's business?"

"What?" Willa tenses again and then relaxes. "Oh, I see. You think someone harmed Nina. Do you know you are the first people who even considered she may have been a victim and not the villain? You are just as morally sound as 60 Minutes made you out to be."

Biddy nods. She only wished the rest of Pooka understood this.

"Nina had two other partners. One was Tom Hettersmith. I actually like him. He's this nerdy guy Nina met in college. I think he had a little crush on her and was a good influence. The second was Brad Overlin—he was head of sales and marketing. That guy was laser-focused on making money. There was nothing he wouldn't give up to make a sale. He's rather distasteful," she says while wrinkling her nose. "But highly effective."

There, Biddy thinks, is the next place to dig. But the revelation about Nina's identity is overwhelming her thoughts. Sister Dymphna is Nina McKellan, the missing tech entrepreneur with millions of dollars and a tragic past.

Biddy thanks Willa for answering all her questions and enjoys the rest of her visit, during which she gets the name of Willa's landscaper. The moment they depart and both slam the car doors shut, Ruby looks at her.

"Sister Dymphna is Nina!"

Biddy is so proud that her friend figured this out. And still kept her mouth shut!

"We have to tell Willa where her sister is," Ruby says. "Did you see how heartbroken she looked talking about Nina?"

Biddy shakes her head. "We can't blow Sister Dymphna's cover. Not yet. Sister Dymphna has a right to know first…And Shelia. Can you imagine how this will make them feel?"

"Just awful." Ruby's smile slips from her face. "They've become friends. Can you believe Shelia's dad killed Willa and Nina's parents?" Ruby asks. "She must feel terrible."

Biddy starts the car, her mind racing. "I don't know that I believe it. Something about Carl Ryan taking the blame for that fire doesn't add up."

Ruby frowns. "Why? It sounds pretty cut and dried. There were witnesses."

"There were just witnesses that he was in the neighborhood, not that he set the fire. I'm telling you, his dismissal from his job seems unlikely. Suddenly, after decades of working at Lucifol and with a family to care for, he becomes a drunk? It doesn't add up. His daughter had a scholarship and was on her way to bigger things. He wouldn't have risked all that." Biddy glances over at her friend as she turns onto the main road. "I think we need to find out what really happened that night and why Edward McKellan let Carl Ryan go from Lucifol. Because if Carl Ryan didn't set that fire, then someone else did. Someone who's been getting away with murder for decades and maybe wants to hurt Sister Dymphna… Plus, we owe the truth to Sheila."

"Oh, Biddy, what if you are wrong?" Ruby's protests fill the car. "Think of what this will do to Sheila—reopening these old wounds."

"But what if I'm right?"

Biddy can't shake the image of Sheila she saw in the newspaper article. The brilliant child holding her scholarship award and the proud, serious father behind her. Then she's suddenly orphaned, surrounded by scandal and blame, with nowhere to turn and no one to trust. No wonder she'd ended up in a profession where at least the transaction was honest—money for companionship, no pretense of love or loyalty that could be stripped away without warning. If Carl Ryan was innocent, then Sheila had suffered for nothing. And someone else—someone who destroyed two families was still out there.

Ruby studies her face. "You feel strongly about this, don't you?"

Biddy nods. Her friend sighs.

"Fine, I'll help look into this. But we keep this line of questioning to ourselves. All we tell everyone else is who Sister Dymphna is. We say nothing about Carl Ryan and his potential innocence. Let's not get Sheila's hopes up when we have no proof."

17

Sheila

Sheila stares at Biddy. Biddy stares back. And three other pairs of eyes watch them. The Pooka Women's Club sits in Biddy's living room and she is the focus of attention. That normally is right where she wants to be. But at this moment, she'd rather be anywhere else. Even the convent.

"Sister Dymphna is Nina McKellan." She repeats the words back to Biddy.

Biddy nods.

She wants to say this couldn't possibly be true, but the moment Biddy tells her, it clicks into place. This is how Sister Dymphna looks so familiar. In the next instant, Sheila realizes, with great sadness, that her friendship with Sister Dymphna will be over. The moment Sister Dymphna knows their true identities, she is going to hate her.

"I can't believe Sister Dymphna is the heiress of the Lucifol fortune," Amelia says.

The rest of the club is clearly oblivious to Sheila's connection to the McKellan family. Sheila is grateful for that. But Biddy knows. Sheila can see it in her eyes.

"There is no fortune," Biddy says to Amelia. "They lost it all."

"I don't think the death threats have anything to do with her being an heiress, rich or broke," Megan says. "I think this is about the fourteen bodies in the church."

Sheila brushes her wimple out of her face. She's found the nun's clothing surprisingly comfortable. She's actually happy at the convent. She and Sister Dymphna have become friends. She's going to miss that. But the best thing she can do is to pretend that none of this is affecting her. She's never cared about what people thought of her before. She's never had friends before. She shouldn't start now. She is president of this club, and she should carry on acting as such. She uncaps her marker.

"Let's write everything we know." She looks at Biddy. "You first."

She doesn't really want to hear more from Biddy, particularly about the McKellans, but there would be hell to pay if Biddy didn't go first. And better to just get this over with.

"Thank you." Biddy tugs on the sleeves of her navy tweed suit to make sure they are straight. "Ruby and I went to visit Willa McKellan yesterday. While we were there, we saw a recent photograph of her with her sister. There's no doubt— Sister Dymphna is Nina McKellan."

Amelia rubs her increasingly sleepy eyes and looks at Biddy. "What do we know about the McKellan's?"

Biddy glances at Sheila, but Sheila doesn't flinch. Biddy looks back to Amelia.

"Nina and Willa's parents founded the Lucifol business in Albion and made a tremendous fortune with their cleaning products. They employed most of the town and their donations funded many of the public services, including the library, schools, and a medical center."

"So what happened to it?" Megan asks. "I've never really heard of that brand of cleaning supplies."

Sheila feels Biddy's eyes shift back once again to her, and senses the dreaded pity in them. She chooses not to meet them.

"There was a fire in the factory," Biddy says, "that killed both of the parents. Their lawyer sold off the company after that and used the money to settle a bunch of lawsuits from employees claiming that the chemicals had caused cancer."

"That's awful," Amelia says. "For the employees, the parents, and the kids. Do they know what caused the fire?"

Sheila takes a deep breath. She doesn't wait for Biddy to eye her this time. "It's not what. It's who. My father, did." The words feeling like a knife ripping her throat as she utters them. "He was angry about getting laid off and started the fire."

The silence that follows is deafening. Sheila feels the weight of their stares. Ruby's eyes water. Megan looks stunned. Even Amelia is completely alert.

"It's not your fault," Ruby whispers.

Not with the pity again. Sheila steels herself to withstand it.

"That's why Sister Dymphna looked familiar to me," Sheila just wants to get the story over with. She wonders if her friends will ever look at her the same. "I went to school with her when we were kids. Before the fire. Before my father destroyed her family and mine."

"To be fair, no court convicted him of this," Biddy says. "He was just a suspect."

Sheila shakes her head. She does not believe in false hope.

"The only reason he wasn't convicted, was that he ran away before they could arrest him."

"Sheila—" Biddy starts.

"No," Sheila cuts her off. "You need to understand. Nina McKellan lost everything because of my father. Her parents, her home, her sense of security. She had to rebuild her entire life from nothing, and then when she finally made something of herself, she has this terrible accident and lost even that. We have to help her." Then she adds, "It's the least I can do."

"Your father's actions aren't your responsibility," Amelia says gently.

"Aren't they?" Sheila can feel her anger rising. She wants to accept the blame she is due. "Willa and Nina lost their parents because of me. Then they lost their fortune. Now Nina ends up with amnesia, hiding in a convent, with all her money gone yet again. None of this would've happened without that fire. This is as far from the life she was supposed to have as you can get. How is that fair?"

"And how is it fair that you also paid the price for someone else's actions? Life isn't fair," Biddy says quietly. "You aren't responsible for fixing everything that went wrong. Plus, for all we know, Nina McKellan brought her current troubles upon herself. We know nothing about her since she's grown up."

"She didn't," Sheila says firmly. "I know she didn't. I'm going to make this up to her. And I won't let anyone say anything bad about her. Not after what she's been through."

Ruby clears her throat. "Maybe we should discuss something else. What else have we learned?" She looks around the group and her eyes settle on Megan.

"I found bodies," Megan says, with more excitement than

the gruesome topic warrants. However, Shelia is so grateful to have the focus turned to something else, she lets her run with it.

"Yesterday, when Sheila and I were investigating the church crypt, we found fourteen bodies. All women. All hidden in a secret chamber beneath the crypt."

Ruby's coffee cup shakes in her hand. She's probably regretting calling on Megan.

"The police have the bodies now," Megan continues. "They're being examined by the coroner, but early indications are that they appear to be from the 1950s. All young women, and…" she pauses to choose her wording. "They didn't die naturally."

"Not again," Amelia's voice is barely above a whisper. "Can't we just solve a mystery without a murder?"

"I'm pretty sure we can't," Sheila says.

"The positioning of the remains suggests they died in terror," Megan continues, the only one unbothered by the discovery. "And the location suggests someone was trying to hide them."

Sheila feels sick about this, too. Sister Mary Bernice had not been happy with the discovery. Journalists have already started accusing the church of a coverup. Sheila can't help but relate to the old nun's problems, remembering the journalists camped out in front of her home all those years ago after the fire.

"Sister Mary Bernice claims to know nothing," Sheila says. "She says the church has no records of any women being buried there, no history of anything like this."

Megan looks at her. "Of course, she'd say that. But Sheila, you're living there now. Have you noticed anything strange?"

"Like Sister Mary Bernice sneaking out in the middle of

the night with a shovel and a body?" Sheila shakes her head. "No! Sister Mary Bernice is a perfectly nice, albeit slightly judgmental woman who would never harm anyone, or cover it up."

"Still, do you think she knows more than she's saying?" Biddy asks.

"I think everyone in this case knows more than they're saying," Shelia replies.

"Including Nina," Megan says.

"Yes," Sheila says. "But it's not her fault. She has amnesia."

"So what do we do?" Ruby helps herself to another petit four. When the going gets tough, Ruby goes to the desserts.

"We need answers," Biddy says. "From Nina, from Sister Mary Bernice, from whoever's behind these attacks." She looks at Shelia. "I can talk to Nina and break the news of her identity to her."

This is a kind offer. And Sheila desperately wants to accept it.

"No," Sheila says. "I should be the one to tell Nina who she really is. I'm president of this club and I owe her that much. Since I know her past, I'm also the best person to fill in some gaps for her."

Biddy nods. It surprises Sheila to see that the look on her face is almost one of approval. Almost.

"Plus," Sheila continues, "I'm already staying at the convent. I can watch for any signs of her memory returning, see if she remembers anything about why she came to Pooka or where she might have hidden the money from her business sale."

"How much money are we talking about?" Amelia asks.

"According to Willa," Biddy says. "Nina made millions from the sale of her tech company. That money disappeared the same night she did."

"That's a lot of motive for murder," Megan observes.

"Which brings us to our next step," Sheila says. "We need to talk to Nina's business partners. Find out who else knew about the money, who else might have wanted it."

"I can help with that," Amelia says immediately. "I've been doing book-keeping for a law firm, and I've gotten pretty good at digging into business records and financial documents."

"And I can help coordinate," Sheila says. "We need to be systematic about this. Nina's life depends on us getting it right."

Biddy nods. "What about the church? Someone needs to keep investigating what happened there, what those bodies have to do with Nina's current situation."

"I'll stay on that," Megan says. "I want to know what Sister Mary Bernice is hiding. Fourteen women don't just disappear without someone noticing."

"The church will not be happy about this investigation," Amelia warns.

"I don't really care," Megan says. "There are dead women to help."

"Biddy and Ruby, what are you going to do?" Sheila asks.

Biddy shrugs as if she does not know. This makes the hairs on Shelia's arms prickle. If there is one thing about Biddy Bramley that you can count on, it is that she always has a plan.

"Since we've already built a rapport with Willa, maybe we'll dig a little more into Nina's past. See if there is anything else we should know from those years after you knew her."

The idea is good, but Shelia can't help but get the feeling Biddy is looking for something specific. Still, she has a difficult conversation with Nina ahead of her, so she lets it go.

"We have to find out the truth," Sheila says. "For Nina, for her family, and for those fourteen women whose bodies were hidden away like they didn't matter."

The words sound noble, but Sheila knows she is not. Now, she needs to go tell Sister Dymphna who she really is, and that Sheila ruined her life.

18

Sister Dymphna

I'm sitting on the narrow bed in the convent, staring at the vase of fresh flowers I placed there this morning—yellow chrysanthemums mixed with sprigs of rosemary. I thought it'd be an interesting juxtaposition of sweet and spicy in visual form. Although, how I know words like juxtaposition and the art of decorating, I still do not know.

I've taken to putting the flowers in all three of our rooms—Sister Mary Bernice's, Sheila's, and mine. The scent should be calming, but nothing about this moment feels calm. Sheila sits across from me in the chair at my desk, and there's something in her expression that makes my stomach clench. She knows something. About me. I instinctually don't want to know. I worry that I'm about to lose this life.

Sheila's been staying at the convent for a few weeks now, and I've grown to love her presence. She has a way of making everything a little lighter. Meals with Sister Mary Bernice have never been so amusing. The two debate practically everything, but especially a woman's place in society. Surprisingly, they're both more aligned than they'd admit. I like these women who've become my family. I like this life here. I don't want to lose it. Not even if it means that I never remember my past.

"Nina," Sheila says, and then stops. "I mean, Sister Dymphna. We need to talk."

"Who's Nina?" I ask. Dread descends over me. I recognize the name somehow. "About what?"

Sheila reaches into the pocket of the long black habit that seems to be her outfit of choice these days and pulls out several photographs. "About who you really are."

I hesitate. I wonder if I can ask her to just put them away and go on with my day.

"You can't avoid it," Sheila says. "But if it makes you feel better, you were a good person."

That does make me feel better. I force myself to take the first picture. It's the faded photograph the women's club found in the crypt—of two little girls in matching coats, standing in front of their parents with a large brick building in the background.

"That's you," Sheila says softly, pointing to the younger girl. "And that's your sister, Willa."

I stare at the photograph of me, and recognize nothing. The young blonde girl smiles impishly back. I try to remember something—anything—about her and these other people who are supposedly my family. The man in the charcoal suit has kind eyes and a proud smile. The woman in the floral dress looks elegant and happy. They should feel familiar. They should trigger some spark of recognition.

They don't.

"I don't remember them," I whisper.

"I know." Sheila's voice is gentle but firm. There is no escaping this discovery of who I was. Who I am. "But they're your parents, Edward and Constance McKellan. And that building behind you is the Lucifol factory in Albion. Your family owned it."

She hands me another photograph, this one more recent. Two young women in their twenties, arms around each other, laughing at something outside the camera's view. One is clearly me and the other…

The other has my face. My eyes. My smile. My hair. But she looks more serious.

"Your name is Nina McKellan," Sheila continues. "You're from a wealthy family. You went to college, started a tech company in Silicon Valley, and made millions of dollars. You have a sister named Willa, who still lives in your childhood home in Albion."

Nina McKellan. The name feels foreign in my mouth when I try to say it, like speaking a language I don't know. Am I nice? Am I likable? Do I have lots of friends or am I a loner like I am now?

"Why don't I remember any of this?" I ask. "All I feel are hints of familiarity."

Shelia shrugs. "I don't know."

I stare at the pictures. "What about my parents?"

Sheila takes a deep breath, and I can see her steeling herself, as if she has some awful news to deliver. "Something terrible happened to your family when you were a teenager. Your parents died in a fire at the factory. Someone burned it down."

Fire. Suddenly I can smell smoke, can taste ash in the back of my throat. My nightmares—they're always about fire. But when I reach for the memory, it slips away.

"I was there," I say.

"You weren't," Shelia says. Again her voice is firm. It's like she somehow knew me. "It happened at night…It was arson."

"By who?"

Sheila looks down at her hands. When she looks back up, her eyes are pleading. I don't understand any of this.

"My father set it. Carl Ryan. He killed your parents."

I stare at her, trying my very best to make sense of this. Shelia and I knew each other before now? Her father murdered my parents? I sit back on my bed.

"Why? Why would he do that? What did my parents do to deserve that?"

I wish someone else had told me this story. It's unfair that I have to process this with the person connected to it right in front of me. The person who has recently made me feel so safe.

Tears form in Sheila's eyes. "Your family did nothing to deserve that. No one deserves that. My father had been laid off from the factory and was angry about it. I was told he'd been drinking, making threats." Sheila's hands clutch each other so tightly her knuckles are white. "But Nina, my mom and I never saw this coming. I'm so sorry. If we'd known, my mom and I would've said something. I swear."

How could she and her mother have missed the signs?

"Is he in prison now?"

Sheila shakes her head and looks down again. I'm pretty sure this is the worst conversation of my life.

"He ran away before they could investigate."

I close my eyes and try to visualize my family. Try to remember my parents, their faces, their voices. Instead, all I see are flames consuming everything in their path, and with the image comes a wave of guilt so intense it takes my breath away. Why would I feel guilty? Why would I have memories of a fire I wasn't present for? This is Sheila and her family's burden to bear.

I shake my head, trying to clear it. It's all so much. "This still doesn't explain what caused my amnesia."

Sheila pulls out another paper from her stack, and this one makes my stomach drop. It's a newspaper clipping with the headline "Tech Entrepreneur Vanishes After Fatal Crash." Below it is a photo of a car, crumpled against a tree, surrounded by emergency vehicles.

Headlights. Blood. Screams. Money.

"You had a car accident in Los Angeles," she says. "A family was involved. A mother and child died."

Dear God. I take the photo and stare at it. I did this. Deep down, I knew I was an awful person. I just knew it. I'm as bad as Sheila. No wonder why we get along.

"I killed them," I say numbly.

"Not on purpose," Shelia says. She's trying to comfort me, but killers don't deserve comfort. "It was an accident. You were drinking, but it was an accident."

"I was drunk." The words taste bitter. "I got drunk and got behind the wheel and killed a mother and child."

"Nina—"

"Don't call me that."

"Alright. Sister Dymphna, you can't blame yourself for something you don't even remember."

"How long ago?"

"A little over a year. Right before you showed up here with amnesia."

A year. The same time I've been resting comfortably at the convent, being fed and cared for. And all this time, there's been a family somewhere grieving because of me.

"What happened after the accident? How did I end up in Indiana?"

Sheila shrugs, and she shakes her head. It's the first time today, she hasn't had all the answers. But then again, she hasn't known me as an adult.

"You just disappeared. The police were looking for you, but you vanished. Along with the money from selling your company—millions of dollars that should have been split with your business partners."

I stare at her, trying to reconcile this image of myself as a wealthy, successful businesswoman who fled the scene of a fatal accident in Los Angeles with stolen money to the person I've been here at the convent.

"So I'm a killer and a thief," I say. "I'm no different than your father."

Sheila flinches. "You aren't the same. You had amnesia. You didn't run on purpose. You're simply someone who made terrible mistakes."

It's sweet of her to thread that needle, but it's hard to find comfort from the person whose father killed my parents and is now a hooker. I'm not entirely sure she's on the right path of morality, either.

"No wonder someone is trying to kill me."

"You don't deserve to die," Sheila says forcefully. "Never say that. We will help you figure out what's going on. There is probably a lot more to this story than meets the eye. What if you ran from that accident for a good reason? What if you kept the money for a good reason?"

I look down at the photographs in my lap. This smiling, confident young woman stares back at me, and I can't connect her to the person I now think of myself to be. She feels like a stranger. But yet, I'm still responsible for her sins.

"I can't remember any of it," I say. "Not my parents, not my sister, not starting a company or selling it. I can't remember the accident or taking the money or coming to Indiana. All I remember is fire."

"Maybe your mind is protecting you from memories that are too painful to bear."

"Or maybe I'm exactly the type of person who would drink and drive and kill innocent people and then steal money and run away." I set the photographs aside and look at her. "What if the amnesia isn't trauma? What if it's guilt? What if some part of me knows I don't deserve to remember the good things because of what I've done?"

"That's not how amnesia works."

"How do you know? How does anyone know? Maybe this is my punishment for being selfish and reckless and—"

"Stop." Sheila's voice is firm again. "I've watched you for the past week. I've seen how you care for Sister Mary Bernice, how you tend to the garden and put bouquets in our rooms, how you pray for guidance to be a better person. That's not the behavior of someone who's selfish and reckless."

"But it is the behavior of someone who's trying to atone for something terrible."

We sit in silence for a moment. Outside my window, I can hear the normal sounds of late afternoon—birds in the oak trees, cars passing on the distant road. The world going about its business while my carefully constructed new life crumbles around me.

"What happens now?" I ask.

Sheila hesitates and her eyes meet mine. "You need to turn yourself in to the police. Face the consequences of what happened."

I don't point out the laughable irony of Sheila telling me to turn myself in when her father ran to escape the consequences of killing my parents. Still, even knowing how awful it feels to be the victim of a crime to which no one claimed responsibility, my immediate instinct is to shake my head, to refuse. To keep being Sister Dymphna. But how could I be Sister Dymphna if I don't do the right thing?

"How is it fair that I'm going to be punished for something I don't remember doing?" I whisper.

"Sister Dymphna." This time the voice isn't Sheila's.

I look up and see Sister Mary Bernice standing in the doorway. She wears her full habit, with a boot on her foot. I do not know how long she has been there. But it really doesn't matter. I'm sure she already knows my story. She is as all knowing as God himself.

"You need to do as Sheila says."

All of it is unfair. But I nod. If I trust anyone, it is Sister Mary Bernice.

"What about my sister, the business partners, the money—"

Sister Mary Bernice shakes her head. "I think dealing with the accident is enough for one day. Let's take it one step at a time, shall we?"

I'm grateful for this bit of generosity. I pick up the photograph of my parents again, studying their faces. They look kind and loving, the sort of parents who would have been proud of their daughters' accomplishments and devastated by their mistakes. I wish I could remember them. I wish I could grieve for them properly instead of feeling this hollow sense of loss for people who feel like strangers.

I look at Shelia. "I think you should leave now. I'd prefer to be alone while I figure out how to mourn my parents."

She looks at me with hurt in her eyes but stands up and leaves. Sister Mary Bernice takes her place beside me and holds me in her arms. I grip her tightly. I know it seems unfair to throw out Sheila, but how can you befriend the person whose family killed your family? You simply cannot.

19

Megan

Megan and Amelia carefully walk down the rotted wooden steps into the hidden earthen room beneath the crypt. Between them is Sister Mary Bernice, who leans heavily on Megan's shoulder as she navigates the stairs in her boot. The space is still musty with its mud walls and low ceiling, but the police rigged up spotlights at various corners, which at least makes it more navigable. Because of the lights and the removal of the bodies, Megan realizes the room no longer feels creepy. It just feels sad. These women were people. With lives and families. Their stories need to be remembered, told, and celebrated. She just needs to figure out what happened to them.

At least, Megan acknowledges, they are getting closer to doing this. Thanks to science, they know the women died in the 1950s. And thanks to the myths of screams in the night, they know the women most likely lived at the convent before dying. Pooka police reports show no missing women, so they also are most likely not native to the area.

When they reach the bottom of the stairs, Megan wanders

from empty cot to empty cot, studying them. Amelia pulls out her notes to review the research she has done. Sister Mary Bernice simply stands on the landing and stares. She insisted her ankle healed enough to make the trip down the stairs to see the space. But now that she's here, she doesn't seem as shocked as the other people viewing the room for the first time. It's almost as if she's seen it before, Megan realizes.

Amelia pulls a bit of apple out of her hair, considers flicking it to the floor, but then eats it. Then she reads from her notes. "In the early 1950s, there was a woman named Sister Agatha Benedict who ran the convent."

Both Amelia and Megan look at Sister Mary Bernice.

She glares back. "I don't know how old you two think I am, but I did not know her. That said, no nun in my order is capable of insidious behavior. I'm sure she's not behind this."

"We didn't mean to imply that," Megan says quickly. At times like this, she feels lucky to have a prickly mother. It's taught her how to navigate difficult conversations. "But maybe your order knows who these women were. Given the rumors of noise coming from the convent, they seem to have been staying here. The 1950s were a time when churches housed unwed mothers and put their children up for adoption. Maybe that's what brought these women here, and that's how they died?"

This only angers the nun further.

"I know about the 1950s and the practice of forcing unwed women into giving up their babies. I know you are also being too polite to mention the often unsafe and abusive environments they faced. My order would never take children against their mother's will or abuse women in need," Sister Mary Bernice insists. "Never."

She looks at the cots and shakes her head with a sadness in her eyes. "Myself and my sisters have devoted our lives to doing God's work as best we can. I ask that you both discontinue this line of inquiry. My sisters are good people. The best. Whoever these women were, they deserve our prayers. Not accusations."

She turns on the heel of her good foot and heads up the stairs, her habit billowing behind her. The sound of her footsteps, one genteel and one a clomp of her plastic boot, fades, leaving Megan and Amelia alone, staring at the fourteen empty burial platforms and a growing list of questions.

"Well," Amelia says after a moment, "that went well."

"She knows something," Megan says. "The way she re-acted… she was overly defensive. Plus, she didn't seem that shocked or curious about this room. It's as if she knew it was here. Maybe that is why she kept the crypt locked up tightly."

"Sister Mary Bernice wouldn't harm anyone."

Megan isn't so sure of that, but she knows how to tread lightly in situations like this. "I didn't say she would. I simply said that she knows more than she's saying."

Amelia tucks her notes back in her bag and looks around.

"I can't stop thinking about them," she says quietly.

"Me neither." Megan runs her hand over the dusty board that supported a body. "Whoever they were, they deserve better than being forgotten in a hole under the church."

"At least someone cared enough about them to put them in separate burial sites," Amelia says.

She's right. The bodies weren't just thrown on the floor. Someone laid them on individual platforms. Megan bends to examine the construction of one more closely. Whoever built these shelves arranged the platforms like bunk beds, stacked five high. Although the vast majority of the platforms supported bodies, some had not been used. Megan doesn't know whether to be pleased or depressed by that.

"How sad that they had planned for more than they needed," Megan says.

"Or maybe," Amelia says, "they just ran out of time before they could fill them all."

This is a dark thought, especially for Amelia.

"Do you really they think they were pregnant?" Amelia asks. "Or were you just taking a guess when you suggested that to Sister Mary Bernice?"

"I spoke with the coroner. The evidence is not definitive, but there are signs all the women had delivered babies. The pubic bones often separate after birth and a groove on the pelvis becomes more pronounced from the stretching of ligaments. All the women showed signs of this."

Amelia grimaces. "Mine is probably notched as deep as the Grand Canyon by now."

Megan smiles despite the circumstances. She's never really given any thought to how Amelia feels about motherhood. She thinks of Amelia the same as her own mom—just a mother. In some ways, she can't imagine either of them in their lives or bodies before children.

"Did you always want kids?" Megan asks.

"Of course," Amelia says. "I love my children." She pauses, running her hand along one of the empty platforms. "I just wish I had a little time for myself. To remember who I was before I became someone's mother." She smiles. "But that's why I have the Women's Club."

For the first time, Megan realizes the importance of the club to Amelia, even when she can barely hold her eyes open.

"And I'm sure I'll have more time for myself as they get older. At least, that's what I tell myself when I'm scraping Play-Doh out of the carpet at midnight."

The ultimate joy and the ultimate sacrifice, Megan thinks as she looks around the space. How did the women hidden in this room feel about becoming mothers? Had anyone cared about them or just their new role in life?

Then she sees something on the wall. Deep grooves in the dirt above a cot. Markings that appear more regular and intentional than typical striations in sediment.

She leans in closer and runs her fingers over it. The marks are fine, as if carved by a needle-like instrument. She pulls out her cellphone and shines the flashlight at them.

"What do you see?" Amelia asks, moving closer.

"I'm not sure…" They both peer at the space lit by Megan's flashlight.

"It looks like words," Amelia says.

"'Forever in our hearts,'" Megan makes out.

"It's an inscription!" Amelia gasps. "Do you think the others have them too?"

They move from platform to platform, using Megan's phone light to examine the walls. "'In loving memory.' 'Rest in peace.' 'Beloved and Remembered.' 'Gone but not forgotten.'"

Each burial site has something inscribed, and it warms Megan's heart that someone loved these women and laid them to rest. But it also raises new questions.

"If these women were here against their will," Amelia says, "who was writing these inscriptions? Who cared enough to carve these messages?"

"Maybe other women who were here? Maybe they formed a community, took care of each other?"

"Or maybe," Amelia suggests, "not everyone here was complicit in whatever was happening. Maybe some people were trying to help."

The two split up to investigate and photograph each resting area.

"Megan," Amelia calls from the far end of the room. She's leaning over a bottom platform, most likely the most recent of the burials. "This isn't a quote. It's a name!"

Megan hurries over and crouches beside her. "'Sarah Hope.'"

"If these bodies are from the 1950s, that isn't that long ago," Amelia says excitedly. "She could still have family that remembers her."

"She could have a child," Megan whispers.

They continue their examination, finding more names scattered among the inspirational quotes. Mary Catherine. Elizabeth Rose. Dorothy Mae. Each one a real person, not just an anonymous victim.

"Wait," Megan says, stopping at a platform near the entrance to the chamber. "Look at this."

The inscription here is different—fresher somehow, carved more recently than the others. It simply reads: "The truth will surface."

"Well, it finally did," Amelia says.

"But this carving doesn't look as old as the others." Megan runs her fingers over it. "This is maybe months old, not decades. Sediment hasn't filled it in. It's more pronounced."

"You think someone else has been down here recently?"

"I think so," Megan says slowly. "Is it possible that Sister Dymphna—Nina—might have found this place before we did? She had a pretty strong reaction to visiting the crypt."

They look at each other as the implications sink in.

"Remember where we found that photograph of the McKel-lan family?" Amelia asks.

"Right above this chamber. Nina could have dropped it while trying to open the trapdoor."

"But she would have needed a key to get that trap door open. And why would she come down here? How would she even know this place existed?"

Megan examines the fresh carving more closely. "What if she was looking for a hiding place for her money? We saw the marks on the tomb upstairs. What if she couldn't get it open and then saw the trapdoor? Just like us, she figured out it was a secret room. What if that's why someone is trying to kill her? That she knew about bodies someone wanted to remain hidden?"

"I just can't believe someone in the church would be behind threatening a nun," Amelia says firmly.

Megan barely hears her protest because now she sees something else. "Amelia, look at this."

Carved into the wall, beneath the "Truth will surface" message, is an arrow pointing to a loose stone in the wall.

Megan carefully works the stone free and peers into the small cavity behind it. "There's something here."

She reaches in and pulls out a small, waterproof envelope. Inside is a piece of paper with writing in what appears to be Nina's hand.

"What does it say?" Amelia asks.

Megan unfolds the paper. There is no writing. Just thirteen digits.

"Well that's not helpful," Amelia says.

"It could be an account number…"

"It could be anything…"

"It could be why someone wants her dead," Megan finishes.

Megan puts the paper in her pocket and the two agree to keep it a secret from the outside world until they have time to discuss it at their next women's club meeting. They head up the stairs and out of the building. Megan can't help but look back at the beautiful stained glass windows and peaceful exterior. How many secrets is this place hiding? How many people have died to protect them?

20

Biddy

Biddy is in the parking lot of what was once the Albion Police Department. It is now a deserted crumbling brick building with boarded windows and weeds growing through cracks in the asphalt. The sign out front still bears the department's name, but it's faded, spray-painted with a word Biddy can't even decipher, and hanging at an angle, much like everything else in this forgotten town.

"Are you sure about this?" Ruby asks, clutching her purse tighter as she eyes the building. "I don't think it's such a good idea to break into a police department."

Biddy frowns. "It's not a police department. It's a former police department. I'm telling you, something is fishy about the accusation against Sheila's father. And don't you think it's a little suspicious that the McKellan family donated a brand new police building right after the fire that killed their parents? Usually, people donate a park or a statue or a church window in those circumstances."

"Only in your world," Ruby says. "In my world, they just bury their parents. I can't understand the thought process behind rich people."

Biddy has to admit the abandoned police station has an ominous quality in the gray afternoon light. But this is where the records from the Lucifol fire investigation were kept. She doubts anyone was careful enough to move solved-cases to the new building. With the crime rate skyrocketing, solved case documents could have been left behind.

Ruby shifts uncomfortably. "What if we get arrested for breaking and entering?"

"We're not breaking and entering. We're conducting historical research. In a historic building. Megan says that all the time before invading someone's privacy." Biddy adjusts her wool coat, climbs out of the car, and strides toward the building with more confidence than she feels. Ruby, as always, follows. Biddy looks over her shoulder and smiles encouragingly at her. "Besides, who's going to arrest us? There's no one here."

The front door is locked, but a side entrance yields to Biddy's persistent pushing. The hinges protest with a screech that makes Ruby jump.

"Maybe we should call someone to get permission first," Ruby suggests. "Like the mayor or—"

"Ruby, the mayor of Albion is probably the person manning the gas station we passed on the way in. This town has a population of three hundred people and a median income that wouldn't cover Sheila's monthly shoe budget. It's an empty building. They won't care."

They step into what was once the main lobby of the police department. Dust motes dance in the shafts of light filtering through dirty windows. The reception desk still holds an ancient computer monitor and a coffee mug with "World's

Greatest Dad" printed on the side.

"This is depressing," Ruby observes.

"It's a gold mine," Biddy corrects, spotting a sign labeled "Records Storage" down a dim hallway. "Twenty years ago, this was a functioning police department investigating a major arson case. Those files have to be here somewhere."

"I bet they moved them to the new station," Ruby says.

"And your optimism that people always do the right thing is my favorite thing about you," Biddy says. "I bet not. They probably thought they'd never need them again."

They make their way down the hallway, their footsteps echoing in the empty building. Most of the office doors are open, revealing rooms stripped of everything valuable but still containing the detritus of abandoned bureaucracy—empty filing cabinets, broken chairs, yellowed paperwork scattered across the floor. This confirms Biddy's suspicions. Much did not make the trip from here to the new station.

"Here," Biddy says, stopping in front of a heavy door marked "Records Storage." She tries the handle. Locked.

"Well, that's that," Ruby says with obvious relief. "We tried our best, but—"

Biddy pulls a bobby pin from her hair. "Sheila isn't the only one with useful skills from a questionable past."

"Biddy Bramley, again? I thought you'd become a society lady."

"So did I," Biddy says, working the bobby pin into the lock mechanism. "But apparently you can't walk away from who you once were."

The lock clicks open. Biddy smiles proudly.

"I'm pretending I didn't see that," Ruby mutters.

The records storage room is larger than Biddy expected,

with metal shelving units stretching from floor to ceiling. Most of the shelves are empty, but boxes and files are still scattered throughout the room, apparently abandoned when the department closed.

"How is this stuff still here?" Ruby asks. "It could've been important!"

"I'm sure they come back for it when they need it," Biddy lies.

She's already scanning the boxes, looking for dates and case numbers. She finds what she's looking for in the back corner: three banker's boxes labeled "Lucifol Arson Investigation - 2004." Her heart races as she lifts down the first box and sets it on a nearby table. She opens the box to reveal folders thick with police reports, witness statements, and photographs.

Ruby peers over her shoulder as Biddy spreads the contents across the table. "I don't know what you're looking for. Even Sheila thinks her father did it."

But Sheila was only a child then, Biddy thinks. And her mother was sick. She would hardly have been following the investigation.

The first document is a police report detailing the discovery of the fire at 4:17 AM. Biddy scans the details: the factory was fully engulfed, two bodies were found in the administrative offices, and arson was suspected because of accelerant patterns. Nothing new here.

She pulls out another document and flips through it. "These are witness statements placing Carl Ryan near the factory." Her heart sinks. She was hoping this wasn't true.

Ruby reads over her shoulder. "Martha Henderson saw a man matching Carl Ryan's description walking toward the factory around 2 AM. She was returning from her shift at the hospital."

"But the fire didn't start until after 4 AM," Biddy notes. She's determined to hold out hope. "What was he doing for two hours?"

She continues reading through the witness statements. Three different people claimed to have seen Carl Ryan near the factory between 2:00 and 2:30 AM. But none of them saw him still there at 4 am. Or witnessed him actually starting the fire.

"This is interesting," Biddy says, pulling out another file. "Look at this."

The file contains statements from Carl Ryan's coworkers, several of whom mentioned that he'd been asking questions about the factory's financial records in the weeks before the fire. None of them mentioned a drinking problem.

"'Carl kept saying something wasn't right about the layoffs,' Biddy reads aloud. "'He said the factory was making more money than ever, so why were they cutting workers?'"

"Maybe he was investigating something," Ruby suggests. "Maybe he thought they were hiding money before the employees' unsafe working conditions lawsuits were filed."

"Maybe he was." Biddy continues reading.

Biddy opens another folder, this one containing financial records that had been subpoenaed during the investigation.

"And look at this—the police found irregularities in the company's books. Significant amounts of money were being transferred to accounts that couldn't be traced. That's what they did with the money instead of paying employees."

"If Carl was investigating financial fraud, that gives someone else a motive to silence him," Ruby says.

"And what better way to silence him than to frame him for

murder?" Biddy continues reading through the files, looking for more evidence. What she finds in the next folder makes her blood run cold.

"Ruby, look at this."

It's a statement from Carl Ryan himself, given to police two days after the fire. But it's not a confession—it's an alibi.

"I was at the factory from approximately 2:00 to 2:45 AM, looking through Edward McKellan's office for evidence of financial irregularities," Biddy reads. "I left when I heard someone else coming. I walked to Brady's Tavern and remained there until closing time at 4:00 AM. I then walked home and was there the remainder of the night."

"He had an alibi," Ruby breathes. "He was at the tavern when the fire started."

Biddy flips through more documents, looking for follow-up on Carl's statement. What she finds is a single note from the investigating detective: "Tavern owner confirms Ryan was present 2:45-4:00 AM. Alibi verified."

"He had a verified alibi," Biddy says, her voice rising with indignation. "The police knew he didn't set the fire."

"Then why was he charged?" Ruby asks.

Biddy continues reading, looking for an answer. She finds a handwritten note dated three days after the fire: "District Attorney requesting charges against Ryan despite an alibi. Political pressure from McKellan family attorneys. Need quick resolution for insurance."

"They charged him anyway," Biddy says flatly. "Even though they knew he was innocent."

"But why would he run if he had an alibi?" Ruby asks.

Biddy shakes her head. "That's a great question. And I think we need to find the answer."

21

Sheila

Police stations are among Sheila's least favorite places. Nevertheless, she sits in the hard plastic chair of the Pooka Police Department's conference room, watching Sister Dymphna fidget with the sleeves of her habit.

"I really don't need your help," Sister Dymphna says to her, the third time today.

"You really kind of do," Sheila says firmly. "You're in a police station. I know police stations."

Things have been strained between them since Sister Dymphna discovered that Sheila's father killed her parents. But Shelia won't let this impede protecting her. It is the least she can do. And if doing so means taking Sister Dymphna's anger, she'll do that too.

"Perhaps we should focus on the matter at hand," Sister Mary Bernice whispers, while keeping her attention on the two police officers across the table from them.

Detective Martinez from the LAPD looks tired from his red-eye flight to Indiana, but professionally alert. His partner, Detective Chen, has her laptop open and a stack of files spread across the scratched conference table. Both detectives have the weathered look of people who've seen too much and believed too little, but Sheila notices a hint of gentleness in their eyes when they look at Sister Dymphna. This is, at least, promising. Sheila is sure that the habit is not hurting Sister Dymphna's cause. As she always says, apparel makes the person.

"Thank you for coming forward, Ms. McKellan," Detective Martinez says. "We know this can't be easy."

Sister Dymphna flinches at the use of the name unfamiliar to her, but she clasps her hands tightly. "I'm ready to take responsibility for what I did."

Sheila cringes at the words, but Sister Mary Bernice nods her approval.

"We understand you believe you were involved in a fatal traffic collision on March 15th of last year," Detective Chen says, consulting her notes. "Can you tell us what you remember?"

"That's just it," Sister Dymphna says, her voice shaky but determined. "I remember nothing. Not the accident. Not running away. Not coming to Indiana. My first clear memory is waking up in the hospital here with amnesia."

Sheila watches the detectives exchange glances. She can see them questioning the veracity of this statement and trying to decide how to handle a confession from someone who can't actually remember committing the crime. Even in Sheila's wealth of police interactions, this is new for her.

"The bartender at Whiskey River in LA confirmed you'd been drinking heavily that night," Detective Martinez says carefully. "Do you remember that?"

Sister Dymphna shakes her head.

Perfect. Just answer the question. Never give more details

than necessary.

"But you believe you were driving under the influence?"

"It doesn't matter what she believes," Sheila interjects quickly. This question is clearly a setup. "She has no memory. She'd just be guessing. And I'm sure you already know the answer to that. You've talked to the bartender."

Detective Chen looks at her. "Are you a lawyer, in addition to being a nun?"

"No," Sister Mary Bernice says, "she isn't."

"It's okay," Sister Dymphna says. She practically wrinkles her nose at Shelia as if her defense of her is distasteful.

"The evidence suggests it." Sister Dymphna says to the police. Sheila can hear the self-loathing in her voice. "It seems apparent that I had been drinking. That I got behind the wheel. And a mother and her seven-year-old daughter died because of my choices."

Once again, Sister Mary Bernice nods her approval at the words, and Sheila bites her lip. She can't help but think Sister Dymphna is taking advice from the wrong person. Sister Mary Bernice may know how to avoid hell, but Sheila knows how to avoid prison.

"Ms. McKellan," Detective Chen says gently, "I need to share some information with you about the accident investigation."

Sister Dymphna straightens in her chair, bracing herself.

"Our forensic team conducted a thorough analysis of the accident scene, including tire mark patterns, impact analysis, and witness statements. The evidence shows that the other driver, Sarah Hoffman, had fallen asleep at the wheel. She had spent a long night in the hospital emergency room with her baby, who had a fever. Her vehicle crossed the center line and was traveling in your lane when the collision occurred."

Sister Dymphna blinks. "I don't understand."

"The tire marks show you attempted to swerve to avoid the collision," Detective Martinez says. "You tried to get out of the way, but there wasn't enough time or space."

"But I was drinking," Sister Dymphna protests. "I was impaired. If I had been sober, maybe I could have reacted faster, maybe—"

"You had been drinking, and that was wrong," Detective Chen says. "But nothing would have changed. Mrs. Hoffman was traveling at approximately fifty-five miles per hour when she crossed into your lane. You had less than two seconds to react. Even a completely sober driver would not have been able to avoid the collision."

Sheila's heartbeat quickens. She can hardly believe it. Sister Dymphna is not responsible for the deaths of the mother and child. She watches Sister Dymphna process this information too, sees hope warring with months of assumed guilt. This girl deserves this break, she thinks. After everything that had happened during her childhood.

"Since you ran away before we could test your alcohol levels," Detective Martinez continues, "we can't even charge you with a DUI. However, the accident itself was not your fault."

"Then why did I run?" Sister Dymphna asks, her voice breaking.

"We have no idea," Detective Chen says. "Based on witness statements, you were conscious and walking after the accident. You simply walked away. Maybe you panicked because you knew you were intoxicated. Or maybe you were in shock. Head injuries can cause confusion and disorientation."

"What about the hit and run charges?" Sister Mary Bernice asks suddenly, speaking for the first time since they sat down.

Both detectives look at her with mild surprise, as if they'd forgotten she was there. Sheila also looks at her, surprised at the very good legal question.

"There will be consequences for leaving the scene of an accident," Detective Martinez says. "But given the circumstances—the head injury, the amnesia, and that Ms. McKellan has voluntarily come forward—the DA will work with us on a plea agreement."

"What kind of plea agreement?" Sheila asks.

"Probably community service and mandatory counseling," Detective Chen explains. "The goal is accountability and healing, not punishment for someone who was clearly as much a victim as she was a participant."

No cop has ever expressed that goal to Shelia for her crimes, but again, she'll take it.

"I still took the money," Sister Dymphna says. "I stole millions of dollars from my business partners."

It's like she wants to get arrested, Sheila thinks. She needs to stop talking.

"That's a separate issue," Detective Martinez says. "And one that's outside our jurisdiction. We don't even know of that case."

"We'll close the missing persons case," Detective Chen says, making notes in her file. "And we'll be in touch about the plea agreement."

Tears stream down Sister Dymphna's face at this unexpected grace.

Shelia puts her hand on Sister Dymphna's arm to squeeze it, but Sister Dymphna pulls her arm away.

22

Biddy

"Are you trying to get us arrested today?" Ruby whispers. "Breaking into the police station wasn't enough for you?"

"Former police station."

Biddy stands next to Ruby in the shadows of the overgrown boxwood hedge that surrounds the former District Attorney's house. District Attorney Harold Morrison was the person who had requested that the police charge Carl Ryan, despite his alibi. She has also learned another fun fact about him. Before becoming DA and demanding that Sheila's father be prosecuted, he was the family lawyer to the McKellan's.

His colonial-style home sits on a quiet street in what was once a prestigious neighborhood in Albion. Like everything else in the dying town, it has seen better days. Paint peels from the shutters, and the wraparound porch sags slightly under the weight of neglect. This is good news, though. Neither he nor any of his neighbors live here any longer.

"I can't believe I'm doing this," Ruby whispers beside her, clutching her flashlight like a weapon. "Breaking and entering is a felony, Biddy. A felony."

"Well," Biddy tries to shrug this off, even though she knows her friend is right. "You already did it once."

"I did not. The police station had been abandoned. The police don't own it anymore. You said we were just trespassing. Not breaking and entering."

Biddy did say that, but she isn't entirely sure that is how that works. Nevertheless, it no longer matters. They didn't get caught.

"This is the same. Morrison moved to Florida three years ago. So this house is abandoned too."

"It's not abandoned. He still owns it."

"It's close enough." Biddy steps out of the shadows and starts walking toward the house. She is guessing that a man like Morrison keeps a paper trail of misdeeds to cover himself. She bets he has files on everyone—dirty politicians, judges, and business people. Evidence of their guilt is insurance to him, in case anyone tries to cross him. And those files aren't items you'd take to your vacation home in Florida.

They make their way around the side of the house, staying close to it to avoid being seen by neighbors, not that there appear to be any. Anyone with money fled this area years ago.

Harold Morrison's backyard is overgrown with weeds and volunteer trees, providing excellent cover. Biddy notes with approval that the nearest streetlight is broken, making it unlikely there are working cameras.

"This is insane," Ruby mutters, but she follows Biddy up the steps to the back door. She really is the best friend ever.

Biddy pulls on latex gloves and examines the lock. It's old and simple—the hardware that was standard when the house was built in the 1960s. She selects one of her picks and inserts it into the keyhole.

"How are we are in our sixties and still picking locks on a regular basis?" Ruby says.

Biddy laughs. "The nuns always said that our childhood years would prepare us for the real world." The lock clicks open. And Biddy smiles. "I guess they were right."

They slip inside, finding themselves in Morrison's kitchen. Late afternoon sunlight filters through the windows, revealing dusty cabinets and countertops. Underneath the film of dirt, Biddy spots marble. Morrison did well for himself.

"Where do we start?" Ruby whispers.

"His office." Biddy points toward the front of the house. "If Morrison kept the files I think he did, that's where they'll be."

They make their way through the deserted rooms, their flashlight beams dancing across furniture covered in sheets. Morrison's office overlooks the street. It's a wood-paneled room with built-in bookshelves and a large desk positioned to face the door. Like the rest of the house, this room still contains furniture that appears to have been there a lifetime—along with filing cabinets, boxes of documents, and law books, too heavy or worthless to move to Florida.

"Jackpot," Biddy breathes, surveying the filing cabinets that line one wall. Some are so full, the doors can't even close.

She starts with the cabinet closest to the desk, pulling out drawers and scanning the file labels with her flashlight. Most contain routine legal documents—case files, correspondence, court filings. But the bottom drawer is locked.

"Ruby, hand me the crowbar. It's in my handbag."

"Biddy, are you sure about this? If you use a crowbar, they're going to know someone was here."

"I bet these houses get broken into all the time. They'll just think it's some kids looking for liquor." Biddy wedges the crowbar into the gap between the drawer and the cabinet frame. She tells herself not to let Ruby's sensible advice deter her and pulls down. "Besides, we've come this far."

The drawer pops open with a satisfying crack. Inside, Biddy finds exactly what she was hoping for—files marked with names she recognizes from Albion's elite. McKellan. Ryan. Henderson. Each folder is thick with documents and photographs.

Where to start? She looks from the McKellan file to the Ryan file. Both are likely to contain useful information—one about Carl Ryan, Sheila's father, and one about Nina's. She pulls out the Ryan file simply because it is thinner. She opens it on Morrison's desk.

"Goodness," she whispers, staring at the contents.

The file contains dozens of documents—police reports, witness statements, financial records. All of them point to Carl Ryan's guilt in the arson case that killed the McKellans. Her heart falls…she'd been so sure.

But then she sees a smudge on one paper and rubs at it. It flakes off, revealing writing underneath. Biddy bends down to exam it more closely. It's been altered. If she looks closely, she sees the telltale lines where original information has been whited-out and typed over. That means these hard copies that were filed at the courthouse differ from the original documents which were typed at the police station.

"Look at this," she says, showing Ruby a police report dated two days after the fire. "This version says the witness saw Carl Ryan at the factory at 4:00 AM, right when the fire started. But the original report we found at the police station said 2:00 AM."

Ruby peers over her shoulder. Her eyes widen, for Ruby

would never dream someone capable of lying. "Someone changed it."

"Morrison changed it before filing it." Biddy flips through more documents. "Here's a witness statement from the tavern owner, saying Carl never showed up that night. But we know from the police files the same witness confirmed Carl's alibi."

Ruby frowns. "So Morrison falsified evidence to make Carl look guilty."

"That's exactly what he did. And he probably paid the police off so that they said nothing." Biddy pulls out another folder, this one marked "Insurance - Lucifol Fire." Inside are correspondence and financial documents showing payments from various insurance companies totaling millions of dollars. "And here's why."

Ruby examines the insurance documents. "Morrison was getting kickbacks from the insurance settlements?"

"Not just kickbacks. He was orchestrating the whole thing." Biddy points to a letter from an insurance adjuster. "Look at this—'As discussed, quick resolution of the arson case will expedite claim payments and minimize investigation costs.' Morrison wasn't just covering up the real killer—he was profiting from it."

They continue searching through the files, uncovering more evidence of Morrison's corruption. Bribes from developers who wanted to buy the burned factory site for pennies on the dollar. Payoffs from competitors who benefited from Lucifol's destruction. A web of financial crime that stretched far beyond the factory fire itself.

But it's the next file that makes Biddy's blood run cold.

"Ruby, look at this."

The file is marked "Contingency - Ryan Family" and contains documents that make Biddy sick to read. Falsified police reports accusing Carl's wife of multiple drug arrests. Fake witness statements describing Sheila as a member of a violent gang. School records altered to show failing grades and disciplinary problems. Even photographs that appear to show Sheila in compromising situations with known criminals.

"This is all fake," Ruby says, examining a police report claiming that Sheila had been arrested for assault. "Sheila would never do this! She was an honor student. She never got in trouble."

"Of course it's fake." Biddy presses her lips together as she studies it. "But if Carl had fought the charges against him, Morrison would have leaked these files to the press. Planted them in official records. Destroyed Sheila's reputation and her mother's ability to work again." Biddy's hands shake as she reads through the fabricated evidence. "Carl didn't run because he was guilty. He ran because Morrison threatened to destroy his family's lives if he fought the charges."

"So he chose exile over fighting back."

"He chose to protect the people he loved, even if it meant sacrificing himself." Biddy photographs each document with her phone, building a comprehensive record of Morrison's crimes. "Sheila has spent years blaming herself for her father's supposed crimes. She gave up everything she worked towards because of his guilt. But he was innocent. And he left because he was protecting her."

They continue searching through the files, finding evidence of Morrison's involvement in numerous other cases. Witness intimidation. Evidence tampering. Bribery and extortion on a scale that's breathtaking in its audacity.

"How did he get away with all this?" Ruby asks.

"Because he was careful. Because he had powerful friends. And because anyone who tried to expose him ended up like Carl Ryan—destroyed or driven away." Biddy closes the file and looks around the office. "But he made one mistake."

"What?"

"He kept records of everything. Morrison was so paranoid about someone turning on him he documented every crime, every payoff, every threat. He thought these files were his insurance policy, but they're actually evidence of his guilt."

As Biddy reaches for the McKellan file, Ruby grabs her arm.

"Do you hear that?"

Biddy freezes, listening. In the distance, she can hear the wail of sirens, getting closer.

"Police?" Ruby whispers.

"Or fire department. Or ambulance." Biddy says as nonchalantly as she can manage. She doesn't want Ruby to know her heart is pounding. The sirens are distinctly from a police car. "Any which way, we should go."

The sirens are getting louder now, and Biddy sees flashing lights through the office windows.

Well, that's not good.

"They're coming here," Ruby says, panic in her voice.

"That's impossible. No one knows we're—" Biddy stops mid-sentence and looks up. In the corner above the door is a small camera with a red blinking light pointed directly at the desk.

How could she forget to check for cameras? That's a rookie mistake.

"There's a camera. It's probably motion triggered." She quickly gathers up the most incriminating files, pauses, and then decides to take the McKellan file as well. She stuffs them into her purse. "Let's go."

They hurry toward the back door, but the sound of car doors slamming and voices getting louder stops them cold. Through the kitchen window, Biddy sees flashlight beams already begin to sweep the backyard.

"We're trapped," Ruby whispers.

Biddy's mind races, looking for options. She hears the voices outside shouting instructions.

"The basement," she says suddenly. "There might be a way out through the basement. The house is built on a hill."

They find the basement stairs and hurry down into the darkness. The basement is partially finished, with a family room area and what appears to be an exercise room. More importantly, Biddy can see a small window that might be large enough for them to crawl through.

"There," she says, pointing to the window. "If we can get outside and hide in the bushes, we might be able to avoid detection."

As they work to open the window, footsteps pound across the floor above them. Someone is searching the house, and it's only a matter of time before they check the basement.

The window is stuck, painted shut years ago. Ruby finds a screwdriver on Morrison's workbench and starts chipping away at the paint while Biddy keeps watch.

"Almost got it," Ruby whispers.

Above them, the footsteps are getting closer to the basement stairs.

The window finally gives way, swinging open to reveal a view of the side yard. It's a tight fit, but they might squeeze through.

"You first," Biddy whispers.

Ruby wiggles through the window opening, dropping to the ground outside with a soft thud. Biddy hands her the purse full of documents and then climbs through herself.

She's halfway out when she hears footsteps on the basement stairs.

"There's someone down here!" a voice shouts.

Biddy pushes herself the rest of the way through the window, scraping her back on the frame but making it outside. She and Ruby run toward the hedge that separates Morrison's property from the neighbors', but the beam of a flashlight finds them.

"Freeze! Police!"

Biddy and Ruby stop running and put their hands in the air. But before she does so, Biddy pitches her purse containing the precious files into a thorny bush.

23

Megan

Megan and Amelia are in Amelia's minivan, driving towards some teeny tiny town three hours from Pooka. Megan brushes a few Cheerios from her seat and glances through the heavily fingerprint smeared window to her right. They are lost.

"We aren't lost," Amelia says without her even voicing her concerns.

"How can you tell?" Megan asks. "No matter what road we're on, all you can see are cornfields."

"For one, we are using GPS and two, the woman gave us directions on the phone. This is the road she said to take."

"So, then we should be there," Megan says. "It's been three hours."

"Maybe we are here," Amelia says.

Dear God, Megan thinks, but does not say. What a terrible place to live.

Amelia snatches the cellphone with the map from Megan and glances at it. She must like what she sees because five minutes later, she pulls off the main highway on an exit.

"I told you we were here," she says.

"Mommy is always right!" pipes up a high-pitched voice from the third row. A few more Cheerios come sailing past Megan's ear and lands on her seat. Did Megan forget to mention that Amelia brought the kids since couldn't find a babysitter?

"Mommy knows everything," says a solemn girl in the second row.

"She doesn't know Minecraft," says the 10-year-old boy.

"I'm watching YouTube videos about the game," Amelia says. "I'll figure it out, Liam."

"Could we just focus on finding the house?" Megan asks. Her research trips have taken on a markedly different appearance since her exit from Harvard. Yet, she finds herself excited.

"I'll look for the house," says the chirpy voice from the back. "Is it pink? That's my favorite color."

And definitely more colorful.

To give credit to where it is due, Amelia is the one who found the likely daughter of Sarah Hope. The real challenge wasn't finding a person named Hope. It was finding the right Hope. Amelia had organized a spreadsheet with names and then had narrowed it to five based on age and geographic location. Lucy Hope was born in 1956, making her 69. But even more exciting than her age, is that her birth certificate listed her mother as unknown.

"I think I see it," Ann says from the second row. "The address is 1213, right?" She points to a house on the left. It's a little ranch with flowers spilling from window boxes.

"I have to go to the bathroom," Birdie, the one with the chirpy voice, says from the back.

"I'm sure Miss Hope will let you use hers." Amelia pulls the car against the curb on the far side of the street and puts it in park. "Liam, would you like to come in or wait in the car?"

"Car," Liam says.

"Car," Ann says, pulling a book out of her tote bag.

Megan prays to hear the word 'car' a third time.

"In!" Birdie shouts.

Megan shrugs. How different can Birdie be from her student interns? Except that she's five. And wears two wispy pigtails held by different colored bows. Other than that, her unbridled enthusiasm and distinct lack of skills are exactly the same.

Amelia, Megan, and Birdie climb out of the car and, to Megan's surprise, Birdie puts her sticky food colored hand into Megan's and tugs her across the street.

Amelia whispers that she's sorry and holds out a wipe but Megan says it's okay and surprisingly it is.

"Why are we here?" Birdie asks.

"We are trying to figure out where Miss Hope was born," Megan says.

"That should be easy," Birdie says. "We'll just ask her. I know I was born in the Pooka Medical Center."

"It's a little harder than that," Amelia says. "Her mom didn't tell her, so she may not know. We have to ask lots of questions to figure it out."

Birdie's eyes light up. "Like twenty questions?"

"Yes," Amelia says. "Like twenty questions."

Megan rings the doorbell while Birdie hops from foot to foot, her hand still in Megan's. Megan really hopes that Lucy Hope likes children.

The door opens, revealing an attractive older woman. She has white hair, likely set in rollers and a long, lithe figure. She wears a yellow sweater with a knee length blue skirt and walks with a cane.

"Can I use your bathroom?" Birdie asks.

The woman looks down and smiles. "Sure."

Birdie drops Megan's hand and before anyone can say anything, she runs into the house and starts opening doors in the hallway until she finds the right one. She hurries in and slams it behind her.

Lucy looks back at her remaining two guests. Megan extends her hand.

"I'm Megan Bramley and this is Amelia Reagan. Thank you for seeing us."

"Of course," Lucy says, taking her hand between her own. "It's such a pleasure to have visitors. Especially young ones. I never had children of my own."

This, Megan thinks, is good to hear.

Lucy leads them into a small living room to the right of the entry. A plate of cookies, a pitcher of lemonade, and a stack of glasses sit on the coffee table. Lucy offers them to Amelia and Megan, who shake their heads and then watches with a smile as Birdie races into the room, helps herself to a napkin and stacks it four high with cookies. She sits beside Lucy and swings her feet as she bites one.

"We're going to play twenty questions," she announces to their host.

"Actually," Megan says quickly, "we want to see what you remember about your birth mother."

Lucy looks at Birdie. "I don't think that was phrased in the form of a question, do you?"

Oh for God's sake.

Birdie shakes her head, flinging crumbs in all directions.

"Definitely not."

Megan takes a breath and reminds herself that it is Amelia's hard work that got them here.

"Do you know who your mother is?"

Lucy shakes her head. "No."

"Darn," Birdie says.

"Do you know where you were born?" Amelia asks.

"No."

"My turn." Birdie jumps to her feet. "Did you ever consider painting your house pink?"

Lucy inclines her head. "No, but I should."

What a waste of a question, Megan thinks…until she realizes this isn't actually a game of twenty questions. It's an interview.

"How did you come to be adopted?"

"That's not a yes or no question," Birdie says.

"Birdie, it's okay," Amelia says quietly.

"No, it's not," Lucy says. "Rules are rules."

Megan wonders if all children are this unhelpful.

"Did someone you know bring you here?" she asks.

Lucy smiles. "Yes."

"Good one!" Birdie says to her with a smile, and Megan actually feels a sense of achievement.

"Is she still in your life?" Amelia asks.

Lucy's smile widens. "Yes."

"Is she a stork?" Birdie asks.

"A distant relative," Lucy says.

Megan doesn't really care if she's a hippopotamus.

"Can we meet her?" she asks.

"Yes."

Amelia looks around the room and Megan sees her eyes settle on a picture of a young girl with curls not dissimilar to

Birdie, standing between two stern looking adults. Amelia nods at it. "Did they raise you?"

"Yes."

"Are they your parents?" Birdie asks.

"They became my parents," Lucy says. "But really, they were my aunt and uncle."

"What happened to your mom?" Birdie asks.

Megan is mildly irritated that Birdie took her turn, but this is a good question and she thinks the little girl will get farther asking a non yes/no question than she will.

"Well." Lucy looks at her. "My mom died in childbirth and Rachel…a friend of hers…brought me here. She told my aunt and uncle that I was family and that they needed to step up and take me in."

"Did she say where she came from or how she knew your mother?" Amelia asks.

Lucy shakes her head. "No."

"Was Rachel pregnant when she brought you?" Megan asks.

Lucy's eyes widen. "Why yes. How on earth would you have guessed that?"

"She's actually pretty good at this game," Birdie says.

"It seems like she's had a bit of practice," Lucy says. "I googled her before she came and her background is quite impressive."

"I know," Birdie says, "she was on TV with my mom."

"Well, that is impressive," Lucy says. "Unfortunately, I'm not sure how much more help I can be. I really know little more than I've told you. Rachel has stayed in my life over all this time and comes to visit for every single one of my birthdays. But she refuses to tell me anything about my past other than that my mother really loved me and wanted me. I don't know how the two knew each other or where I was born."

Megan is about to stand up.

"Wait," Birdie says. "I still have a question."

Lucy smiles at her. "Okay."

"Did someone make that bracelet for you?"

Lucy fingers the beaded bracelet on her left wrist, the beads strung on a fraying slip of pink thread. "Yes. Rachel said it was my mom's, but my aunt and uncle don't remember it."

Megan holds her breath.

"Can I see it?" the little girl asks.

Lucy passes it to Birdie and Megan leans over her shoulder as the child fingers it. The beads have little markings on them that look like decorative crosses. The color is a beautiful shade of deep green.

Megan inhales.

"I've got it!" Birdie announces, passing the bracelet to Megan. "You're from Pooka. Every second grader makes these in religion class for their sacrament of Reconciliation."

Megan stares at the beads in her hands. This bracelet isn't a bracelet at all. It's rosary beads with a cross hanging from the top. The beads are Irish marble, the traditional color of Sacred Heart of the Woods.

"You're right," Megan whispers.

"I'm pretty good at this game too," Birdie confirms.

"Pooka?" Lucy says. "I've never heard of it."

Amelia nods. "Pooka," she says, kindness filling her voice. "It's about three hours from here, and I think we may have found your mother's grave."

Lucy's eyes tear. "Really? You found my mother? I've spent my whole life wondering who she is."

Megan is about to tell her more, but then her cellphone

rings. She listens briefly and then puts it back in her bag.

"Unfortunately, we have to go," she says to the women as calmly as she can. "There's been a bit of a family emergency."

"Is everyone okay?" Lucy asks.

Amelia looks at her questioningly.

"They are," Megan says. She adds the words 'for now,' in her head. This is the second time in a year, her mother has called her to bail her out of a jail. "I'm so sorry to interrupt this conversation. Can we call later and set up a time to talk further and maybe have you come visit Pooka? We'd also love to speak with Rachel."

"Please do. I really want to learn more." Lucy fingers her bracelet. "My mother!" Her voice fills with wonder.

Megan nods to Amelia and both mother and daughter stand up. Amelia hugs Lucy goodbye and drags Birdie towards the door…Birdie's pockets bulging with cookies.

<h1 style="text-align:center">24</h1>

<h1 style="text-align:center">Biddy</h1>

Biddy is not stupid. She uses her one phone call to let Megan know where she is, which is the right thing to do. But she has Ruby use her phone call to call Shelia, the person you really want with you when stuck in the cogs of the justice system. Therefore, it is no surprise when Sheila follows a uniformed officer to the holding cell of the Albion police department. Sheila is still wearing her ridiculous nun's habit, and Biddy can't believe she is thinking this, but Sheila was better off when she was dressing like Biddy.

"Bless you, my son," Sheila says to her escort and winks at Biddy. "May the Lord be with you in your good works."

This is taking things too far, Biddy thinks. But the man nods his thanks and smiles a little more kindly at Biddy and Ruby, so maybe it isn't a terrible choice after all.

Sheila looks at the hodgepodge of women congregated in the cell and then at Biddy and Ruby, who huddle at the corner of a bench. The smell of body odor is overpowering and only one out of every four fluorescent lights seems to work. Drug addled shouts and screams echo throughout the space.

"You realize that prison in Albion is not the same experience as prison in Pooka?" Sheila says.

"We do now." Biddy stands up from the metal bench, brushes off her black slacks, and walks to meet Sheila at the bars. Before she gets there, a redhead with a bouffant of matted hair steps between them. The woman wears five-inch platform stilettoes, a tank top, and something that looks like denim underwear.

"Sheila?" She peers at Sheila through the bars. Then she throws her head back and laughs. "You became a nun?"

"How are you Gabs?" Sheila asks. "Still on the corner of 7th and Lex?"

"Yep." The woman shakes her head. "But business isn't what it once was. Prices have tanked."

"All the good customers left," Sheila says. "Simple supply and demand. You should make a move."

Biddy can't believe she is listening to this economics lesson. She also really hopes Sheila doesn't suggest that this woman move to Pooka.

"You should try Florida," Sheila advises. "That's where all the rich people are and better weather."

Thank goodness.

The woman nods, and her eyes are so sad, Biddy suddenly sees beyond the thick rings of mascara and feels sorry for her.

"I know. It's just that this is home. You were right to get out of the business. Although I don't know that the church pays much better. Anyway, it was nice seeing you."

The woman walks away, and Shelia's eyes return to Biddy and Ruby.

"You know each other?" Biddy asks.

"Gabs and I went to grade school together."

Biddy flinches, trying to picture the woman as a seven-year-old.

"Anyway, that's doesn't matter. What does matter is why you are here. What were you thinking?" Sheila asks them.

Biddy does not want to talk about what she discovered in this place. If the DA was dirty, there's no telling if the cops are too. "I wanted to investigate something, and the records were in that house we broke into," she says. "Trust me, getting arrested was worth it. Did you bail us out?"

"No, I didn't bail you out." Sheila looks surprisingly angry. "I want to know what you were investigating first. I'm the president. I'm in charge. And you did this behind my back. Plus, you could've gotten yourselves killed. Albion is not the place for people like you."

Biddy flinches again. People like you. Not people like us. She hates that Sheila sees herself as different from them. But didn't Biddy think the same thing a few minutes ago when she sat in this cell with Sheila's classmate and hoped she didn't move to Pooka?

"It was Biddy's idea," Ruby says.

The words feel a little traitorous, but Biddy figures Sheila probably could've guessed that on her own.

"Mom, what were you thinking?"

Uh oh.

Megan storms towards the holding cell with Amelia and three children trailing behind her. If Sheila seems angry with them, Megan is positively livid. Biddy had been hoping that Shelia would've gotten them out of this cell before Megan arrived.

"It smells in here," announces the youngest of the three children. Her hair is in pigtails, and her shirt boasts a sparkly rainbow. The other children say nothing. Their eyes widen and they push closer to their mother.

"I think we'll wait in the car," Amelia says. Her arms encircle her children and she heads out much more quickly than she had entered.

"This is the second time you've been arrested," Megan says. "You are sixty-eight years old. This isn't normal."

"Oh, this isn't the second time," Ruby giggles. "It's way more than that. You just didn't know her in high school."

This doesn't appear to sit well with her daughter.

"So," Sheila says, "I hate to agree with Megan, but what were you doing?"

Biddy has about had it with Megan and Sheila lecturing her.

"I was thinking your father's case deserved another look, and I found—"

"So this isn't even about Sister Dymphna?" Sheila interrupts. "This is about me?"

Now she looks furious.

"My life is none of your business. I'm not a case for you to solve. You are supposed to be my fellow club member. My mentor."

"I told you not to meddle," Megan says.

"That's low," Gabs says. She leans against the bars on the left-hand side of the cell and shakes her head. "Investigating your friend."

"I wanted to help you. You were valedictorian of your class. You had gotten a full ride to Princeton! You don't deserve this life."

"I think being a nun is a fine life," Gabs says. "I've never heard of someone trying to save a person from a career in the church."

"This is exactly why I didn't tell you about my past," Sheila snaps. "It's because you somehow think all that makes me a better person. I'm the same person no matter what path I took. You don't respect the career I built for myself. You want me to change."

"Amen to that, sister," Gabs says.

Ruby giggles and starts singing "Amen."

"Don't give me that," Biddy says. "I thoroughly respect who you are. Look where you came from." She waves her arms around the cell. "And look who you've become despite all that. You did what you needed to do. But I don't think you should feel stuck with that career for the rest of your life. You deserve options."

"Biddy…" Ruby says.

"I still don't think being a nun isn't all that terrible," Gabs says.

"Mom…" Megan says.

"I don't need options," Sheila says. "I deserve respect. I'm exactly who I want to be."

"Are you?" Biddy grips the bars separating them. "What if none of it happened? What if your dad hadn't set the fire?"

"No. I won't even pretend that." Sheila shakes her head. "The one thing you and I have in common, Biddy, is that we accept reality. My dad is an arsonist and murderer. My mom got sick. And I did what I needed to do to provide for her. I don't question how the world could have been different. I've learned to live with everything that happened. And I'm not ashamed of who I've become. Unlike you, apparently."

"I'm not ashamed of you, and you shouldn't be ashamed either," Biddy says. "You should be angry."

"Angry?" Sheila grips the bars as well. "Angry at who? My

dad for killing two people in a fire and then deserting us? My mom for dying? Or you for not letting things be?"

"At the police," Biddy whispers, still well aware of her surroundings. "Your dad didn't start the fire. The District Attorney set him up."

Sheila's face goes white as a sheet.

25

Sheila

Sheila is numb, a buzzing, hollow numbness, as if every nerve just stopped functioning. She tells herself not to believe Biddy's words. They are too good to be true. Even she doesn't think a lawyer would stoop that low. She fights off various emotions, wanting to surface. Rage. Relief. Vindication. Grief so sharp it cuts clean through her ribs. Instead, she insists on disbelief.

She turns on her heel and walks back towards the front desk, the fluorescent lights humming overhead, the smell of old coffee and disinfectant clinging to the air. Her body moves on routine, muscle memory taking over where thought cannot. She pays the bail for Biddy and Ruby...and then adds Gabs to her tab. She signs the women out with a hand that doesn't shake, thanks the officer on duty with a voice that sounded perfectly normal, and ten minutes later, ushers everyone outside like this was just another normal visit to the police station.

They cross the parking lot, gravel crunching beneath their shoes, the late afternoon sun hanging low and carrying a coolness with it.

Gabs looks at the quartet of quiet woman. "I think I'm going to go. Thanks Sheila."

Sheila nods and watches Gabs walk away. Then she turns to face Biddy.

"I don't believe you."

The words rip out of Sheila before she realizes she's speaking. Her voice is tight, brittle, the sound of something stretched too far. She starts walking again and is moving fast—too fast—her strides long and angry. She's not walking so much as stalking. As if she can outrun the announcement in there.

Biddy, in her sensible shoes and tailored coat, has to take quick little steps to keep up. Ruby runs after her friend and Megan trails quietly behind them all.

"You're like my mother," Sheila says to Biddy, the comparison flaring hot and uninvited. "You just want that to be true. You need it to be true. But it isn't." She stops abruptly and spins, forcing Biddy to halt with her. "I've learned to accept that my father is guilty. I had to. So leave it alone."

For decades, Sheila has lived with this story. Her father is a criminal. A coward. A man who chose fire and destruction instead of his family. She built her adulthood on that foundation.

Biddy shakes her head, slow and deliberate. She looks... certain.

"I can prove it," Biddy says.

The words hit Sheila like a slap.

Before she can respond, Megan steps forward, her brow furrowed. "You know what?" Her voice is careful. "Why don't Ruby and I go home with Amelia, and you two can...talk this out?"

Ruby nods immediately, eyes darting between Sheila and Biddy. She looks like someone who has wandered into a family argument by accident and isn't sure on which side she is supposed to stand.

Sheila nods.

They split off in the lot, goodbyes muttered, promises to check in later, hanging awkwardly in the air. Biddy climbs into the passenger seat of Sheila's car and folds her hands neatly in her lap.

How can she be so calm? Sheila wonders.

"So," she says as she pulls out of the parking spot, the engine sounding too loud in the silence. "Where's your so-called evidence?"

"I'll show you."

The drive is quiet. No radio. No small talk. Just the hum of tires on asphalt and Biddy's occasional directions—left here, right there—guiding them away from downtown and into a part of Albion Sheila hasn't driven through in years.

They pull up in front of a colonial-style home set back from the street, white siding dulled with age, black shutters symmetrical and severe. The lawn looks like it hasn't been touched all summer.

"Park here," Biddy says.

Sheila does. Turns off the engine. Waits.

"Let's go for a walk," Biddy adds, already opening her door.

Sheila stares at the house.

"This is the house you broke into?" she asks.

Biddy nods.

"Whose is it?"

"Former District Attorney Harold Morrison," Biddy says.

"A close friend of the McKellans. And a very grateful recipient of their donations."

A memory stirs—a man in a dark suit with too many questions showing up on their doorstep.

Sheila climbs out of the car and follows Biddy. Dusk is settling in, the sky bruising purple and gray. Biddy moves with purpose, like someone retracing familiar steps. Their shoes crunch on the pockmarked road as they head toward the side of the house, shadows stretching long and thin.

"What exactly did you discover?" Sheila asks.

She's been dying to ask all afternoon. Ever since Biddy spoke those words in the police station, certainty ringing through them. She wants—desperately—to believe her. God help her, she does. But wanting doesn't make something true. Biddy has to be wrong. There is no other option. The alternative is too big, too cruel.

"When both of Sister Dymphna's parents died in the fire," Biddy says, "she and her sister were still teenagers. They were too young and too traumatized to make decisions. Someone else must have stepped in."

Sheila's stomach tightens.

"That someone," Biddy continues, "was their lawyer and family friend. Harold Morrison. He also happened to be the district attorney at the time."

The memory comes crashing back without warning.

The images on TV of press vans lined up outside the McKellan house. Nina and Willa sealed inside, curtains drawn. Then the uncle arriving from Pennsylvania, his face set, telling the press there would be no comment. And of a lawyer standing beside them all. The girls were gone to Pennsylvania with their uncle by nightfall. The lawyer stayed and did all the TV appearances after that.

And her father—missing.

He didn't come home that night. Or the next. Or the next.

Then the knock at the door. The uniformed police. Her mother's cry, raw, when they told her what they'd found. Then her adamant denials.

"The police found my father's fingerprints all over the gasoline cans," Sheila says firmly. She refuses to believe this. "The accelerant. They also had witness statements."

"They were planted," Biddy says with equal conviction.

Sheila laughs. It's short. Humorless. "How could you possibly know all this?"

"Because there's a file."

Biddy crouches next to a row of thorny bushes separating Howard Morrison's home from the neighbor's and starts swearing as she thrusts her arm into them.

"You tossed evidence?" Sheila asks incredulously.

"Well, I didn't want to have to break back in again."

Even in the depths of her emotions, Sheila can't help but think Biddy Bramley would have made an excellent criminal. She has a certain practicality about her, an efficiency that borders on alarming.

Sheila sighs and joins her, fingers stinging as thorns scrape skin and fabric. She tells herself she's humoring Biddy. That she is doing this just to end it, once and for all.

"I've got it!" Biddy announces, holding up a bag, her cashmere sleeve snagged and shredded. "We should go somewhere else to read it."

Sheila nods. She desperately wants to open the files and see what is inside, but Biddy's already been arrested once here. It can't happen again. She thinks about locations. Megan is at Biddy's house, and she doesn't want an audience for this. There is only one other option.

"My apartment."

The drive back to Pooka feels endless.

"Sheila, your father—"

"Please," Sheila snaps. "Just wait."

Her apartment feels smaller than usual. But then again, there are two of them in it. Now that she thinks about it, she doesn't think she's ever had a guest here before. She flips on the lights and watches Biddy take it in—the mismatched furniture, the stacks of papers on the table from the Sister Dymphna investigation, the Marilyn Monroe poster she bought years ago and never took down.

"The poster's a bit much," Biddy says mildly.

Oddly, she seems approving of the rest of the decor. And even more oddly, Sheila finds she likes the approval.

"Can I see the file?" Sheila asks.

Biddy reaches into her bag, fishes around and hands her a file labeled Ryan, Carl. She stands at the kitchen table and flips it open, page after page blurring as her heart pounds and tears form in her eyes. Financial records. Statements. Memos. Names she recognizes and ones she doesn't.

Then she reaches the section labeled *Contingency.*

Her breath catches.

There, in neat type, is a version of her life she has never lived. False records. Fabricated histories. Lies about her mother. About her.

She gasps.

"Why?" she whispers. "Why would he do this?"

Biddy shrugs. "It's hard to know without talking to Harold, but as best as I can tell, he got kickbacks for the large insurance settlement. In order to get that, they needed to close the investigation into the fire and determine its cause. Your father was the perfect fall guy."

"But who was giving him the kickback? It certainly couldn't be the insurance company. They wouldn't want to pay."

"I think I know the answer to that." Biddy reaches into her bag again and this time pulls out a folder labeled McKellan, Edward. She puts it on the table and starts flipping through the contents.

"I think it was Edward McKellan. Nina's parents were trying to save their wealth. The chemicals at the factory were likely making the employees sick, and they realized they could lose everything if the employees sued. So they got ahead of the problem by getting as much money as they could out of the business. They slowly transferred the money from their business accounts to their personal accounts. They started laying off employees to maximize the money they could take. Then your father sensed something was wrong."

Sheila remembers her father being gone at all hours of the night. She secretly worried he was having an affair, but her mother seemed to harbor no such doubts. "He realized they were skimming money from the business."

Biddy nods. The documents in front of her are proving out this theory. "They fired your father to get him off their trail and then they burned the factory down to collect the insurance money. The plan was almost perfect. They could walk away with all that cash, and since the building burned down, there would be no financial books to study and no business to sue. The only thing they were missing was someone to blame the fire on. And Edward McKellan saw the perfect opportunity to kill two birds with one stone. He could frame your father for the arson, discrediting any claims he may have made of fraud. The DA was always dirty. Paying him off was simple."

"All this was for money," Sheila whispers.

"Someone wise once told me that all crime is about money," Biddy says gently.

"So why did Edward McKellan kill himself in the fire?"

Biddy shakes her head. "I don't think he meant to. I think the fire got out of control and he and his wife couldn't escape as planned. I don't know that we will ever figure out for sure what happened that night."

"So, what happened to my father?" Sheila asks.

Biddy shrugs. "From these documents, it looks like he originally stayed to fight the charges. He had a solid alibi and documentation of the business accounts being raided. But then Harold Morrison forced the police to change the evidence. My guess is that Harold met with your father and threatened to destroy your mother and you if he didn't accept the blame. So he left."

"And deserted my mother and I?"

"He thought he was doing what was right."

Sheila can't believe it. Her whole history—all those years of guilt over what her father had done, giving up everything to take care of her mother while she was ill, figuring out a way to pay for her treatments and put food on the table—all of that was because of the McKellan's. It can't be true. None of this can be true.

"I want to talk to Nina," Sheila says. She realizes this is the first time she's called Sister Dymphna by her real name. But knowing this, she doesn't think she'll ever be able to think of her as Sister Dymphna again.

"She was just a child," Biddy says gently. "She won't know anything. This isn't any more her fault than it was yours when you thought your father was guilty."

"She knows something," Sheila insists. "I know she knows something. She keeps dreaming of fire."

Biddy shakes her head. "She may dream of fire, but she can't remember why. It probably is from her car accident. She wasn't at the factory that night. It was just her parents. Talking to her won't help. Besides, we must be cautious."

"Why?"

"Because someone is watching. There were cameras in that house. Harold Morrison may be in Florida, but he's still keeping an eye on things here. Now, he knows what we've found. Talking to Sister Dymphna about this could put her in more danger."

Sheila nods, but she does so only to get Biddy off her back. Biddy's logic makes perfect sense, but how can she not face the person tied to her father's framing? How could she not want to dig for the truth?

26

Sister Dymphna

There is an assumption you make when you decide to join a convent. And that is that your life will be predictable. Some think this is a boring proposition. I think the opposite. In my recent experience, unpredictability has a way of leading to trouble, and trouble is something convents are supposed to avoid. So I'll take predictability.

After my visit to the police station, I try my very best to push all thoughts of my real identity from my head. I try not to think about who I was. Who my sister and parents were. Of why I would take money that belonged to others and run across the country with it. Of why I came to Pooka. Instead, I just try to be Sister Dymphna again.

Dinner seems as good a place as any to begin. We eat at the same time every evening, in the same room, seated in the same chairs, with meals that follow a rotation so dependable I can recite it backward in my sleep. Lentil soup on Mondays. Chicken casserole on Tuesdays. Fish on Fridays, prepared in a manner best described as reverent rather than flavorful.

This night, it is lentil soup, and so, even though I don't like it, I make it. I've become an adequate cook. I'm guessing this isn't something I did often in my past life. But the lentils soften properly, the onions are not scorched, and I add bay leaves at precisely the right moment. Making this meal feels very much like Sister Dymphna's life and as far as I can get from Nina McKellan's.

Sister Mary Bernice sits across from me and nods her approval. Sheila has respected my wishes for her to keep her distance and does not eat with us anymore. I can't help but look at her empty chair and miss her. She would tell me my soup could use more spice.

I am just taking my third spoonful—always the one that tells you whether the meal will be remembered kindly—when the front door bangs open.

I freeze.

My spoon hovers midair.

The soup steams gently.

How did I not remember to lock the door? Sheila has tacked a post-it note beside it to remind me of the task in her absence.

Sister Mary Bernice looks at me with wide eyes.

Footsteps creak towards the dining room and then Amelia appears, an unknown older woman with kind eyes next to her.

Both Sister Mary Bernice and I exhale with relief.

"Sorry for the noisy entrance," Amelia says. "The door got away from me with the wind."

Amelia is dressed neatly but hastily, her coat buttoned crooked, her limp hair in something approximating a ponytail. She has the look of someone who was mid-dinner herself with evidence of whipped sweet potatoes on her sleeve. She also wears an apologetic look on her face.

The older woman is her exact opposite. Her hair is perfectly tamed into a curled silver coif and she appears to be in her Sunday best in a dress, wool coat, and low heels.

"Hi," I say to her.

"I'm sorry to intrude," she says. "I know this should have waited until morning. But I couldn't stop thinking about Megan and Amelia's visit. I finally called Amelia and here we are."

I smile politely, welcoming, as a nun is taught to do, but none of this is helping me understand her presence.

"Sister Dymphna," Amelia says, "this is Lucy Hope. She is the daughter of one of the women in the crypt."

Oh.

I immediately feel bad. I naturally assumed this was about me. These days I think everything is about me. But it isn't. This is a convent, and the attention is supposed to be on the community. And here is a person in need.

I turn to look at Sister Mary Bernice for guidance, but she is just staring at the woman. Her face is white as a sheet.

I guess I'm on my own.

"I'm so sorry for your loss," I say. "I recently learned that my mother has passed as well."

"It's never easy," Lucy says, "even when you don't even know them."

"No," I say, "it isn't."

And just like that, I feel better. I've had the hardest time trying to figure out how to mourn someone I can't remember. Of feeling inadequate to her memory. But Lucy's words resonate. Whether or not I ever remember, she was my mother and I can still love her and mourn her. After all, loving someone who lived and died for you despite not knowing them is one of the church's greatest lessons.

"I'd like to see where you found her," Lucy says. "I'd like to pay my respects."

Now, this isn't good. The crypt has all the charm and reverence of a torture chamber. It is not the place you want to take a grieving daughter to remember her mother. I look again at Sister Mary Bernice, but she just stares at the woman as if stunned. I guess this will fall to me.

"Perfect," I say, even though it isn't. I'll fib just a little. "She was buried in our crypt, a sacred burial spot."

This is directionally true. Her mother was just found a little farther beneath it in the scary cave.

"We have a lovely grotto for vigils right above the crypt, in the church. I'll be happy to show you to it."

Even this is a fib. Technically, the grotto is for the clergy buried in the crypt, but I'm sure if they knew about the girls also buried there, they'd be happy to share.

"If it's alright," the woman says carefully, "I'd like to see the exact spot they found her."

My eyes meet Amelia's. I can see she agrees with me.

The woman senses our hesitation.

"I never got to meet her. I know it sounds stupid, but it would make me feel closer to her."

I close my eyes and think of my mother, who I can't remember. I nod. I'd do anything to feel closer to her, too. In fact, I can sympathize with her wishes. I suddenly want to see where my mother died and is buried as well.

As Sister Mary Bernice would say, there is no other way but through, although at this moment, she still isn't saying anything. The older nun is visibly upset by the guest, and I can't blame her. How to explain to a grieving daughter her mother was buried in a secret chamber of a church is not a pleasant cross to bear. Nevertheless, I will shoulder it. Somehow, I am tied to this as well. My initials were carved down there too.

I pluck my coat from the coat stand and lead Amelia and Lucy back out into the night. There is no need to borrow the key from Sister Mary Bernice, as I somehow still have one in the pocket of my sweater. I've become almost comfortable with things just appearing and disappearing randomly in my life. It's become my normal.

The falling leaves swirl around us as we walk past the graveyard to the church. Above us, soars the black shadow of the grave marker of Eileen Delancy. I remember finding it tacky when I first arrived. But now I see it for what it is. A monument of love. I wish I was taking Lucy to something equally honorable for her mother.

"Why was she buried in the church?" Lucy asks, as we approach the side door to the crypt. "Did she work here?"

"We don't think so."

Sister Mary Bernice could find no record of these women working at the church or even being parishioners.

"I don't understand," Lucy says.

"I'm afraid we don't either," Amelia says. "Your mother was the first we could identify. We are still sorting it out. I'm sorry we can't share more."

I insert the giant skeleton-like key into the repaired lock, twist, and open the door. "Are you ready?"

Lucy takes a breath and nods. We step inside and I fumble for the switch to light the candelabras. The space emerges gradually—not ominous, just old with a distinct tone of reverence. Stone walls. Arched ceilings. Names carved deep into raised marble burial vaults. This, at least, is a space that is comforting. It is not a place of secrets so much as a place of memory, honor, and quiet dignity.

Lucy walks to one tomb and runs her hand over the marble surface. "This is lovely. I'm glad someone cared enough for her to honor her in this way."

Amelia's and my eyes meet. It would be so easy to let Lucy think this is where we found Sarah Hope and then end this little visit right here. But I can't. I can't lie to her. She has a right to know the truth about her mom.

"Actually," I say gently, "this isn't where she was buried. She was in a small plot beneath this."

"Beneath this?" Lucy walks towards me. "There's something beneath this?"

I lead her to the trapdoor and take out my key set to insert the smaller of the two keys. I turn it and then tug hard to pry up the heavy piece of stone.

"Good God," Lucy says.

We stare into the black hole, the first rickety wooden steps, the only thing that is visible.

"Lucy," Amelia says, "it really isn't pleasant down there and there isn't much to see. The police are investigating to discover why your mother may have been found down there. Perhaps it'd be better to remember her up here or at the grotto in the church?"

"No," Lucy whispers. "I want to see."

My heart falls.

I lead the way down the stairs, my cellphone flashlight guiding me. Lucy follows, with Amelia trailing behind. We reach the bottom and I flick on the spotlights rigged by the police. Lucy peers around the earthen space, her eyes taking everything in. Then she sees the empty wooden cot-like platforms lining the walls.

"Which one was hers?" she whispers.

Amelia nods at the one in the bottom, far left corner. Lucy walks over and runs her hands along it.

"Here," Amelia says, shining her cellphone light on the wall, "is her inscription."

The roughly hewn name of Sarah Hope, ever so carefully preserved into the dirt, becomes recognizable. Lucy stares at the marker.

There it is. Her mother's name. Neat. Permanent. Entirely unconcerned with Lucy's feelings on the matter. She stands still.

I have learned, over the last year, that there are many kinds of silence. The convent has trained me to recognize them. This one is the kind that comes just before grief rushes in. Sure enough…

"Why was she here?" Lucy wails. "Who did this to her?"

Or, in this case, anger.

"We don't know," I say with all the calmness I can infuse in my voice.

Lucy stares at me. "How could you not know? This is your church. It is your job to know."

I wince. This is not entirely fair, as I wasn't even born when all this happened. But I understand that I'm representing the church. And my sisterhood. "I'm aware."

Lucy crouches slightly, tracing the letters carved into the dirt.

"Was she hurt?" Lucy asks. "Before she died. Was someone doing something to her down here?"

"No," Amelia says quickly. Megan's investigators blessedly

had detected no evidence of torture. I am grateful that Amelia leaves her answer to this and doesn't mention the expressions of fear on the skeletal remains.

Lucy's shoulders ease just a fraction.

"Then why hide her?" she demands. "Why not tell her family?"

Before I can say the words 'I don't know' one more time…it is a phrase I am rather good at uttering after all…footsteps sound on the stairs and we all peer through the shadows towards them.

Sister Mary Bernice appears, gripping the railing with one hand. Another woman, even older than Lucy, is just behind her.

"Rachel?" Lucy says.

"Why didn't you tell me you were coming here?" the older woman says. She doesn't look around the space. She doesn't react at all. To the empty bunks. To the stench. To the tomb-like quiet that sucks all noise and light from being.

Lucy stares at her. "You knew."

Rachel stops short. "Lucy—"

"You knew," Lucy repeats. "And you didn't tell me."

Rachel opens her mouth, closes it again, and then tries honesty. "I was afraid you'd come down here and have to see all this. I didn't want you to remember your mother this way. She wouldn't have wanted you to remember her this way."

"She's my mother! I have a right to know where she was buried. How she died."

Sister Mary Bernice steps forward. "Rachel was trying to do the right thing. This is bigger than just your mother."

Now it's my turn to be shocked. Sister Mary Bernice knew

too? In some ways, though, this doesn't surprise me. Sister Mary Bernice has been acting strangely. Plus, it is hard to swallow that she wasn't aware of something happening in her church.

"Why was she here?" Lucy asks Rachel. "Was she scared?"

Rachel hesitates too long.

Lucy notices.

"She was scared," Rachel says finally. "But not of anyone here. She was pregnant. Out of wedlock. Against her will."

Tears form in Lucy's eyes, and I can practically read her thoughts. *This is my fault. I'm the reason she died here.*

"At that time, single woman didn't have babies. The doctor and her parents were going to abort it. She didn't want that. Sacred Heart of the Woods was a safe haven for women like her. Like me. I met her here. The nuns in this order hid us from the world and cared for us. Then, after we gave birth, they helped us start a new life with our children so they wouldn't be taken away from us. They did their best to deliver our babies safely. But it was hard. I lost my baby a month before she was due. And Sarah lost her own life."

Tears are now streaming down Lucy's face.

"We buried the women we lost here and survivors continue to visit their graves and tend to the space, even after all these years. They were never alone and they were never forgotten."

"She should have gone to a hospital. She should have just forgotten about me."

Rachel smiles sadly at this. "She never could have forgotten about you. She loved you to the end. She made me promise to always care for you."

"Then why not just tell the police all this when we found the burial site?" Amelia asks Sister Mary Bernice. "Clearly, the women weren't being held against their will. You were helping them. Times have changed. Why not let the truth surface?"

"Times haven't changed so much. We are still helping women in need. Women who are in danger. No one can know about this place for their safety."

Suddenly, a voice echoes down the stairs.

"Nina!" The name, although faint in the dirt tomb, is clear. The voice is Sheila's.

I stiffen, especially at the use of my old name. My instinct, like always, is to avoid her. However, it is time that I face Sheila. It is time that I forgive her. I realize it is no more Sheila's fault that my parents were murdered than it is Lucy's fault that her mom died in childbirth. The fault lies solely with her father.

I head up the stairs and hear the others trailing after me. Amelia is particularly close to my heels. I walk through the crypt to the outside door a little more quickly now, as Sheila continues to shout my old name, its echo very apparent in the marble walled crypt. I emerge outside to a chill wind and an unexpectedly angry looking Sheila.

"You let me believe it was my fault," she screams at me. "For all these years."

"I don't know what you are talking about," I say.

I don't understand this. If anyone should hate the other, it is me.

"My father," Sheila continues, "was framed. By yours."

Before I can ask what on earth she is talking about, a car roars up Main street and drives across the church's front lawn. Headlights sweep across my face, blinding me. I put my hand up to shield my eyes. Sheila twists to see the source of the lights. Their glare blinds both of us.

"No!" Rachel screams.

She and Lucy are off to the side of our group and not in the car's bright headlights.

There is a click. I freeze. I sense the threat, but I still can't see a thing. I don't know where to run.

Rachel is already in motion. She throws herself in front of me.

The shot rings out.

Rachel falls.

And the convent, which has seen many things, more than we ever would have imagined, falls silent.

When we kneel beside her, Rachel's eyes flutter open.

"This is all my fault," she whispers. "I was the one moving your things around. I wanted to scare you away. To keep our safe house a secret. I'm sorry."

And then her eyes close.

27

Sheila

The next day, the Pooka Women's Club gathers in Biddy's living room, all a little shell-shocked from the prior night's events. Ruby sinks into the sofa so deep, Sheila knows it will take a tug from Biddy to get her out. Amelia sits forward on a folding chair, hands clasped, her expression serious and surprisingly alert. Megan leans back in her chair, arms crossed, watching everything with that thoughtful frown she gets when she's trying to make sense of something that refuses to be sensible. And then there's their guest speaker. Sister Mary Bernice sits very straight in Biddy's favorite chair, hands folded in her lap, calm as a lake that has never once been tempted to ripple.

Sheila finds a certain comfort in Biddy's living room these days. It is soothing in its exacting arrangement and proper upholstery. The floral sofa, alone, Sheila estimates, has survived at least three decades and one regrettable phase involving tassels. Framed photographs line the mantel—Biddy at various charity events, Biddy with dignitaries, Biddy with people who look vaguely famous but might also just be well-dressed dentists. Sheila wishes the entire world followed Biddy's rules and decorum. Because the world outside of her purview seems quite a mess.

Sheila stands near the fireplace, fingering the sleeve of an old sweater she's kept from her high school days. She isn't feeling very presidential at the moment. In fact, she feels she has more questions than answers. She doesn't even know where to focus her attention. Every time she closes her eyes, she sees headlights from the car last night. Hears the gun aimed at Sister Dymphna. But then, she opens her eyes, and it's her father she envisions. The fire in the factory burning years ago. The dirty lawyer pointing his finger at her father on behalf of the McKellans.

Sheila clears her throat and gently lowers her gavel on a coaster so as not to chip the marble table and incur Biddy's wrath.

"I call this meeting to order. Thank you all for coming," she says. "I know it's... been a lot."

"Especially for you," Ruby says sympathetically.

Sheila does her best not to tear up at this kindness.

"It's time we get some answers." Sheila nods at Sister Mary Bernice. "I've invited Sister to our meeting to help clarify what happened at the church last night."

Everyone's eyes swivel towards the elderly nun.

"The convent," Sister Mary Bernice begins, "has served as a place of refuge for over a century. While its methods have evolved, its purpose has not."

Sheila bites her lip to keep from snapping at the nun. Can't anyone just get to the point and spit out the truth?

Sister Mary Bernice pauses, letting the weight of her words settle. Sheila pauses to count to ten before she erupts.

"For generations, Sacred Heart has quietly helped women escape danger. At first, for women like Sarah Hope, it was a safe haven from angry families who disapproved of their pregnancies. But now it takes in women avoiding abuse, exploitation, and trafficking."

"But this is just a small church in the middle of nowhere, Indiana," Megan says. Everyone looks at her and her face turns red. "I didn't mean that to sound so demeaning. It's a great church. But how many trafficked women are in this community?"

"That's what makes it so useful," Sister Mary Bernice says. "No one would suspect it. The women don't come from here. They come from all over. Sisters at other churches, many in big cities, send the women here. Indiana is central in the US and accessible from all directions. Some come to us with nothing and want to start over. Some cannot safely be known to exist at all. For their protection, we keep our services secret. We get new identities for them. Find new homes for them and then send them back out to a new location. To a new life. We're a halfway house of sorts, teaching these women a new way of life. But all of it is done in secret for their safety and the nuns who send them to us."

Megan exhales slowly. "So you didn't tell the police when they discovered the burial ground because—"

"Because secrecy keeps people alive," Sister Mary Bernice says simply. "That's also why Rachel didn't tell Lucy about where her mother was buried."

Silence settles over the room.

She looks at Sheila. "That day you thought the crypt was broken into, it wasn't. That was Rachel arriving to feed a few women passing through. They hid in the secret burial space until the police left."

Sheila immediately regrets her shortness with Sister Mary Bernice. This is one of the most noble undertakings she has heard. She watches Amelia absorb the words, watches Ruby's jaw tighten as understanding dawns. Watches Megan's ever distrustful expression soften, her anger finding somewhere else to land.

"And Rachel?" Amelia asks quietly. "How is she?"

Sister Mary Bernice folds her hands more tightly. "She survived emergency surgery last night. She is in a coma."

The words hit Sheila harder than she expects. That woman had saved Sister Dymphna's life. She'd taken a bullet for her. She grips the edge of the mantel.

"Lucy hasn't left her side," Sister Mary Bernice adds.

Of course she hasn't, Sheila thinks. Lucy Hope may have lost her mother before she knew her, but her mother had left Rachel in her staid.

Ruby breaks the silence. "So… where does that leave Sister Dymphna's case?"

Sheila straightens. This, at least, is familiar ground.

"I recognized Rachel as the woman who broke into the church and framed Sister Dymphna for leaving the wine cabinet unlocked."

Sister Mary Bernice presses her lips together. "I honestly had no idea Rachel went to that extent to protect our underground network. I never would have approved of her actions—of making Sister Dymphna think she was going crazy. But I can assure you she is not behind the murder attempts. I am confident in that."

"I agree," Sheila says. "She only broke into the church because she was bringing food to women in hiding," Sheila says. "And the bodies in the church appear to have nothing to do with Sister Dymphna…unless she is one of the women you are protecting?"

Sister Mary Bernice shakes her head. "I genuinely didn't know her. She had amnesia, and I took her in. Just like I've said."

"The bullet came from a passing car," Sheila continues. "It was someone outside the church, unconnected to this operation the convent is running."

Megan tilts her head. "Not necessarily. Could it be someone else's angry husband? Or someone connected to trafficking?"

Biddy, who has been quiet until now, sets her teacup down with purpose. "Whoever is behind this, pointed the gun at Sister Dymphna. All the attempts have targeted Sister Dymphna. If the shooting was related to the convent operation, it wouldn't make sense to target just her. Why not Sister Mary Bernice? Why not Rachel? No—Sister Dymphna and only Sister Dymphna is the target."

"I agree," Sheila says. "And that someone is still trying to hurt Sister Dymphna. We still need to stop them."

She takes a breath. A deep one. What comes next is hard for her to say.

"I'm stepping down as president."

The room erupts at once.

"You're doing what?" Ruby demands.

"That's ridiculous," Amelia says.

Megan blinks. "Is this—are we voting on this?"

Biddy just stares at her.

Sheila puts her fingers to her lips and whistles. The sound is loud, shrill, and immediately stops the ruckus. She learned this trick from someone at a jail one night.

"I can't lead this investigation. Not now. I'm too personally involved. I just learned Sister Dymphna…Nina's family framed my father. And I know I should be professional and rise above it as a president should, but I'm angry. You could do better than me."

Biddy stands and that silences the room instantly.

"As President Emeritus," Biddy says, "I refuse to accept your resignation."

"Can she do that?" Sheila asks Megan.

The back door bangs open. Everyone jumps. Sheila grabs a poker from the brass fireplace tool set.

Charles the goat charges in from the kitchen, chewing something pink and thorny. He plants himself beside Biddy, lifts his head, and bleats loudly.

"Naaah."

Sheila lowers the poker and stares. "Do you really still have that goat?"

Ruby claps her hands delightedly. "Look! He just voted no to your resignation!"

Megan shakes her head slowly. "I genuinely no longer understand how any rules of order—Roberts or otherwise—apply to this club. But I agree with the goat. I don't think you should step down."

"I second that," Amelia says.

Biddy places one hand on Charles' head and her other on Sheila's arm. "You are made of firmer stuff than you realize. No matter how you feel about Sister Dymphna, I know you will give your all to helping her."

She gestures decisively. "We voted, and your resignation is not accepted. You are president. In order to ease your concerns, I will partner with you for the rest of this investigation and make sure you are being impartial. Ruby can work with Amelia."

Megan looks pained and then raises her hand. This, in itself, is odd, because Megan never volunteers for stuff. "I can't believe I'm offering this, but I can take your place at the convent with Sister Dymphna. I'll stay with her and watch over her so you don't have to see her every day. I can understand how that would be awkward."

Sheila is almost touched. "I can loan you my—"

"I refuse to dress like a nun," Megan adds. "I draw the line there."

Ruby giggles. "You'd make a terrible nun with your cheek-bones."

Sheila doesn't know what cheekbones have to do with being a nun, but she lets this comment go as she is wont to do with a few of Ruby's insights.

"What do we tell Sister Dymphna?" Megan asks. "We never told her that her family set Sheila's dad up for a crime he didn't commit."

"I think we hold off on that," Biddy says, her eyes not on Megan but on Sheila. "We need to solve the current attempts on Sister Dymphna's life before we visit past wrongs."

This time, Sheila nods at Biddy's suggestion and is grateful for the guidance on how to proceed. She had acted out of anger yesterday, storming over to the church to accuse Sister Dymphna. That action had almost got her killed.

Amelia glances around. "Well. Now that we have settled all that… what are we investigating next?"

Everyone looks at Sheila.

Sheila feels something steady itself inside her. Her compass knows where to point.

"Murder is always about one thing," Biddy reminds her.

Sheila nods. "Money."

She looks at her team. "Ruby and Amelia, you two need to focus on those numbers we found on the paper stashed behind the stone in the crypt. They have to be an account number, or a password, or a combination to a lock. If Nina hid the money somewhere, we need to find it."

She turns to Biddy. "We'll visit Nina's business partners. If she ran off with the money, they'd be furious. They might want to kill her."

"What about her sister?" Biddy asks. "Willa?"

"I think she came back here to give the money to Willa. It would explain her presence in Indiana. She was going to help her sister repurchase Lucifol."

This part makes Sheila feel sick. Everything is about money. The family business. And no one in the McKellan family appears to care who gets hurt in the process of pursuing their wealth and family legacy. Nevertheless, she looks at Biddy and is reminded of her belief that Sheila can rise above her anger and do the right thing.

"I think we should reintroduce them. Willa is no threat to Sister Dymphna and they deserve to be reunited."

Biddy nods approvingly.

"Oh goody!" Ruby claps her hands. "A reunion! Can I be in charge of this? I'll throw a party."

"I don't know that Sister Dymphna is ready for a party," Biddy says. "Maybe just a quiet re-introduction someplace?"

"No, no, it needs to be a party. We need to celebrate something happy like this," Ruby insists.

The room hums with purpose now. And unity.

Sheila feels it—solid, grounding, unmistakable.

The Pooka Women's Club is back in motion, for better or worse.

28

Sister Dymphna

It's been a week since the shooting and I keep replaying it in my head. The entire thing lasted only two minutes…not even that…but so much was packed into that little time. I remember being in the hidden room and hearing Sheila call my old name. I came up the stairs and out the side door of the crypt to see her. Sheila shouted something at me then. Something that got lost in the shooting's frenzy. She shouted my father had framed her father.

But this makes no sense. What did she mean? My father died because her father started a fire. I've asked everyone and no one will tell me what she meant.

"She was upset," is all Amelia will say, which is true in the same way that calling a hurricane "windy" is also technically accurate.

"She didn't mean it the way it sounded," Ruby adds without meeting my eyes, which suggests strongly that she meant it exactly the way it sounded.

Sister Mary Bernice simply pats my hand and says, "All things in time."

I'd ask Sheila herself, but she is gone. Completely. She doesn't visit. She doesn't reach out to me. She no longer lives at the convent. Megan does.

Everything has changed since that night. People who used to speak freely around me now pause. Conversations stop when I enter a room. Words are weighed before they are offered. Megan treats being here like a job assignment. She does everything correctly. She locks the doors. She checks the windows. She keeps track of schedules and visitors and asks sensible questions like, *Did you take your medication? And Are you sure you don't remember anything else?*

Sheila used to ask questions too, but hers sounded different. Like she didn't care what the answer was. Just what I thought. She treated being at the convent like a privilege. She even wore that silly habit when Sister Mary Bernice told her she needed to conform to our ways of doing things at the convent. I don't think the habit was what Sister Mary Bernice was talking about, but Sheila always went above and beyond. Megan doesn't think living here is a privilege. It is a burden to her. A favor she is doing.

I miss Sheila. I sincerely hope she is wrong about her accusation and that my family and I are not responsible for hurting her or her family.

And now Ruby is insisting that I meet her at her pub. It's the last thing I feel like doing at the moment, but I will not say no to a group of women who have done so much for me.

I walk out of the convent and down the road to Main Street. Ruby's pub glows mid-block, with its windows fogged, and the door propped open with a flowerpot that once might have held something alive. Laughter spills out in a way that feels indecently loud after the hush of the convent. I pause, my hand tightening on my bag.

I haven't been to a pub since I arrived at the church. I have zero desire to drink. Even if the accident and the death of that woman and child were not my fault, I never want to put myself in a situation where it might be. I've learned my lesson. But Ruby was adamant we meet here. It had to be here. So here I am. I walk through the door.

"SURPRISE!"

Ruby's voice rings out alone in the dim pub. Everyone else stares at me as if a show is about to begin. The pub is nearly empty—just the Pooka Women's Club arranged awkwardly around the place like a community theater production and a few town residents leaning over their beers at the bar, looking at me curiously.

Then I see Sheila. She's here. I'm not sure if this is the surprise Ruby means, but I'm grateful to see her. I take in her appearance. She stands by herself in the corner wearing a black dress like she's at a funeral. Her hair hangs limp as if she hasn't curled it. And she has no makeup. She won't meet my eyes. She looks awful. So why is she here? Why am I here? What's the surprise?

I look to Amelia, who perches on a barstool in a floral dress that belongs to April, not October, with what is definitely a cherry stain on its shoulder. She gives me a small wave that seems to say, "I don't know why I'm here either."

Then I notice Megan standing awkwardly to the side, holding a video camera pointed directly at me. The red recording light blinks accusingly. She mouths "sorry" but keeps filming, which rather defeats the purpose of being sorry.

And Biddy—sensible Biddy—frowns from her position near the bar with the expression of someone who tried to stop a train wreck and was overruled by enthusiasm.

That leaves Ruby as the ringleader. I look back over to her standing in the middle of the pub and it is then I notice the woman standing next to her.

We stare at each other. She's perhaps thirty-five, with hair pulled back so tightly it must be giving her a headache. She is wearing an elegant forest green sheath with long sleeves and a peter pan collar. It's a little formal for a pub. Especially one in Pooka.

"Nina!" she screams and launches herself at me.

I stand frozen as arms wrap around me and tears dampen my shoulder. Lavender perfume mixed with joy fills my nose. This is Willa. My sister. I recognize her from the photos the women's club showed me. I try terribly hard to remember her, but I can't.

"We found your sister!" Ruby announces, as if I haven't worked this out for myself.

As a nun, it's hard to want to throttle someone, especially when that someone is the ever sweet Ruby, but I'm coming dangerously close. This feels like an ambush.

Willa pulls back from her hug. I try to mirror her joy so as not to hurt her feelings.

"Nina," she whispers, her hands coming up to frame my face. "My God, Nina, where have you been? Why are you wearing a nun's clothes?"

I am thrilled to meet her. I really am. She's my sister. And I'm thrilled to discover that I have a loving relative. It's just that this is—a lot. In the mirror behind the bar, I catch sight of us—two women with matching faces, one crying, one looking like a deer in headlights. The problem, I realize, isn't her. It's me. She wants to be reunited with Nina. But I am no longer

Nina. I'm sister Dymphna.

"I… I am a nun."

"No, you're not." Willa's face crumples like tissue paper, but then recovers. "It doesn't matter," she says. She grabs my hand and pulls me towards a booth, sliding in so that I can fit beside her. "You're here now. That's all that matters."

But clearly it's not, because she immediately launches into a flood of memories. Words pour out like she's been saving them up—which she has. I can see her love for me. She shares stories of our childhood, shared adventures, family dinners, jokes I don't understand. Around us, the party limps along. Sheila orders drinks no one touches but herself. Ruby flutters between tables like a moth who can't find the right lamp. Amelia sips water, checking her watch.

"Remember when you got arrested for that pool party you threw in college? You broke into the President's backyard and invited the whole school while he was out of town. Or the time you made Page Six for the best tech launch party in the city?"

I flinch but nod along to all these stories. I am ashamed. Nina sounds wild and exhausting. Adventurous, Willa calls her. Fun loving. But I can't imagine having the energy for that much chaos. These days, I consider it adventurous to decorate the church altar with succulents instead of chrysanthemums.

"Why did you run away?" Willa whispers, tears in her eyes. "That night, after everything happened… why didn't you come to me?"

I can only shake my head. I don't know. I know how hard my amnesia is to believe. But the night in question is a void in my memory, black and complete. I stare at my sister, who radiates love and compassion. I want to please her. I can feel

I loved her, too.

"I think I was trying to come to you," I say. "I think that's why I came to Indiana."

This must be true. Why else would I have come here?

She nods. "Of course you were. Well, we can put all this behind us now. I found you. And what matters is our future. Our plans. We had big ones. Do you remember?" Her eyes light up. "You were going to use the money from your company sale to rebuild Lucifol with me. We were going to restore our family business."

Lucifol. The factory. The fire. I feel a wave of nausea.

Willa squeezes my hands. "We can still do that, Nina. Together."

But I don't want to, I realize. I don't want my past. I want to be a nun.

The evening drags on. Willa talks about the business strategies I apparently had developed. Megan's camera captures every uncomfortable moment. Ruby orders food no one eats—the shepherd's pie sits between us like a prop.

Biddy finally convinces Megan to put the camera down with a look that could strip paint. "This isn't a documentary, Megan."

"Ruby said—"

"I don't care what Ruby said. Put it down before I feature you on it."

The camera disappears, but the damage is done. Somewhere in the world, there's now video evidence of me standing like a mannequin, not remembering my only living relative.

"I have so much to show you," Willa says as the pub empties, real customers giving our sad party a wide berth. "Tomorrow, I'll take you around town. Show you all our old places. Maybe it will help you remember."

Dread pools in my stomach. I won't remember. I'll never remember. I'm sure of this after all this time. Tomorrow will be a tour of memories I don't have and I'll disappoint my sister over and over with blank stares and apologetic shrugs. I am a terrible sister and from Willa's stories about my wild past, I'm guessing I've always been one.

"I should get back," I say. "Sister Mary Bernice will wonder where I am."

"Sister Mary Bernice?" Willa looks confused. "You're still planning to stay at the convent? You can come home with me!"

Home. My home is my narrow bed at the convent, fresh flowers on the nightstand, a different arrangement every week. My new sister. Sister Mary Bernice.

"Let's talk about it tomorrow," I say, which seems safe and noncommittal. "I'm so tired…my head injury…"

"Of course!" Her face turns to contrition, and she hugs me again. "Poor you. All you've been through. Take the time you need. We'll take this slowly. Hopefully, tomorrow's tour will jog your memories."

"Hopefully," I say.

I hug her and promise myself that I will get to know this person and love her, whether or not I ever remember our time together before.

"Eight o'clock tomorrow morning," Willa calls as I escape toward the door. "I'll pick you up at the convent. Wear comfortable shoes—we have a lot of ground to cover."

Outside, I breathe in the night air greedily. My body aches as if I've been holding an unnatural pose for hours, which I suppose I have—the pose of a sister who remembers, of someone who has a past worth touring.

Back in my small room at the convent, I kneel beside my bed and try to pray, but all I can think about is Willa's face when I didn't remember her. Our family. Like I'd forgotten her birthday and Christmas and every shared moment of our lives, which I suppose I have.

Tomorrow she'll come with her comfortable shoes and her memories, dragging me through a past that might as well belong to someone else. She'll point at buildings and street corners expecting recognition to bloom like forced flowers. She'll tell more stories about Wild Nina, Party Nina, Nina-with-plans-for-glory.

I lie in my narrow bed wondering if it's possible to disappoint someone just by existing as yourself instead of who they remember. The convent settles into its nighttime quiet—pipes creaking their evening song.

This is my home, I realize. This place of scheduled prayers and morning, noon, and night rituals. But tomorrow will come anyway, bringing comfortable shoes and a sister's desperate love and probably more stories about Nina-who-was.

29

Biddy

"That was quite a party last night," Biddy says to Sheila.

This is something she's heard young people say to each other, and Biddy is trying desperately hard to make conversation. They are sitting in Biddy's car and Sheila has said nothing to her other than hello.

At least this gets a response. Sheila looks at her as if she's nuts. "It was terrible. Sister Dymphna looked like she wanted to crawl into a hole."

Okay, so maybe it wasn't just Biddy who had a terrible time last night.

The car falls back into an uncomfortable silence.

Biddy has always believed that road trips reveal more about a person than an interview. No one can sit in a car for four hours straight and hide themselves. She supposes this holds true, even at this moment. For Sheila isn't hiding herself. She simply doesn't seem to know who she is anymore.

Sheila is wearing jeans. Not nice jeans. Not skinny, tight, rhinestone studded jeans that draw attention to every curve. Not *deliberate* jeans. Just… jeans. A sweater. Flat shoes. Her hair is straight, parted simply, and tucked behind her ears like she is auditioning for the role of *Approachable Woman Who Explains Things Clearly*.

She looks perfectly normal. Just like she did at last night's party.

And Biddy hates it.

"That sweater makes you look like a kindergarten teacher," Biddy announces, because someone has to say it.

Sheila glances down at her beige cable-knit sweater as if seeing it for the first time. "What's wrong with kindergarten teachers?"

"Nothing, if you are one. Which you're not."

Sheila rolls her eyes. "There is no pleasing you. I thought you didn't approve of what I am."

"No," Biddy turns to look at her. "I don't approve of what you do for a living. There is a difference. I have found that I quite like who you are."

Sheila turns away from her to stare out the window at the Indiana countryside rolling past—endless fields of corn stubble and the occasional billboard promising salvation or discount mattresses. Her hair, usually a wild corona of curls that defies both gravity and good sense, lies flat against her head like a defeated flag.

"Did you even wash your hair?" Biddy asks.

"Lots of people skip a day."

"You aren't lots of people. In fact, you've made a point of stressing that."

"Well I am now."

"Since when?"

"Since I decided to stop looking like I've been electrocuted."

Biddy takes the exit for West Lafayette with perhaps more

speed than necessary. "You know what your problem is?"

"I'm sure you're about to tell me."

"You've given up. One setback and suddenly you're dressing like you sell insurance."

"It's not one setback, Biddy. I just found out that everything I gave up and everything I've had to do because of the guilt I felt over my father was for nothing. The McKellans stole my family from me. They stole my future from me. And now I'm still trying to do the right thing by interviewing Nina's business partners to see if they also might like to kill her." Sheila's voice rises with each point. "I'm sorry that my hair is the least of my concerns."

"Your hair is a metaphor." Biddy says calmly.

"My hair is hair."

"Your hair is surrender."

"Can we just focus on the case and get this over with?"

Biddy shakes her head. "Fine," she says, even though it's not. She turns her attention back to the job at hand and the reason for their road trip.

Sheila found Nina McKellan's two business partners through an internet search. Discovering their identity wasn't too difficult, seeing as they just sold their company for millions of dollars. But what was surprising was that they were not in LA. They are currently in Indiana giving a lecture at Purdue University for a conference. This puts them within driving distance during the attempt on Nina's life last week.

Biddy pulls into the parking structure near Stewart Center, and she has to admit, if only to herself, that Purdue's campus is impressive. It's not Harvard, of course. But all that red brick and confident architecture, crawling with young people who think they're going to change the world, makes her feel both ancient and oddly hopeful.

"Tom Hettersmith and Brad Overlin are speaking in Fowler Hall," Sheila says, checking her phone. "Their talk started twenty minutes ago."

"Perfect. We'll catch them after, when they're high on their own importance and eager to talk to anyone who'll listen."

They climb out of the car, and Biddy is surprised that Sheila is suddenly shorter than her. She looks down and sees she's wearing tennis shoes.

"Oh honestly!" she says.

Sheila just shakes her head and keeps walking.

The Stewart Center is at the heart of the campus and does an admirable job of blending modernization with history. Housing multiple meeting rooms and two auditoriums, it plays host to many conferences, including today's technology conference. The main area is a vaulted two story open space filled with fall light flooding through the soaring windows and bouncing off the patterned tile floor.

Sheila leads them towards a staircase where a large board announces the lectures and corresponding rooms.

"Sheila? Sheila Ryan?"

Both Biddy and Sheila turn at the sound of Sheila's name to see a perfectly coiffed blonde woman in leg hugging dark denim with a blazer and scarf topping it.

"You have another female friend?" Biddy asks. Between Gabs in the prison and this woman now, Sheila may have been popular at one time. Although Biddy cannot see Gabs and this woman in the same social circle.

"These are not my friends," Sheila says between gritted teeth. "They are just people I used to know. If anything, I'm starting to think I already have too many friends."

The blonde woman's face lights up as she and a friend walk towards them. This, Biddy thinks, will be interesting.

"It is you! Oh my God, I can't believe it. I'm Brittany Ashford—well, Brittany Kensington now. We were at Albion Academy together?"

Ah. A friend from the private high school.

Biddy watches Sheila's face cycle through several expressions before landing on something that might generously be called a smile.

"Brittany. Hi."

"I'm not surprised to see you here at all." Brittany turns to her companion, a brunette who looks bored. "Sheila was first in our class. Full ride to Princeton. We all knew she'd end up at these tech conferences. So what are you doing now? Let me guess—Silicon Valley? Startup? We should exchange information. I'm dying to break into the West Coast."

Sheila opens her mouth, and Biddy can see from her defeated look that the truth is ready to fly out—without Sheila's typical pride and panache.

"She's in…marketing," Biddy interrupts smoothly. "She owns her own firm. Very exclusive clientele. Turning down work left and right."

Brittany's eyes widen. "Of course. God, some people just have it all figured out, don't they? Well, I could certainly use your help if you have room in your schedule." She fishes in her bag, pulls a business card out of her wallet, and hands it to Sheila. "Well, great seeing you! We should grab drinks sometime and catch up properly! Please do call. I'd love to discuss hiring you."

She click-clacks away on heels that cost more than Biddy's car, dragging her friend with her.

Sheila turns to throw the card in a nearby trash can.

"Don't you dare," Biddy says, snatching it and shoving it in Sheila's open bag. "If you are using this moment to reconsider your career choices, then this is something you might want."

"I don't do marketing."

"Oh? You should tell that to Maude because I'm pretty sure she's gotten rich off your ideas. Just the other day, she suggested Megan reach out to you for resume help."

This seems to cheer Sheila a little.

"Now let's find Nina's two partners, shall we?"

They find Fowler Hall just as the talk is ending. Tom Hettersmith and Brad Overlin look exactly like their photos—both aggressively casual in the way only tech millionaires can achieve, with sneakers that cost more than most people's rent and three-quarter zips with fleece vests that somehow look both sloppy and expensive. Biddy would've never let her husband embarrass himself in such things. These events were meant for suits.

After the applause dies, the crowd disperses, leaving the two men surrounded by a small cluster of admirers. Biddy watches Sheila straighten her shoulders, and for a moment, there's a flash of the old Sheila—the one who role-played Joan of Arc for a fundraiser that made Sister Mary Bernice question her entire understanding of French history.

"Mr. Hettersmith? Mr. Overlin?" Sheila's voice is steady, professional. Biddy feels reassured. The real Sheila is still in there somewhere. "I wonder if we might have a word?"

Both men turn, warm smiles on their faces. The nice thing about conferences is that people come ready and willing to talk about themselves.

"Certainly. Are you hoping to break into the field?" Overlin asks, his smile not quite reaching his eyes.

"We're not students," Sheila says. "We're here about Nina McKellan."

The transformation is immediate. Both men's faces shift from openness to wariness, with just a touch of confusion.

How interesting, Biddy thinks.

"Nina," Hettersmith breathes. "Is she—have you found her? Is she okay?"

"She's alive," Biddy offers, watching their reactions carefully. "And well. Relatively speaking."

"Thank God." Hettersmith actually sags against the podium. "We've been worried sick. After everything that happened…"

"You mean after she stole millions from your company and disappeared?" Sheila asks, and Biddy mentally applauds. The girl's still got it.

Both men exchange confused looks, this time there is no wariness at all.

"Stole?" Overlin's forehead creases. "Nina didn't steal anything. She paid us every penny we were owed from the sale."

Now it's Biddy and Sheila's turn to look confused.

"She showed up at my house after the party celebrating the sale of our company," Hettersmith explains. "Brad and I had come to my house to play Minecraft. Nina had planned to go to an after-party with some of her friends. But, apparently, she was in some car accident. She had a cut on her forehead, looked like she'd been through hell. She said she'd realized what a terrible life she had led, and that it was time to make things right."

"She gave us both our checks," Overlin adds. "The full amount she owed. But what was weird was that she asked us not to tell anyone we'd seen her. Including her sister. She said the press wouldn't leave her alone, and she needed to disappear for a while."

"Did she say where she was going?" Sheila asks.

"Home," Overlin says. "She said she was going home to confess a wrong and give someone her share of the money. She said it would never make up for what she'd done, but she hoped it would help."

"What wrong?" Biddy asks. "What had she done?"

Both men shrug.

"She didn't say," Overlin says. "But she looked—" he pauses, searching for words. "Haunted. Like whatever it was, had been eating at her. Frankly, I wasn't so surprised. All that drinking and partying, she did? She seemed to be running from something."

Hettersmith grimaces. "We saw all the reports that she was missing and that she'd stolen our money, but we kept our mouths shut like she asked. We knew she'd disappear for a while, but we thought it would be weeks, not over a year. We didn't know what to do."

Sheila thanks the men for their help, promising that Nina will be in touch with them soon. As they walk away, Sheila's phone buzzes. She pulls it out and Biddy can see a picture of Megan on the screen, a crown photoshopped on her head. Biddy will have to speak with Sheila about the inappropriateness of this later.

Sheila punches the button to accept the call and puts it on speaker.

"Sheila? Thank God." Megan's voice is tight with panic. "Nina's missing. We think she's been kidnapped."

30

Sister Dymphna

My day starts normally. I had not slept well, so somewhere around 4 am, I give up trying. The thought of spending the whole day with my sister, pretending to remember things I don't, is too much stress for sleep. So, instead, I head down the creaky stairs and into the kitchen. Unfortunately, Megan is already there, pouring coffee.

"Good morning," she says. "You're up early. Excited to see your sister?"

I nod because it's easier than telling the truth, and Megan steps aside to let me access the coffee pot. She watches me pour the hot liquid into the mug.

"Have you given any more thought to the list of numbers we found behind the stone? Any memory would help," she says lightly, stirring her coffee. "A shape. A pattern. A feeling."

I take my coffee to the table and flop into a seat. Unfortunately, she follows. I stare at the bread basket. At the small chip on the edge of my cup.

"I don't know," I say. "They're just… numbers."

Megan nods, but I can tell she's disappointed.

Everyone is disappointed.

I feel like a book someone keeps opening, hoping the missing chapter will suddenly appear. And I decide it is time to make that happen. I can't keep living this way, even if it's keeping me safe.

So after I finish my coffee, I tell Megan that I am going to my room to practice Latin until my sister arrives. She takes me at my word. In fairness to her, nuns aren't supposed to lie. I suppose I'm the exception.

I wait until I hear her go out the front door and then hurry to my window to watch her walk to the church and descend the side stairs to the crypt. The women buried there fascinate her. She treats it like an archeological discovery. Once she goes down those stairs, I know she won't reappear for hours.

I grab my coat and head out of my room. The Virgin Mary statue watches me from her alcove, and I give her an apologetic shrug. "Sorry," I whisper, "but a girl's got to do what a girl's got to do. Even if that girl is technically a nun."

Once I'm outside, I breathe easier. The fields have that early morning mist over them where the cold air meets the warm ground. It provides a shroud of cover and comfort. I gulp in the cool air and finally feel free. I know exactly where I want to go. For I now know of one person who has been watching my every move. One person who may be able to tell me why I came here.

The hospital at dawn has its own kind of hush, different from the convent's sacred silence. This quiet thrums with the business of keeping people alive—machines beeping, wheels squeaking, the soft-soled shuffle of tired nurses making their final rounds before a well-deserved break. I head to the nurse's station.

"Visiting hours are—" the desk nurse starts, then stops when she sees my habit. "Oh. Sister. How kind of you to visit our patients."

"It's my pleasure. I'm actually here to see someone specific. I wanted to check in on Rachel Epblaum. She was injured at the convent."

"Certainly. The nurse taps on her keys. She's in Room 302."

I nod and head down the hall in the direction the nurse indicates.

Rachel's room smells like industrial disinfectant trying to cover something sadder. She looks smaller than I remember, though she will always be larger than life in my head after taking a bullet for me. Her face is all angles and shadows under the fluorescent lights, tubes and wires connecting her to machines that breathe for her, measure her, keep track of all the living she's not quite doing.

My heart falls a little. This is not a woman who will be able to share her secrets anytime soon.

I settle into the visitor's chair, which has a well worn divot in it. That of Lucy, I'd guess.

I don't know what I'm waiting for.

I watch the machines. I watch her hands. I wonder if I'm supposed to feel something specific when I look at her.

She saved my life. She also tried to ruin it by scaring me away from the convent.

"I don't know who I'm supposed to be mad at anymore," I tell her softly. "You or myself or Sheila or my family or the world at large."

She doesn't answer.

Eventually, I do the only thing I know how to do with certainty.

I pray.

Not for me. Not for answers.

Just for the poor woman lying in front of me who selflessly took a bullet for me.

"Hail Mary, full of grace," I begin, keeping my voice low. "The Lord is with thee. Blessed art thou amongst women…"

I'm halfway through the second decade of the rosary when Rachel's eyes flutter open.

I grip my beads and stare into her face. She stares back and then she smiles. I spring up. "I'll call the—"

"No." Her voice is tissue-paper thin but firm. "No doctors. Not yet."

I glance at the door, then back at her. The right thing to do is to call for a doctor.

"Please," Rachel adds, and something in her eyes decides it for me. I sit back down.

"Water?" I ask, gesturing to the pitcher on her bedside table. She nods, and I help her take small sips through a straw.

"You came," she says finally. "I hoped you would."

"You said this was all your fault. Before you…" I gesture vaguely at her bandaged torso. "I need to know what you meant. What you've seen."

Rachel closes her eyes for so long I think she's fallen back asleep. Then she tells me that Sacred Heart of the Woods isn't just a convent.

I lean forward.

"It's a safe house," she continues. "Has been for decades. For women who need to disappear. Abused wives, trafficking victims, anyone who needs sanctuary while they figure out their next move. It started as a haven for girls with unwanted pregnancies in the fifties and sixties. I was one, and Lucy's mother was another. The nuns of Sacred Heart of the Woods did what they could to help us. We've carried on the kindness to women today with more modern troubles."

My brain tries to process this. "Who knows about this?"

"Very few. Mostly the women we help. They often work with us to repay the kindness. And Sister Mary Bernice." A ghost of a smile crosses her face. "That woman could keep a secret in her grave."

"But not me."

"No. You weren't supposed to know." Rachel's fingers pluck at her blanket. "The night you showed up at the convent, I'd left a key hidden outside the church. For a new arrival. But you found it first."

I try to remember finding a key, try to remember anything about that night. It's like fishing in ink. But it explains how the key came to be in the pocket of my jeans.

"I don't know what you did in the church," Rachel continues, "but I heard you trying to pry open a marble tomb. When that didn't work you managed to find the hidden room. You looked desperate to locate a safe space. You kept glancing over your shoulder. Looking at the street. When you came out, I panicked. We couldn't have random people stumbling into what we do. So I tried to scare you off."

"Scare me?"

"I made a loud noise. You panicked." She winces, though I can't tell if it's from pain or memory. "You ran. But you slipped on the stairs. You fell."

The words hang between us.

"You hit your head on the foundation. Hard." Tears track down her cheeks now. "I didn't know what to do. I couldn't take you to the hospital myself without explaining why we were there. So I… I moved you. To the road, where someone would find you."

"You're the reason I can't remember anything."

"Yes."

I wait for anger to rise, but it's like waiting for a bus in a town that doesn't have public transportation. Instead, there's just this odd, empty contentment with the truth.

"But you didn't try to kill me," I say. "The shootings at me—"

"God, no!" She tries to sit up, gasps, and falls back. "I never wanted to hurt you. Even after… I just wanted you to leave. My mission is to save women, not destroy them. I moved things around that you owned, little scares—I thought if you got spooked enough, you'd go somewhere else."

"Instead, the nosiest women's club in history started hunting you down."

She almost laughs, then clutches her side. "They really are something."

We sit in silence for a moment. Somewhere down the hall, someone's monitor beeps frantically, followed by the quick slap of rubber soles on linoleum.

"So my family," I say slowly, "what Sheila said about them setting up my father—"

"I don't know anything about that." Rachel's eyes are getting heavy again. "All I can tell you is it looked like someone was chasing you and that you needed a place to hide something. My only concern was protecting the women who need Sacred Heart."

"And now?"

"Now?" She manages a weak smile. "Now I'm hoping you'll keep our secret. These women, Nina, they need somewhere to run to. Somewhere that doesn't officially exist. I'm starting to think you may understand that as well as the rest of us do."

I think about the empty rooms in the convent, about Sister Mary Bernice's careful way of not quite answering certain questions, about how sometimes I've heard footsteps in the night that shouldn't have been there.

"Your secret's safe," I tell her.

I don't think she hears me. Her eyes have already fluttered closed again and her chest rises and falls rhythmically in sleep. I'll alert the nurse to her recovery on my way out.

I stand.

"Rachel," I whisper. "Thank you for saving my life."

She doesn't respond, but I hope our conversation has brought her peace. Honesty and forgiveness have a way of doing that. I want to tell Sheila that I forgive her family, but now I'm wondering if it is she who needs to forgive me for something.

The conversation helped. I now know how I got amnesia, but I still don't know what brought me to Indiana from LA or what brought me to this church specifically. Why would I be venturing into its crypt? What do those numbers mean I hid? Who was I hiding them from? These are questions I need answered.

The hallways are still quiet as I make my way to the exit. The rising sun is just burning off the fog of the morning. And the parking lot is empty. It's still too early for visitors and the third shift has not ended yet. I fish in my pocket for my keys when I reach the car. Then I realize I forgot my phone. The nurse had collected it when I checked in, as Rachel's room had sensitive monitors. I turn to go back into the building.

A hand clamps over my mouth.

The world goes sideways, then dark.

* * *

The cold is the first thing that registers—seeping through my black habit, numbing my skin. Then comes the pain, sharp and insistent, pulsing somewhere above my left temple. I try to lift my hand to touch it, but I can't move my arm. My hands are tied behind my back.

Then there's the blood. I can feel it trickling down the side of my face, warm against the chill of wherever I am. The metallic taste of it fills my mouth, and I fight the urge to gag. My eyes won't focus properly, the darkness swimming with spots of color that shouldn't be there. However, I seem to be alone.

I think hard to determine how I got here. The memory of the hospital parking lot surfaces like a bubble through murky water. I'd been walking to my car after visiting Rachel. The morning air had been crisp, autumn leaves crunching under my feet. I'd forgotten my phone. Then—a hand. Strong fingers closing around my arm. A sharp pain at the base of my skull. Nothing.

But that isn't actually what scares me now. What scares me is that I suddenly remember *everything else*. This second knock on my head cleared up my amnesia.

I realize the dream that has haunted me for over a year isn't a dream at all. It is a memory, crystal clear now, as if someone has wiped clean a fogged window. I can see it all—every detail, every moment that has been locked away in some protective corner of my mind.

My name is Nina McKellan. This time the name doesn't taste foreign to my tongue. It is mine. It has always been mine.

I close my eyes and let the memory take over. Fire. Screams.

The scent of gasoline. I stop the vision and force my mind to rewind. To start from the beginning this time.

I am sixteen years old, padding down the hallway of our colonial house in my pink nightgown with the lace collar. The grandfather clock in the foyer has just chimed midnight, its deep bongs echoing through the sleeping house. But I'm not sleeping. Nor is anyone else. I'd heard the garage door open, heard my parents' hushed voices as they prepared to leave.

This isn't unusual. The factory is their second home—sometimes it feels like their first home, with our house merely serving as a place to sleep and change clothes. Lucifol has been in our family for three generations, and my father wears the responsibility like a king wears a crown. Heavy, but necessary.

I watch from my bedroom window as they load something into the trunk of Dad's Mercedes. Mom keeps glancing back at the house, her movements quick and nervous. Now, this is unusual. Mom never gets nervous. She is the one who faced down the board of directors when they tried to push Dad out during the recession. She is the one who organized charity galas for five hundred guests without breaking a sweat.

Then I see another figure slip out of the house. Willa. She is still in her pajamas too—the ones with tiny horses printed on them. She ducks behind Mom's rosebushes as our parents pull out of the driveway, then follows them on foot.

None of this is normal. But if Willa is going, I am going. Since when is she the one to break the rules? That is my job.

The October night is cold, and I wish I'd thought to grab my robe. But there is no time. Willa is already disappearing around the corner, her shiny blonde hair catching the streetlight. I run after her, my quickly thrown on tennis shoes slapping against the pavement in the quiet night.

The factory is only six blocks from our house—close enough to walk but far enough that we usually drive. As I approach, I see the lights blazing in the administrative offices on the third floor. The production floors below are dark, the machines silent. But the offices are lit up like Christmas.

I know this place like I know my home. Better, maybe. I'd taken my first steps in Dad's office. I'd colored at the conference table while he ran meetings. I'd hunted for Easter eggs between the filing cabinets and sat on Santa's lap in the employee break room. This is Lucifol, and the McKellans are its heart.

But tonight feels different. Wrong, somehow. The shadows are deeper. The familiar shapes of machinery through the windows look like crouching monsters. Even Willa seems to sense it. She stopped at the employee entrance, her hand hesitating on the door handle.

"Maybe we should go back," I whisper.

She turns to look at me, and I see my uncertainty reflected in her eyes. But then her jaw sets in that stubborn way I know so well. "You need to go home."

"I'm not going home. You should go home."

I don't even know what we are arguing about, but it is a general rule that siblings must disagree with siblings, especially if they are telling you what to do.

But she doesn't take the bait and continue the fight. She shoves me away. Then she goes inside and locks the door. *Go home*, she mouths through the glass.

I shrug, turn around, and start walking away. I turn back and see she's disappeared. Then I go to the door at the back of the factory and let myself in there.

The back stairs are narrow and dusty—used mostly by the

factory employees. My footsteps echo on the metal steps, despite my attempt to be quiet. It's three flights up to the executive floor. My legs burn by the time I reach the top.

The smell hits me first. Sharp and chemical, it makes my nose wrinkle. It doesn't belong here. I know that smell from helping Dad fill up the lawnmower. Gasoline.

Through the glass panel in the stairwell door, I can see into the main hallway. Dad is there, a red gas can in his hands, methodically pouring its contents over everything. The carpet, the walls, the potted plants that Mom had picked out to make the place feel less industrial. His face is set in grim lines. His movements are precise and deliberate.

Mom is in his office. She pulls things from his desk drawers, shoving them into a large duffel bag. Photographs, files, small pieces of art. And money. Lots of money that was hidden in a safe. Her hands shake as she works.

"What are they doing?" I whisper, even though there is no one to hear me or answer me.

I can't make sense of what I'm seeing. Why would they burn down the factory? This is our legacy, our life. Three generations of McKellans had poured their blood and sweat into this place. It employs half the town. It is who we are.

Then Willa bursts through the elevator door in front of them.

"Stop!" she screams.

Willa doesn't look surprised at the sight that greets her. She just looks angry. How did she know this was happening tonight? But then I think about it. She is Mom's little shadow. A socialite in training. She must have overheard something.

Both our parents freeze. Dad nearly drops the gas can. Instead, gasoline sloshes over his shoes. Mom's hand goes to her heart.

"Willa?" Dad's voice is strangled. "What are you...? Oh, Christ."

He must figure out how she knows, too.

"This is not who we are!" Willa's voice cracks with emotion. She is crying now, tears streaming down her face. "Whatever's wrong, whatever's happened, this isn't the answer. You need to stop! This will ruin us."

Dad sets down the gas can carefully, as if it is made of glass. "Sweetheart, you don't understand. Sometimes... sometimes you have to destroy what you are to become what you need to be. Like a butterfly. It's how the world advances. How we evolve. We'll all be fine."

"That's bullshit!"

The curse word sounds strange coming from my perfect lady-like sister. "You're destroying our good name! Grandpa's name! Everything we've built! This factory should be mine someday."

"Sweetie, we aren't destroying it. We're saving it." Mom's voice is hollow. "Some employees are claiming we exposed them to toxic chemicals here. They don't understand there are risks to every job. The bad press will destroy us. They could take all our money. This is the only way to protect you girls, to salvage something from the wreckage. We let all those greedy people believe there is nothing left. Then we start again."

"By committing arson? By committing fraud?" Willa is shaking now, but not from the cold. From rage. "You think this protects us? This makes us criminals! This makes us—"

"Enough!" Dad's voice booms through the hallway. He grabs Willa's arm, his fingers digging in. I see her flinch. He never touched her like that before. Never. "You're too young to understand. Sometimes adults have to make impossible choices. Sometimes—"

He looks at his wife. "Constance, let's go. It's time to end this."

He pulls something from his pocket. A lighter. Lucifol branded, the ones we gave away at trade shows.

"No!" Willa lunges for the lighter, her free arm swinging wildly. "I won't let you!"

Everything happens so fast. Willa's flailing hand catches Dad in the chest, pushing him backward. His foot slips in the puddle of gasoline he'd created. I watch in horror as he falls, the lit flame still in his hand.

The flames erupt instantly. Dad's gasoline-soaked clothes ignite like kindling. His screams fill the hallway, high and terrible. Mom runs to him, and the fire leaps to her as well, hungry and vicious.

The heat hits my face like a physical blow. The smoke is already thick, black, and choking. Willa stands frozen, her mouth open in a silent scream as she watches our parents burn.

I don't think. I just move. I run out of the stairwell and my hand closes around Willa's arm. I pull with all the strength in my sixteen-year-old body. She stumbles backward, and I keep pulling, dragging her toward the stairs.

"We have to help them!" She fights me, trying to get back to the flames that are quickly spreading. "We have to—"

"They're gone!" The words tear from my throat. "They're gone, Willa! We have to go!"

Somehow, I get her down the stairs. She's gone limp, shock setting in, and I have to support most of her weight. Three flights down, my legs are shaking, my lungs burning from the smoke. We burst out into the night air, and I gulp it down greedily.

Behind us, windows glow orange. The fire is spreading fast, feeding on all that gasoline, all those papers, all those memories. Then comes the explosion. All those cleaning chemicals.

"We have to call the fire department," Willa whispers. "The police. We have to—"

"No." The word comes out harder than any I'd uttered before. I grab her shoulders, force her to look at me. "They're dead, Willa. Mom and Dad are dead. And you… you pushed him. It was an accident, I know it was an accident, but you pushed him and he fell and—"

"I killed them." Her voice was small, broken. "I killed them."

"No. No, you didn't. It was an accident. But the world won't see it that way. The police, the investigators—they'll say you pushed him. They'll say you caused it. You could go to jail, Willa. Or juvenile detention."

I can't lose her too. I'd just watched my parents die. I couldn't lose my sister. I wouldn't.

"What do we do?" She looks at me like I have answers, like I am the older one. "Nina, what do we do?"

I think of the one person Dad trusted above all others. The one person who knows all the family secrets, who'd helped Dad navigate every crisis.

"We call Mr. Morrison," I say.

The memory fades, and I'm back in the basement, back in the cold and the dark, with blood seeping from my head. I feel sick with hatred for myself. Morrison had arrived within minutes that night, his face grim. He'd made phone calls, pulled strings, told lies. Instead of Willa taking the fall, he pointed the finger at Carl Ryan, Sheila's father. And I instigated it all.

The door at the top of the stairs creaks open, spilling a shaft of light into the darkness. A figure descends, footsteps careful on the concrete steps.

I try to focus through the pain, through the blood still trickling into my eyes. The figure comes closer, and finally, I can make out the face.

My heart stops.

"Hello, Nina," Willa says.

31

Sheila

Sheila grips the door handle of Biddy's Lexus as they speed down State Road 26, the cornfields blurring past in the late afternoon's yellow glow. Her reflection in the side-view mirror shows a woman she barely recognizes—hair unwashed and limp, face bare of the carefully applied makeup that usually serves as her armor.

"I've got everyone on speaker," Biddy announces, her creased hands steady on the wheel despite pushing eighty miles per hour. The car's Bluetooth system crackles to life with the overlapping voices of the Pooka Women's Club.

"Sheila, honey, are you alright?" Ruby's voice fills the car, warm with concern. "This must be so hard for you. I know you were friends."

"I'm fine," Sheila says.

"Ruby and I are at the convent," Amelia adds. "Megan, where are you?"

"Just leaving the hospital." Megan sounds breathless, like she's been running. "Rachel is conscious and talking. She said Sister Dymphna came to see her this morning. The hospital called the nurse who was on duty and she said that Sister Dymphna forgot her phone. She never came back for it."

"Something must have happened after she left the hospital, then," Amelia says.

"We spoke with Nina's partners," Sheila says. "The news reports were wrong. Nina had paid everything she owed them. They are not behind this."

"I think Nina was coming back here to tell Sheila the truth," Biddy says. "I think she wanted to give Sheila her money."

"What do you mean?" Ruby asks.

Biddy straightens in her seat, keeping her eyes on the road. "Nina came back to Indiana after decades of being gone. But she doesn't go to Albion. She comes to Pooka. The only thing in Pooka that overlaps with her past is Sheila. She must have figured out that her parents framed Sheila's dad and wanted to make things right after her near-death accident."

The rage that floods through Sheila is sudden and scorching. Her hands clench into fists. "As if money could make up for what her parents did. As if any amount could bring back my parents. My mother died of cancer, likely from the chemicals in their plant. And my father fled under suspicion of two murders he didn't commit."

The car falls silent except for the hum of tires on asphalt. It is Ruby who speaks first.

"But what would make up for that?" Ruby's voice is gentle even when filtered through the speakers. "What could Nina offer that would be enough?"

The question gives Sheila pause. She wants to say justice, but what would that look like? Nina's parents were already dead. Nina and Willa are the only McKellans left. Did she want to destroy their lives the way Sheila's had been destroyed? Would that make this better?

"Nina was offering you the only thing she could," Ruby says. "She couldn't bring your parents back. She couldn't undo what happened. But she could try to provide some measure of… I don't know. Compensation? Acknowledgment? It's not enough, but it's what she had to give."

Sheila can't disagree with this. The fury that flared suddenly subsides, leaving her feeling hollow again.

"Mom," Megan's voice cuts through the emotional tension. As usual, she is all business. "What if the numbers we found in the crypt were an account number at the First National Bank of Pooka?"

"We already tried that," Amelia says. "There was no account under Nina's name."

"Yes, but this time don't look under Nina's name," Biddy says, accelerating to pass a slow-moving pickup truck.

"Try Sheila's name," Megan finishes for her. "If Nina was planning to give her the money, she might have already set up the accounts."

"On it." There's the sound of rapid typing as Amelia works.

"Any idea what the password would be?"

"The date of the fire," Sheila says. The date their lives changed.

"Give me five minutes."

Biddy turns off the highway onto the county road that leads to Pooka. The familiar landmarks—the fields of brown corn, the two rocks with yellow slashes for eyes standing sentry to the bridge leading to town—pass by like ghosts in the darkness.

"I don't believe this." Amelia's voice bursts through the speakers four minutes later. "There must be a decimal wrong somewhere. Liam makes mistakes like that all the time. I think we should call the bank tomorrow and verify this."

"What did you find?" multiple voices ask at once.

"There is an account under Sheila's name at First National Bank of Pooka. It was opened last year. The website shows the balance as…" Amelia pauses. "Seventy-five million dollars."

The number hangs in the air. Seventy-five million. Sheila can't even conceptualize that amount of money. It's even more than her thriving business brings in.

"I don't want it," she says immediately. "I don't want their blood money."

"It's not blood money," Ruby argues. "It's—"

"It's guilt money. Conscience money. Thirty pieces of silver."

"Jesus, you really were paying attention at the convent," Megan says.

"Right now," Biddy interrupts, her voice sharp with focus, "the important thing isn't that you don't want the money and would rather the truth. The important question is who kidnapped Sister Dymphna? Who would want the money and not the truth?"

The car falls silent as everyone refocuses on Sister Dymphna's plight.

"Willa," Ruby says quietly. "Willa would want the money and not the truth."

"Exactly." Biddy takes the turn onto Main Street too fast, tires squealing. "Think about it. Nina paid her partners and told them not to tell Willa. The only person she hadn't paid was Willa. She was hiding the money from Willa."

"How did she know Willa would disapprove?" Ruby asks.

"She probably told her what she was planning to do," Biddy

says. "Amelia, can you please pull up the police records from Nina McKellan's phone the night she disappeared in LA?"

The police had given these to Sister Dymphna after their meeting in Pooka in case it helped jog her memory. Sheila listens as Amelia rifles through them.

"She called her sister right after the car accident," Amelia says.

"So she told her. And I'm sure Willa was not too happy to learn of Nina's plan to tell the truth and make restitution," Biddy says. "Willa treasures her social standing more than anything else. She'd be furious if that was at risk."

"And she'd be even more furious if Nina gave her money to Sheila instead of repurchasing Lucifol," Ruby says.

The pieces are falling into place with sickening clarity. Sheila can see it now—Nina calling her sister, adamant about finally making things right after witnessing a mother and daughter die in her car accident. Finally unburdening herself of this terrible secret. And Willa… Willa hearing that her family's name, her family's reputation, was about to be destroyed.

"She would never let anyone ruin the McKellan legacy," Ruby says. "Not even her sister."

"The murder attempts started right after Sister Dymphna came to town," Megan adds. "That call explains how. Her sister knew she was heading to Pooka. She was waiting for her and found her."

"And she's been trying to kill her." Sheila finishes. "We need to go to Albion. That's where Nina is."

Biddy turns the car around and heads back to the highway. In about fifteen minutes, Sheila can see the abandoned Lucifol factory. Even in the darkness, Sheila can make out its hulking silhouette, the broken windows like dead eyes. All these years, and it still stands there. A building with secrets like the crypt.

"Where would Willa go?" Ruby asks. "If she has Nina, where would she take her?"

"Her house," Sheila says immediately. "She loves that place. It's her safe port."

"Not the factory?" Biddy asks. "Are you sure?"

Sheila hesitates and then nods. Willa would not want to acknowledge that part of her parents' story. She only wants to remember the good parts.

"Okay," Biddy says. "We're on our way there now."

"I'm calling Chief Halloran," Amelia announces.

Sheila rolls her eyes. "Fine. Let's see how long he takes to get there." If anything, this whole experience has taught her to distrust the police even more.

"Mom, you promised not to do anything stupid again," Megan says. "Going into an armed killer's house is stupid."

"What I promised was not to get arrested again. Helping a woman held hostage would not lead to my arrest. But don't worry, Megan. I have a plan."

"I have a plan too," Megan says. "Let's plan to wait for the police."

"Who will help with my plan?" Biddy asks, ignoring her daughter.

It doesn't take long for everyone to agree, although Megan takes the longest. They'll meet at the corner of Summit and Pine and approach the McKellan house together. Safety in numbers.

Biddy disconnects the call, and suddenly the car is quiet. Sheila stares at her hands, twisted together in her lap. They look plain and stubby without her signature red nail polish.

They look like the hands of her childhood.

"I don't know who I am anymore," she says. "That's why I dressed like this today. I think I've been wearing costumes my whole life."

"Well, I know who you are," Biddy says. "You're Sheila Ryan, esteemed President of the Pooka Women's Club. You're the woman racing through the night to save a woman in trouble, regardless of what sins she's committed or what pain she's caused you. You're doing what's right, even when it's hard. Especially when it's hard. You're the same woman you've always been, perhaps minus a certain element of flair. But we all have our flaws."

She reaches over and squeezes Sheila's hand briefly before returning her attention to the road. It's probably the nicest thing Biddy has ever said to her.

They turn onto Summit Drive, and Biddy cuts the head-lights. The McKellan house looms at the end of the street, the picture perfect Victorian. Every light in the house is blazing, unusual for this time of night. Sheila guessed right. Willa is at home.

Sheila thinks about Nina McKellan, sixteen years old, maybe watching her parents burn, judging from her nightmares about flames. She thinks about the position that little girl was in.

She thinks about her own parents, one dying from cancer, the other living a life on the run, never fully knowing why. Never understanding what corporate sin had demanded their sacrifice.

She thinks about truth and justice and revenge and for-giveness, and how sometimes they're all tangled together, impossible to separate.

"What do I do with the money?" she asks Biddy. "If we save her, if she lives—what do I do with seventy-five million dollars? Give it back?"

Biddy shrugs. "Whatever you want. Give it away. Burn it. Build a memorial. Buy yourself a private island and never think about Pooka again. It's your choice, Sheila. I think that's what Nina was trying to give you—a choice."

The thought warms her. But, she has to acknowledge, only rich people would suggest burning money, even jokingly.

About fifteen minutes later, other cars gather at the corner of Pine—Ruby's ancient orange Ford pick-up, Amelia's sensible Honda, Megan's hybrid. The women of the Pooka Women's Club assemble in the darkness like some strange misfit army.

Through the windshield, Sheila watches Ruby take a rather large pistol from her trunk.

"Ruby has a gun?"

Biddy laughs. "No. Can you imagine? She'd shoot herself in the foot. That's from the wall of her pub. It has a placque declaring it George Washington's favorite."

Amelia fishes in her purse and finds a canister that looks like pepper spray. Megan carries a tire iron. Her friends, her chosen family, are ready to walk into battle.

"Well," Sheila says. "It's time for the women's club to do its job."

"I've told you, this is not what a women's club is supposed to do…" Biddy mumbles, but climbs out her car door anyway. Sheila smiles and follows.

Darkness has fallen, and the air smells like rain, dead leaves, and something else—gasoline, maybe, though Sheila is sure that is her imagination. She's just been thinking about it too much lately.

The women gather in a tight circle under the streetlight. No one speaks, but Sheila can see the determination on every face. These women who have stood by her through thick and thin this year. They elected her president and they are now prepared to stand by her through whatever waits in that house.

"Remember," Ruby whispers, checking her pistol, the plastic mechanism on top cocked. "Willa's dangerous. She's killed before. She won't hesitate to kill again."

"Stop it," Biddy says, pushing the toy gun down. "You're scaring Megan."

"Here's the plan," Sheila says. "Biddy and Ruby know Willa. Willa likes them. They knock on the door and tell her the good news that she is to be featured on 60 Minutes."

"She is?" Ruby says.

Sheila ignores this. "Megan and I go around back and break into the house. We search for Nina. Hopefully, Willa will never even know we are in there."

"What do I do?" Amelia asks.

"You stand guard," Sheila says. "You tell the police if something goes wrong."

The women nod.

Sheila looks at the McKellan house, every window glowing like eyes in the darkness, and makes her choice. Not about the money—that will come later. But about who she is and who she chooses to be.

Biddy is right. She is Sheila Ryan, President of the Pooka Women's Club. She is the daughter of victims, but she has never been a victim herself. She is angry and hurt and confused, but she is also strong and principled and surrounded by women who would walk through fire for her. "Let's go," she says, and walks toward the house.

32

Sister Dymphna

It's hard to focus on my sister with my head throbbing where she hit me. Blood has dried on my temple, sticky and itching. I keep trying to scratch it, but then I'm reminded she tied my hands behind me to this chair—one of the old kitchen chairs from our childhood, the one that always wobbled.

It still wobbles.

Even more upsetting than my physical discomfort, though, is what Willa is doing. She is pouring gasoline everywhere. The scent burns my nostrils.

The overhead bulb casts harsh shadows across the concrete floor, making the puddle of spilled gas shimmer like an oil slick. Willa paces and pours near the stairs, dressed in Mom's pearls and a floral dress that would be more appropriate for Easter brunch than killing your sister in a basement. Even Sheila dresses more sane than this.

"Willa," I say, keeping my voice steady. "You don't want to do this."

She doesn't look at me. She just keeps pacing, one hand in her pocket. I can guess what is in it. A lighter.

"You always talked too much," she says. "Even when we were kids. You couldn't just keep quiet."

I test the ropes on my wrists again. They're loose—Willa was never good with knots—but not loose enough. I need more time.

"I'm sorry," I say. "I'm sorry I convinced you to lie. I'm sorry I made you carry this alone. You were trying to prevent a disaster from happening. We should have told the truth and you would've been fine."

"We made a pact." Her voice cracks. "We promised we'd never tell what happened that night. Now, you want to break that promise. And who will spend the rest of her life in prison? Me. Well, I'm not going back on my word. I'm sticking to the original plan. I'll keep our parents' secret and I'll rebuild Lucifol to honor them. It's the least I can do after what happened. Now, it'd be helpful if you tell me where you hid the money."

I'm immediately grateful I deposited the money in the bank in Pooka that night of the accident. That I saw Willa on the street watching me and that I ran to the church to hide the account number. Rachel's presence must have scared her off. Rachel may have saved my life that night as well.

"The police will not arrest you if we tell the truth."

I don't know how to convince her we were wrong. That Morrison mislead us to get the insurance money. All we had to do was tell the truth. Willa was trying to prevent our parents from committing arson. Then there was a tragic accident that killed them. But that's all it was…an accident.

"The police will understand. You won't go to prison."

The Westminster Chimes doorbell rings upstairs. The formal tone feels out of place given my current predicament.

We both freeze.

Willa's head snaps toward the stairs. Her hand tightens in her pocket.

A woman's voice calls through the door, muffled but cheerful. "Willa? Willa McKellan? This is Biddy Bramley!"

My heart leaps. Biddy. She found me.

"And Ruby!" Another voice, even more enthusiastic.

It's not exactly the rescue crew you'd hope for, but I'll take it.

Willa stands paralyzed, torn between social conditioning and whatever dark plan she's constructed in her mind. The perfect hostess versus the desperate woman with gasoline and a lighter.

She glares at me. "They know I took you."

I shake my head. "How could they? They think we are sisters getting reacquainted. They already knew you and I were spending the day together. They don't know anything is wrong."

I don't tell her that Megan had scheduled regular check-in calls with me. I missed them all.

"We have wonderful news to share!" Biddy sing-songs.

I watch Willa's face cycle through emotions—rage, confusion, that ingrained politeness Mom drilled into both of us. She takes one step toward the stairs.

This is my chance.

I throw my weight sideways, tipping the chair. I hit the concrete hard on my shoulder, pain shooting through my arm. But my plan has worked. The ropes are still tied, but my angle is better to move my arms. Not that Willa can see this.

"Ow," I say. I'm not even faking this.

She frowns. "You deserve that. What a stupid thing to do."

The doorbell rings again. Insistent.

Willa looks at me sprawled on the floor and curses under her breath—actual cursing, which Mom would've fainted over. She heads up the stairs.

My heart hammers. If she answers that door, Biddy and Ruby are in danger.

But maybe that's the point. Maybe they're part of a larger rescue effort.

I scrape my wrists against the chair leg, feeling the rope fray.

Upstairs, the door opens. Biddy's voice carries through the house, loud and overly bright: "Willa! We have the most AMAZING news! You won't believe it!"

"This really isn't a good time," Willa says.

"Oh, but it's about 60 Minutes! They want to interview you!"

There's a pause. I can almost see Willa's face, calculating, suspicious.

"60 Minutes?" she says slowly. They have dangled the right carrot.

"Yes! We told them about your sister's amnesia and your reunion and your plans to reopen Lucifol. They love the story! It's just made for TV."

I work faster at the ropes. The fibers are splitting. Just a little more—

I hear a scraping sound from the window. I look up.

Two faces appear in the grimy glass—Megan and Sheila. Sheila's eyes widen when she sees me on the floor. She points at the window lock, makes a questioning gesture.

I nod frantically.

The window is old, the kind that swings inward. Sheila

works at the latch while Megan keeps watch. The metal screeches softly. They both freeze.

Upstairs, Ruby's voice joins in: "They want to film next Tuesday! Leslie Stahl is doing it herself!"

"I don't think they schedule that quickly," Willa says, suspicious.

"Special circumstances!" Biddy's voice goes even higher. "We showed them the video from your reunion at the pub. They want to capture your efforts to reconnect with your sister. It's like an emergency segment!"

"That's not a thing—"

"Of course, it's a thing. They do it for natural disasters all the time."

There is a crash from above. Something breaking.

"Oh my goodness, I'm so sorry!" Biddy says. "Your lovely vase! Let me help you clean that up—"

The window swings open with a soft squeal of old hinges. Cold night air rushes in, carrying the smell of dead leaves and rain. It helps diffuse the scent of gasoline. I breathe easier.

Sheila climbs through, headfirst. The window is tiny—maybe two feet square. She gets her head and shoulders through, then gets stuck.

"Push!" she hisses at Megan.

"I am pushing!"

My wrists burn as I saw the rope back and forth. It's giving way. I can feel it.

Then there are footsteps on the stairs.

Sheila's eyes meet mine. She's stuck, half in and half out, completely vulnerable.

"Go back!" I whisper urgently. "Get out!"

But it's too late. Willa appears at the bottom of the stairs.

She sees me on the floor, the frayed ropes, and follows my gaze to the window where Sheila is wedged like a cork.

For a moment, nobody moves.

"I knew that was too good to be true. And Biddy Bramley would never break a vase at someone's home."

She pulls the lighter from her pocket.

"Willa, don't—" I start.

She flicks the starter. The flame jumps to life.

Sheila makes a strangled sound. Megan appears in the window behind her, eyes wide with fear.

"Everybody stay still," Willa says quietly. Her hand trembles, making the flame dance. "Nobody move. Nobody does anything stupid."

I don't think we are the ones doing something stupid at the moment. The rope on my wrists finally gives way. But I don't move. Can't move. That lighter is six feet from a puddle of gasoline.

Upstairs, the chaos continues. "Willa? Where did you go?" Biddy's voice, closer now. At the top of the basement stairs.

"Stay up there!" Willa shouts, not taking her eyes off me.

"What?"

"I said STAY—" Willa's voice cracks with frustration.

I use the distraction. I surge up from the floor, hands free, and grab the nearest thing—a paint can on the shelf beside me. I hurl it at Willa.

My aim is terrible. I probably have a concussion from when she hit me. The can sails wide, missing her completely, and crashes into the shelving unit on the far wall. The impact sends the whole structure tipping forward.

Paint cans, boxes of old Christmas decorations, Dad's tools—everything slides off in slow motion, crashing to the concrete floor in a cascade of metal and cardboard.

Willa stumbles backward to avoid the avalanche. Her foot catches the edge of the gasoline puddle. She windmills her arms, trying to catch her balance, and the lighter flies from her grip.

It arcs through the air, still lit, tumbling end over end toward the gas can.

"No!" I lunge forward, diving across the wet concrete.

My fingers close on the lighter mid-air. I have it—I have it—

My momentum carries me into Willa's legs. We both go down hard. The lighter skitters from my grasp, bouncing across the floor. It's still lit. It's one of those antique butane lighters that holds its flame without continuous pressure on the button, more like a gas stove. Willa has really thought this out.

At the window, Megan shoves Sheila from behind. "Move, move, move!"

Sheila pops through the window and crashes onto the washing machine, then tumbles to the floor with a grunt. She scrambles toward the lighter on her hands and knees.

Willa rolls away from me, faster than I expected. She lunges for the lighter too.

We're both crawling across the gasoline-soaked floor, racing for the tiny flame that's skidding toward a pile of paint-soaked cardboard.

Sheila reaches it first. Her fingers close around it just as Willa grabs her wrist.

"Let go!" Willa shrieks, yanking at Sheila's arm.

The lighter slips free like a bar of soap and bounces across the floor again—right toward the puddle.

I throw myself forward, slide on my stomach across the wet concrete like I'm stealing home, and grab it an inch from the liquid.

The flame is so close to my fingers I can feel the heat. I click it closed.

We all freeze, breathing hard.

"Jesus," I wheeze, looking at my sister. "Why can't you use one of those cheap plastic lighter that takes ten tries to start?"

Megan drops through the window and lands in a crouch. She takes two steps toward us, then her foot hits a rolling paint can. Her feet go out from under her and she lands hard on her back with a whoof of expelled air.

"Ow," she gasps.

"Can we come down now?" Biddy shouts.

"Yes," Megan says.

Footsteps thunder down the basement stairs. Biddy and Ruby appear, Biddy wielding a rolling pin, Ruby still clutching her toy pistol.

"We heard—oh my Lord." Biddy takes in the scene. The toppled shelving unit. The paint cans everywhere. The three of us sprawled on the gasoline-soaked floor like we're making concrete angels. Megan flat on her back, groaning.

Willa starts laughing. It's a high, brittle sound that makes my skin crawl.

"It's fine," she says. "Everything's fine. We're all fine. It was just a misunderstanding. A sisterly squabble."

She's definitely not fine.

I push myself up to sitting, still clutching the closed lighter. My hands shake so badly I can barely hold it.

"Willa," I say carefully. "It's over. We need to call the police."

"No." She scrambles to her feet, slipping twice in the

gasoline.

Sadly, I'm one of the few people in America who understands just how slippery gasoline is.

"No, I just—I need a minute. I need to think," Willa says.

She's backing toward the stairs. Her eyes are wild, unfocused.

"Willa, don't run—"

But she's already bolting up the stairs, pushing past Biddy and Ruby.

"Stop her!" Sheila shouts.

I struggle to stand, but my head is spinning. Megan rolls over and crawls to her knees. Sheila is already running for the stairs, but her gasoline-soaked shoes slip on the bottom step and she crashes into the railing.

By the time I make it up the stairs, Willa has run through the kitchen and out the back door. I can see her through the window, running across the dark backyard toward—

"The garage," I breathe. "She's going to the garage."

Where Dad kept more gasoline for the lawn mower. Where Mom stored all those old papers and photo albums. Where everything is dry and flammable and perfect for burning.

I run for the back door, Sheila right behind me. Megan limps after us, Ruby and Biddy bringing up the rear.

The motion-sensor light flicks on as we burst into the backyard. Willa is at the garage door, punching in the code— 1-2-3-4, because Dad never was good with security.

"Willa, stop!" I'm running full out now, ignoring the pounding in my head, the way my vision swims.

The garage door grinds open. Willa disappears inside.

I reach the garage just as she's grabbing the red gas can from the shelf. But she's moving too fast, too frantically. The can is heavier than she expects. It slips from her hands and hits the concrete floor.

The cap wasn't on tight. Gasoline glugs out, spreading across the garage floor.

"Willa, leave it—"

She bends to pick it up, her dress dragging through the gasoline. Her pearls swing forward, catching the overhead light.

That's when I see what's in her other hand.

Another lighter. She must have grabbed it from the kitchen drawer—Mom kept a dozen of them for the candles she never lit.

"Don't." I hold up my hands, stopping just inside the garage door. "Please don't."

"I can't go to prison, Nina." Her voice is calm now, eerily calm. "I can't face everyone. I can't have them know what we did."

"Then we won't tell them." The lie tastes bitter, but I'll say anything right now. "We'll keep the secret. Just put down the lighter."

She looks at me, and for a moment I see my sister again. The girl who taught me to ride a bike. Who helped me with my homework. Who held me when I cried after our parents died.

"You're lying," she says softly. "You were always a terrible liar. Although I really never guessed you'd become a nun."

Behind me, I hear Sheila and the others approaching. I hear Ruby on the phone with 911, her voice high and frightened.

"I'm sorry," Willa says. "I'm sorry for everything."

"I'm sorry too," I say.

She flicks the lighter.

The flame catches.

"Willa, NO—"

I lunge forward, reaching for her hand, for the lighter, for anything.

My foot hits the spilled gasoline. I slip, my legs shooting out from under me. I land hard on my hip, sliding across the wet concrete like it's ice.

Willa jumps back, startled by my sudden movement. Her elbow hits the shelf behind her. Tools rattle. A jar of screws tips over, spilling across the floor with a sound like rain on metal.

She stumbles, trying to regain her balance. The lighter is still in her hand, still lit.

Her foot comes down on a rolling screwdriver.

It's almost comical, the way her arms windmill. Her eyes go wide. The lighter tumbles from her grasp.

Time slows.

I see it fall, rotating through the air. See the flame flickering. See Willa reaching for it, missing.

It bounces once on the concrete.

The flame doesn't go out.

It lands in the spreading pool of gasoline.

"NO!" I scream.

The fire erupts with a whomp that steals all the oxygen from the air. Heat slams into me like a physical blow. I'm still on the ground, sliding backward, my hands scrabbling for purchase on the slick floor.

Sheila grabs me under my arms and hauls me backward, out of the garage. "Get out, get out, get out!"

The flames spread fast, racing across the spilled gasoline like a living thing. They hit the wooden shelving units, catch on cardboard boxes, climb the walls.

And Willa—

"Willa!" I scream, fighting against Sheila's grip. I will not lose another family member this way. I will not.

Through the flames, I see her. She's frozen in the center of the garage, watching the fire spread around her in a circle. Her face is blank, shocked. Like she can't quite believe what's happening.

"Willa run!" My voice is raw, desperate. "Move!"

She doesn't move. She just stands there as flames lick at her feet, as smoke begins to fill the space.

I can barely see anything now. The smoke is too thick, the heat too intense. I'm coughing, choking, my eyes streaming tears.

"Nina!" Sheila says to me. She has me by the arm, pulling me back. "You can't help her! We need to get out!"

"I'm not leaving her!" I wrench free and lunge forward into the garage.

The heat hits me like walking into a wall. I can't see. Can't breathe. My hands stretch out in front of me, searching blindly through smoke and flames.

My fingers brush fabric. Willa's dress. She must have moved nearer to the door. I grab it and pull.

She doesn't move.

"Willa!" I'm coughing so hard I can barely get the word out. "Come on!"

I pull harder. She stumbles toward me, then her knees buckle. We both go down hard on the concrete floor. The air is slightly clearer down here, but not much. Above us, the ceiling is fully engulfed.

I try to drag her toward where I think the door is, but I've lost my bearings in the smoke. Everything is gray and orange and choking darkness.

A beam groans overhead. Wood splinters with a crack like a gunshot.

"Nina…" Willa's voice is barely a whisper. "Go. Leave me."

"No." I'm crawling now, pulling her along beside me. But I don't know which way leads out. The smoke is everywhere. My lungs are burning. My vision is going dark at the edges.

I hear voices from outside—muffled, distant. Someone screaming my name. Sheila? I try to answer, but I can't get enough air.

A beam falls somewhere to our left. The crash sends up a shower of sparks.

This is it, I think through the haze. This is how it ends.

Just like our parents.

The pattern completing itself, after all.

My arms give out. I collapse beside Willa on the concrete floor, still trying to pull her with me even though I can't move anymore. Can't think. Can't breathe.

Her hand finds mine in the darkness.

"I love you," she whispers. "I'm sorry. For everything. I just wanted to make it up to mom and dad."

"I love you too," I manage. My voice is barely a rasp. I can't believe how easy it is to find forgiveness for once. "Always…"

The smoke is so thick. I can't see anything at all now. Just darkness and heat and the distant roar of flames.

I close my eyes.

At least we're together.

After everything—all the lies, the pain, the secrets—at least we have each other in the end.

Willa's grip on my hand loosens. Or maybe mine does. I

can't tell anymore.

The world narrows to a single point of consciousness, then even that begins to fade.

Somewhere far away, I hear sirens. But they're too late.

Too late for both of us.

The darkness closes in completely, and I let it take me.

33

Sheila

Sheila watches the lighter fall from Willa's trembling fingers like a dying star, and her first thought is: Really?

The flames leap up instantly where the lighter hits the gasoline-soaked floor, hungry orange tongues that spread faster than her business cards after her portrayal as Joan of Arc for the charity drive. She made them a lot of money that night.

She glances down at her clothes—the oversized sweater and pair of jeans that have seen better decades—and feels a moment of relief. At least she's not wearing any of her expensive clothes. But then she realizes she can't die looking like this. What would people think?

"Biddy! Ruby!" She barks the orders like the leader she is, this is her club and her mission to finish. "Call the fire department. Tell them the McKellan house is on fire."

The flames are spreading in earnest now, following the trail of gasoline. Both sisters have collapsed together. Occasionally, Willa mumbles something that sounds like a conversation with her parents—who are very much dead.

Sheila looks to her right. "Megan, help me with Nina." Sheila surveys the room, her mind cataloging exits just like she does every day on the job, in case of a police raid. Front garage door—blocked by fire. Window—absolutely not happening again; her size has limits. Side door—bingo.

Sheila and Megan rush towards it. They push it open and are grateful to see a path without flames to the women. They each grab one of Nina's arms, helping to support her. The woman's heavier than she looks—probably all that Catholic guilt weighing her down. Blood from her head wound smears across Sheila's sweater. This really has not been her day.

"My sister!" Nina's eyes open and she struggles against them, surprisingly strong for someone who's been bleeding like a fountain pen. "I can't leave without Willa!"

"Your sister is the reason we're in this predicament!" Sheila grunts, dragging Nina toward the door. The smoke is getting thicker. She watches Megan coughing so hard she's doubled up as she supports half Nina's weight.

"Please!" Nina's voice cracks. "She's all I have left!"

They make it to the door and Megan shoves it to open it wider, gulping in the fresh air. Sheila pushes Nina out and then pauses, looking back at Willa huddled on the floor. The flames haven't reached her yet, but they're doing their enthusiastic best. The woman who kidnapped Nina and tried to kill her. The woman who's been living as a ghost for decades, protecting the memory of parents who didn't deserve it.

Sheila decides she is definitely not keeping the money. *Rich girls*, Sheila thinks. *Really aren't that bright.* Biddy excluded of course. Maybe not Megan.

"Megan," she says, making an executive decision that she's

definitely going to regret. "Get Nina out of here. I'll get Willa."

"Are you insane?"

For once, Sheila agrees with the woman.

"You can't—"

"I'm the President of the Pooka Women's Club." Sheila straightens her shoulders, channeling every club meeting she's presided over with her gavel. "I don't leave women behind. Even monumentally stupid ones who can't figure out how to express their feelings without making everyone else suffer."

She fixes Megan with her best confident look and hopes that Megan remembers this moment. She is definitely calling Megan as a character witness next time she is arrested.

Megan opens her mouth to argue, which is actually rather touching, but Nina decides for them by passing out. Megan shoulders her weight and hauls her out into the night and towards safety.

Alone now, except for Willa and the increasingly ambitious flames, Sheila assesses the situation and the enormity of what she has just promised floods her. The fire has spread along the gasoline trails, creating a maze of flame between her and Willa. The smoke is getting thicker, and fear rushes in. What if she can't do this? What if she fails?

"Willa!" she shouts over the roar of flames. "Willa McKellan, you get up right now! You owe me."

Willa doesn't respond, but she's still semi-conscious. Sheila can make out words now—"good daughter," "kept my promise," "sorry, sorry, sorry."

It's like listening to Sheila's own internal monologue over all the years. How could one night have sent them both spiraling down this same path?

The heat is getting intense. Sheila's clothes are sticking to her skin, and she can feel her hair—what's left of it without the clip-in extensions—singeing. She needs to move, needs to find a path through the flames. She doesn't have much time.

There—a gap where the gasoline didn't quite reach. It's narrow, and she'll have to time it perfectly, but she's navigated tighter spots.

She takes a breath—immediately regrets it as smoke fills her lungs—and runs.

The heat is like a physical wall, pressing against her from all sides. She can smell burning fabric and hopes it's the rags scattered around the garage and not her outfit. Her eyes water, her lungs burn, but she pushes through because she's Sheila Ryan, and she doesn't quit. Not when her mother got sick, and she had to support her. Not when everyone blamed her for her father's actions and the deaths of the McKellans. And not now.

She reaches Willa just as another section of the ceiling collapses. Burning timber crashes down, blocking their escape route.

"Well," Sheila grabs Willa and pulls her against the wall. "This is just perfect. Trapped in a burning garage with a murderer. I never get any breaks in my life."

Willa looks up at her, eyes red from smoke and tears. "Why did you come in?"

"Apparently, I make poor life choices." Sheila scans the room, looking for options. "Biddy says it's a character flaw. Like my inability to dress myself appropriately."

The flames are closing in, forming a semicircle around their corner. The smoke is so thick she can barely see, and breathing is…impossible. But there—is that water dripping from the ceiling?

"You have water pipes," she realizes. "Of course. You have a sink in here."

She grabs a piece of fallen timber—hot but not actively on fire—and starts swinging at the pipes above them.

"What are you doing?" Willa coughs.

"Saving our lives, obviously." The pipe dents. Apparently, rich people get copper pipes instead of plastic. "But I want it known that I am furious with you."

Another swing. Another dent. Her arms burn with effort. But on the fourth swing, the pipe bursts.

Water cascades down, not enough to put out the fire completely, but enough to drench them and create a barrier. Enough to buy them time.

Sheila drops the timber and pulls Willa under the spray. "Now we wait for the fire department and try not to die. Do you think you can manage that without setting anything else on fire?"

Willa stares at her. "I set your father up. I ruined your life."

"Yes, well." Sheila adjusts their position to get maximum water coverage. "That's not exactly right. You set my father up. But you did not ruin my life. I have a thriving business, the best of friends, and I'm president of the Women's Club. I've done just fine for myself. And, from the looks of things, better than you."

The water is cold, a shocking contrast to the heat of the flames. It plasters Sheila's clothes to her skin and completes the destruction of her hair. She's going to look like a drowned rat when they get out of here. If they get out of here. But the nice thing, she realizes, is that she cares again.

"I killed them," Willa says quietly. "My parents…"

"Yes, you mentioned." Sheila shifts to avoid a piece of

burning debris. "You'll have plenty of time to confess properly when we get out of here. I'm sure the police will be thrilled to close those cases. Really boost their solve rate."

"You're awfully calm for someone who might die."

Sheila considers this. She is calm. Maybe it's shock. Maybe it's the smoke inhalation. Or maybe it's just that after all these years of carrying guilt like a boulder, she can finally set it down.

The water continues to cascade down, creating a small island of safety in the inferno. It won't last long—the fire's too hungry, and the water pressure's already dropping.

"You know what I realized tonight?" Sheila says. "I'm not just someone things happened to. I'm someone who made things happen. You really missed out on life by not living it."

Sirens wail in the distance, getting closer. It's about time. This is Sheila's hefty tax dollars at work. For she's never fudged her income on tax returns. Not even once. Not even after the government expressed its disapproval multiple times of how she earned her income.

Sheila catches sight of her reflection in a broken piece of glass. "Dear God, I look like a tornado has styled me. What if the firefighters are hot?"

Willa actually laughs—a broken sound, but genuine. "You aren't who I expected you to be."

"No one ever is." Sheila pulls her closer as a beam crashes down nearby. "That's the first lesson of the Pooka Women's Club."

The sirens are right outside now. She can hear voices, equipment being deployed. The cavalry has arrived, and not a moment too soon. The water from the pipe is down to a trickle, and the flames are getting bold again.

"They're going to arrest me," Willa says.

"Probably." Sheila is nothing if not honest. "But you'll survive it. We all make choices. Your parents made theirs. You made yours. Nina made hers. And I'm making mine." She squeezes Willa's shoulder. "I'm choosing to be more than my tragedy. You should try it. Orange jumpsuits might not be flattering, but they're better than this whole Victorian ghost aesthetic you've got going on."

The basement door crashes open. Firefighters pour in like heavily equipped angels, shouting orders and deploying equipment. The flames hiss and retreat under the assault of professional-grade water pressure. A few more minutes and the men will reach them. Sheila feels relief flood her body.

Then a flaming beam lands on their heads.

34

Megan

Megan stands beside the other members of the women's club and watches the flames lick at the windows of the McKellan garage. They stand on the grass in total silence—willing Sheila to emerge.

Sister Dymphna is with them. Blood has dried in rusty streams down the side of her face, and she sways slightly, as if the October wind might blow her over. But she won't allow the paramedics to take her.

"She's still in there," Nina says, her voice hollow. "My sister is still in there."

Megan tries not to be angry. Sheila's in there, Megan thinks. It's Sheila who deserves to live. She thinks about labels and judgments, about how quick she's been to categorize people into neat little boxes. Nuns are good. Successful business women are even more admirable. But a hooker? She's terrible. An embarrassment to the gender.

The thoughts make her flinch now. How easily she'd dismissed Sheila and reduced her to that single word. How easily she'd dismissed Biddy, her own mother. The woman who's currently organizing the emergency response like a bobbed general, making sure the firefighters know about the garage layout, the gas lines, and the best access points. And how little she'd expected of her father, even when he failed to uphold his title of husband.

"I need to go back," Nina says suddenly, taking a step toward the garage.

Megan grabs her arm. "You can't. Sheila told me to keep you safe, and that is what I am going to do."

"You don't understand." Nina turns to her, eyes wild with the desperation that makes people do stupid things. Like run into burning buildings. Like lie about who really started a fire. "Willa's all I have left. This is all my fault. I can't—"

"Sheila will get her out." The words come from behind them, calm and certain. Megan turns to find her mother standing there, still in her Chanel suit from her Purdue trip, looking exactly as unflappable as she had when Megan was sixteen and got arrested for protesting the library budget cuts. Actually, now that Megan thinks about it, her mother looked a little proud that day.

"Sheila's been in there too long," Megan says, the guilt eating at her like acid. She should have stayed. She should have made Sheila leave. She should have done something other than follow orders like she always does, standing on the sidelines while other people fight the fights.

"Sheila Ryan is a survivor," her mother says simply. "She has been since she was a teenager. A fire couldn't stop her then. And it won't stop her now."

Megan wonders what her mother would say about her if it were she in the building. Probably, that she can't take care of herself and someone should rescue her.

Biddy studies the expression on her face. "You aren't going in either."

Megan wants to argue, but Nina, who's started praying, catches her attention. Megan recognizes the words and joins in.

The firefighters are working with efficient chaos, hoses snaking across the lawn like giant tentacles, water arcing into the flames. But it's not enough. The old garage is too eager to burn, fed by whatever accelerants Willa had spread around. Just like the factory decades ago.

Megan thinks about choices, about the small million decisions that lead to moments like this. She thinks about her own choices—waiting to be told what to do instead of shouldering the responsibility and outcomes of her own decisions.

Flames break through the roof. A window explodes outward in a shower of sparks. Firefighters fall back, regroup, and adjust their strategy. Megan's heart clenches. How long has Sheila been in there? How long can anyone survive in that inferno?

"There!" Ruby's voice cuts through the noise. She's pointing at a puddle under the garage door, where water is streaming out. "They broke the pipes! Smart thinking! I did that once, by mistake of course."

Hope flutters in Megan's chest like a trapped bird. But it only lasts for minutes. Minutes where nothing happens. Then the minutes drag by like hours. The firefighters gain ground, then lose it. The roof partially collapses, sending up a shower of sparks that look like ascending souls in the darkness. Megan prays one of them isn't Sheila. Nina's prayers are quicker, more insistent. Even Megan's mother looks worried now, her usual calm cracking at the edges.

"I should go in," Megan says out loud this time. "I should—"

"You should wait," her mother says firmly. "And trust. Sometimes that's the hardest choice of all."

Megan wants to argue. She's spent her whole life waiting on the sidelines. She now realizes this and wants to do better. She doesn't want to be like her father anymore. She doesn't want to be famous anymore. She wants to be like her mother—kind, but no-nonsense, with clearly defined boundaries. She wants to be like the hooker—the bravest, kindest person she knows.

The firefighters disappear into the garage. The waiting stretches, elastic and unbearable. Nina's prayers have shifted to bargaining—offering everything she has, everything she's built, if God will just save her sister. Megan can relate to this. This is a more familiar prayer to her. Ruby paces like a caged animal. Amelia is on her phone, probably researching survival rates for fires. And Biddy... Biddy stands perfectly still, watching the garage door like she can will Sheila through it by force of concentration.

Then—movement. Firefighters emerge, and between them—

"Sheila!" The name tears from Megan's throat as she breaks free from her mother's grip.

She runs across the lawn, dodging hoses and equipment, ignoring the shouts of emergency personnel. Sheila's being supported by two firefighters, soaking wet and looking like she's been through a blender, bleeding from a gash in her head, but alive. Gloriously, impossibly alive.

Megan doesn't think. She just throws her arms around Sheila..

"Do you have a comb I can borrow?" Sheila whispers in her

ear. "All these potential clients and I look like you."

Megan laughs. The joke will not offend her. She's sure it's a joke. "Is Willa…?"

"Being brought out now." Sheila glances back at the garage. "She'll live. Whether she'll want to is another question."

Sure enough, more firefighters emerge with Willa McKellan between them. She looks smaller than she did before, when she held the lighter in her hand. Nina breaks free from the crowd, stumbling toward her sister.

Megan watches as the sisters embrace each other, both crying, both broken, both finally free of the secret that's poisoned their lives. It's messy and painful and nothing like the justice of historical documents. Real life leaves scars. Real life doesn't have clear good guys and bad guys. Except maybe one.

"You saved her," Megan says to Sheila. "After everything she did, you saved her."

"Yes, well." Sheila attempts to smooth her destroyed hair, failing spectacularly. "Your mother would tell you I've made worse decisions."

But Sheila is wrong. Biddy would tell you that Sheila Ryan is admirable. Maybe the most admirable person she knows. Megan can finally see the truth. Sheila Ryan, harlot of Pooka, chose compassion over revenge. She chose to save rather than to let burn. She chose to be more than her tragedy defined her to be.

Megan looks at Sheila through new eyes. And Sheila looks back.

"Now, if you'll let me go," she says, "I need to find a mirror and some makeup before the press arrives. This is bad for business."

She walks away, still imperious despite her soggy keds slapping into the ground with each step. Megan watches her go, then turns back to where Nina and Willa are being loaded into ambulances. The garage continues to burn behind them, but it's controlled now, contained. Still, it is a total loss. All those preserved memories, all those artifacts of a life built on lies—gone.

Maybe that's for the best. Maybe some things need to burn to make room for whatever comes next.

35

Sister Dymphna

It's been three days since the fire and I've made many choices in that short amount of time. Surprisingly, I've found the decisions to be easy. Now, I can sit in silence, at peace. No dreams, no guilt, no doubt. It's what I'm doing right now. I sit on the cold stone steps of Sacred Heart of the Woods Church, my hands folded in my lap, watching the late afternoon sun cast long shadows across the graveyard. The moment is perfect. Until I hear cursing.

I look towards the gravel path leading to the church and watch as a voluptuous blond teeters on stilettos that sink into the soft ground with every step. She is dressed in a fitted black dress that doesn't look like it belongs in a strip club but also wouldn't pass at a Junior League luncheon either. The shoes are still her signature heels, but they are three inches tall, not five, and there isn't a bedazzled platform at the sole. It's the first time I've seen her dressed like this and it suits Sheila perfectly.

"Sister Mary Bernice called me," she says, falling beside me on the steps and wiping dirt from her heels. "She said tomorrow is a big day for you."

My fingers trace the rough fabric of my novice habit. I've decided not to give it up. I'm going to take my final vows tomorrow.

"She shouldn't have bothered you."

"I wanted to come." Sheila's voice carries none of the sharp edges it once held. "I wanted to wish you well."

We sit in silence for a moment, watching pigeons peck at crumbs in the distant parking lot. The weight of everything that's happened between us hangs in the air, but it feels different now—less suffocating, more like a morning mist that will soon burn away.

"How's Willa?" Sheila asks.

I take a deep breath. "She's recovering. The doctors say the burns will heal, but the scars…" I pause, thinking of my sister's face, half-hidden by bandages. "The police aren't charging her for our parents' deaths. My dad's fall was just an accident, not her fault. But the DA is insisting on charging her for what happened this week. He's recommending time in a mental institution for starting the fire at our house and for…" The words are still hard for me to say. "For trying to kill me."

Sheila's hand moves slightly, as if she might reach for mine, then stops. "That must be hard for you."

"I hope it helps her," I say. "She needs to deal with her guilt and grief properly. She's been carrying it alone for so long, letting it poison her. Maybe now she can finally heal."

"Maybe." Sheila shrugs and I can tell she thinks Willa won't recover. But I can also tell she wishes her no ill will despite everything.

"I hear you've been helping with the investigation into Harold Morrison," Sheila says, changing the subject.

I nod. "The Albion authorities have everything they need. Your father's name will be cleared, Sheila. The records prove he was trying to expose my father's embezzlement. That Harold framed him for the arson."

Sheila's jaw tightens. "All these years. All these years without my dad. Feeling like his guilt was my load to bear."

My own guilt pushes on me like a weight. My family did this to her. I did this to her.

"Will you look for him now?" I ask.

She's quiet for a long time, her gaze fixed on the pigeons. "I don't know. It's hard, you know? I built my whole life around that hating him. Learning to let it go, learning to like him… it feels impossible."

"Sheila, I'm so sorry." The words tumble out, inadequate but necessary. "For my part in all of this. For what my family did to yours. Willa and I both agree—you should keep the money. All of it."

A small smile plays at the corner of her mouth. "Good, because I already spent it."

Despite everything, I laugh. It feels strange and wonderful, laughing with her. "On what?"

"Do you know the empty house on Riverside? The big Victorian with the wraparound porch?"

I picture it immediately—peeling paint, overgrown garden, but solid bones. It's right down the road. "The one near here?"

"I bought it."

"Good for you."

"And then I donated it to Rachel and Sister Mary Bernice."

How the entire world doesn't see the gift that is Sheila Ryan is a mystery to me.

"They're going to create a real safe house for the women

who need it. Not a creepy dungeon. And it's not going to be just a temporary shelter, but a place where they can heal and rebuild."

"Sheila, that's…"

"I'm calling it the Hope House after Sarah Hope." She turns to face me fully. "Nina, we've both suffered enough for our wrongs. None of what happened was intentional. Your parents made their choices. Willa made hers. We made ours. But I'm tired of carrying all this anger and pain. Of pretending that either of our current lives is terrible, because it isn't. I want to forgive you." She pauses, her eyes meeting mine. "Besides, I kind of like you."

I feel tears prick at my eyes. "I like you too."

She hugs me and then pinches my habit. "So you're really going through with it? The vows? You could go back to your old life, you know."

I shake my head and think of LA. Of who I was there. "I don't want it. This is who I am now. This is who I want to be."

"No regrets?"

I think about it, really think about it. About the luxury I'm leaving behind, the comfort, the ease. Then I think about the women in the shelter, about the peace I've found in prayer, about the purpose that fills my days now. "No regrets."

"What about you?" I ask. "What will you do now?"

Sheila stretches her legs out in front of her, leaning back on her hands. "I have an idea. A career move I've been thinking about. But I've also learned to love who I've become. I don't want to change who I am just because I can."

"Will you tell me what it is?"

"When I figure out all the details." She reaches into her jacket pocket and pulls out something that catches the light.

"I brought you something. To celebrate your final vows and… our time together in the convent."

She places a rosary in my hands. It's unlike any I've seen—the beads are bright turquoise and coral, interspersed with small silver charms. The crucifix is delicately worked silver, almost luminous in the fading light. But what is unique is that someone has bedazzled the entirety with tiny rhinestones. It's beautiful and bold and completely unexpected.

"Sheila, I can't—"

"Yes, you can. I bedazzled it myself. I know nuns usually have plain ones, but I figured for your personal prayers…" She shrugs. "A little color never hurt."

I close my fingers around the beads, feeling their smooth coolness. It is so Sheila. I realize how much I'm going to miss having her in the convent. "It's perfect. Thank you."

We stand together, brushing dust from our clothes. The bell in the tower rings, calling everyone to evening prayers.

"Will we stay friends?" I ask, not sure what answer I'm hoping for.

Sheila smiles, and it transforms her face. "I'd like that. It might be the strangest friendship in history, but I'd like that very much."

She pulls me into a quick, fierce hug. I breathe in her scent—confidence, a zest for life, and an expensive perfume that is uniquely hers. Then she steps back and heads down the steps. Masses were never really her thing.

"Sheila," I call after her.

She turns, eyebrows raised.

"Thank you. For everything."

"It was my pleasure," she says. "But Nina? When you take your vows, when you become a full sister … for heaven's sakes, pick a better name than Dymphna."

She walks away; her stride confident, her head high. Her heels still getting caught in the gravel. I watch until she disappears around the corner of the convent, then look down at the rosary in my hands. The colors seem to glow in the twilight—vibrant and alive and full of possibility.

The bell rings again, more insistent now. I slip the rosary into my pocket, feeling its weight against my hip, and turn toward the church doors. Tomorrow I'll take my vows, choosing poverty, chastity, and obedience. I'll receive my religious name and begin the next phase of my journey.

But tonight, I carry with me an unexpected gift—not just the rosary, but the knowledge that forgiveness is possible, that even the deepest wounds can heal, that sometimes the most unlikely people can become friends.

I push open the heavy doors and step into the church. The familiar scent of incense and candle wax envelops me. Other sisters are gathering for prayers. They are in town to celebrate my final vows tomorrow. Sister Mary Bernice catches my eye and tilts her head, a question in her expression.

"Everything's fine," I whisper as I pass her. "Better than fine."

I take my place in the pew, pulling out my plain wooden rosary for communal prayers. But I can feel Sheila's gift in my pocket, a bright secret, a reminder that beauty and friendship can bloom in the most unexpected places.

As we begin the opening prayers, I think about transformation. About how the worst moments of our lives can sometimes lead us to exactly where we need to be. Willa is finally getting help. Sheila is free from the burden of hatred. The women in the shelter will have a real home. And I've found my calling.

The familiar rhythm of the prayers washes over me. Tomorrow, everything changes. Tomorrow, I leave Nina behind… and yes, Dymphna too. I become someone new. But I won't forget who I was or what brought me here. The rosary in my pocket won't let me.

When we reach the prayers of petition, I add my own silent ones. For Willa's healing. For Sheila's journey to find her father. For the strength to live up to the vows I'm about to take. For the grace to continue becoming the person I'm meant to be.

The candles flicker in their sconces, casting dancing shadows on the walls. Through the stained glass windows, the last rays of sunlight paint colored patterns on the floor. I'm surrounded by beauty and peace and purpose.

Sister Mary Bernice's voice rises in the final hymn. It's off key, but we respond in unison, our voices blending into one. As the prayer ends, we file out. I walk down the steps where Sheila and I sat and pause for a moment. They are empty now, but I can still feel the echo of our conversation, the weight of forgiveness given and received.

"Thank you," I whisper to the evening air, to God, to the strange twists of fate that brought us all to this moment.

Then I hurry towards the convent, ready to embrace whatever comes next, Sheila's rosary a bright promise in my pocket, a reminder that even the most broken things can be made beautiful again.

36

Biddy

Biddy adjusts the bright blue leather leash in her hand, watching Charles the goat trot ahead with an admirable enthusiasm. The late October sun warms her back as she and Ruby make their way down the dirt path that winds past the Doyle farm.

"I didn't know goats walked on leashes," Ruby observes, her walking stick tapping a steady rhythm against the packed earth. She bruised her hip from the escapades at the McKellan house, but she will be just fine.

"Charles isn't just any goat," Biddy replies, shocked that her friend can't see this. "I'm actually feeling bad about naming him after my louse of a husband. He's infinitely more faithful. Yesterday, Abigail Larter tried to pet him and he screamed like she was trying to murder him and then peed on her foot. New shoes, too."

Biddy can't help but smile at the memory. Now, there is an appropriate response to another woman trying to touch you.

"How nice that you've bonded," Ruby says. "Has Megan learned to love him yet?"

The mention of her daughter brings Biddy back to their difficult conversation after the fire. She can still see Megan's tear-stained face. Her want for everyone to forgive each other and go back to the way things were. But that's not how forgiveness works.

"I explained to her it's important to search your heart for forgiveness," Biddy says, watching Charles investigate a particularly interesting tuft of grass. She wills him to eat it like a normal goat. Anything but her roses. It doesn't happen. "But you also have to love yourself enough to set healthy boundaries."

"And?"

"I forgive my husband. I do. I wish his memory no harm. But I can't play the doting wife and widow when our marriage wasn't real. I won't do that disservice to the institution or to myself." Biddy pauses, remembering Megan's shocked expression. "I told her I'd give her the money for the memorial for her father. I sincerely hope she has one if it brings her peace. But I won't attend. I owe it to myself to be able walk away."

Ruby nods slowly. "That's fair."

"I might be convinced to send flowers," Biddy adds, then looks at Charles, who's now eyeing a patch of wildflowers with intent. "If this Charles doesn't eat them first."

"Maybe your husband Charles would be honored that you named a goat after him."

Biddy smiles. "He'd hate it."

They continue walking, passing the old McKenna farm with its foreclosure sign hanging crooked on the gate. The fields that once grew potatoes and barley lie fallow, weeds taking over where crops once thrived.

"At least the town seems to have moved on from blaming the women's club for its economic downfall," Ruby comments, gesturing toward the abandoned property. "They finally forced Mayor Dillon to resign."

Biddy shakes her head. "While I have no love lost for Arthur Dillon, the town needs to accept responsibility for its own part in this mess instead of always blaming others. First it was the women's club, then the mayor. When will they look in the mirror?"

"I don't think fixing their hair is going to solve their problems, Biddy."

Biddy smiles and doesn't explain to her friend what looking in the mirror actually implies. They walk in companionable silence until they reach the field's edge, where the Pooka rocks rise from the grass like ancient sentinels. The massive boulders, with their yellow eye-like slashes, seem to watch their approach.

Charles trots over to investigate, his little hooves clicking against the smaller stones scattered at the base. Ruby peers at the largest rock, tilting her head this way and that.

"I see a bunny today," she announces. "Look, there are the ears, and that shadow makes the nose."

Biddy watches Charles stretch up to lick the rock's surface, his pink tongue leaving wet streaks on the gray stone. "Charles must see a giant rose bush. Those are his favorite."

"A rose bush?" Ruby squints harder. "I don't see it."

Then Ruby turns to study Biddy with those sharp eyes that miss everything, but a heart that misses nothing. "So what are you going to do now that you've solved the mystery of Sheila?"

Isn't that the question? Biddy fidgets with the leash. "I don't know. Maybe I'll take that butter churning job at Maude's farm."

"Butter churning?" Ruby laughs as if the notion is somehow hysterical. "You? Biddy Bramley? I'm impressed you even know that butter doesn't automatically come out of cows in the shape of swans."

"But wouldn't it be nice if it did?"

Ruby looks at the rock and then at Biddy. "You know, I don't think I see a bunny after all. I think I see a mayor."

Biddy laughs, the sound carrying across the empty field. "Your not looking at the Pooka."

"No." Her curls shake wildly from side to side. "I'm looking at you."

"You want me to run for mayor? No one wants to hear what I have to say."

"That doesn't mean it shouldn't be said. You have a distinct gift for delivering hard truths."

"Ruby, I'm a widow who won't mourn her husband publicly. Instead, I named a goat after him. I got my brother arrested, and I shut down the town's main source of income. I'm pretty sure people have to like you to elect you. I'm not likable."

"Nonsense. The town needs someone who actually understands economics and is practical." Ruby taps her walking stick against Biddy's stomach. "That's you. You say what you think, no matter who you hurt in the process."

Biddy isn't sure that came out as the compliment Ruby intended. "Stop being ridiculous."

"Just think about it."

They stand there a while longer, watching Charles attempt to eat the lichen off the rocks. Biddy is pretty confident that he'll try to eat anything except for grass. Then they head for home. Ruby leaves her at the corner of Main Street, directly across the street from the town hall, with a significant look and a pat on the arm. Ruby has never been subtle.

Alone now except for Charles, Biddy finds her feet carrying her towards it.

"Let's just go see who's added their name to the ballot," she tells Charles, who's more interested in the flower beds surrounding the little potted trees. "I'm not applying. I'm just curious."

She pauses in front of the town hall, where a big sign announces that all who want to register for mayoral candidacy are welcome. She looks at the vacant buildings surrounding her, the paint peeling and the brick crumbling. She could fix this. As she stands there, she can see it all so clearly. The town hall with fresh paint and clean windows. Council meetings where real issues get discussed instead of finger-pointing. A budget that makes sense. Programs to help the displaced workers. Initiatives to attract new business that don't rely on wishful thinking. And maybe a few more beautification projects.

"Mayor Biddy Bramley," she says aloud, testing the words. "It does have a nice ring to it."

Charles chooses this moment to stretch up and delicately pluck a rose from the library garden. He turns and presents it to her with a soft bleat, the red flower dangling from his mouth.

Biddy takes the rose, touched despite herself. "With your blessing, then?"

Charles bleats again and bumps his head against her hip.

"All right then. Let's do this." She squares her shoulders and starts toward the town hall entrance. The registration forms will be inside, probably covered in dust like everything else Dillon neglected. She can fill them out, file her candidacy, start making lists of what needs to be done.

But just as she's about to pull Charles out from the shadow of a nearby tree, the door to the town hall swings open. Sheila steps out, looking determined and slightly flustered, clutching a folder of papers. Biddy steps back into the shadows.

Biddy can see the forms in Sheila's hands. It's the candidacy registration. She thinks of everything Sheila's been through—the loss of her mother, the revelation about her father, the fire. The girl needs to find a new path, something to anchor her. She'd make a great mayor.

"Never mind," she says to Charles. She tugs on his leash. "Come on, you. Let's go home."

She walks away before Sheila can see her, Charles trotting beside her. The disappointment sits heavily in her chest, but she pushes it down. It's not her time.

"Butter churning it is," she tells Charles as they make their way home. "Maude will be pleased."

The goat bleats and tries to eat another rose from Mrs. Murphy's garden. Biddy pulls him away, thinking about paths not taken and opportunities missed. But as they round the corner toward home, she straightens her spine. She's Biddy Bramley. She's survived a faithless husband, raised a daughter, and founded the Pooka Women's Club. She'll survive a little boredom.

Still, as she opens her front gate and watches Charles make a beeline for her own rose bushes, she can't help but wonder what might have been. Mayor Biddy Bramley. It really did have a nice ring to it.

37

Megan

Megan settles into the folding chair in the front row of Pooka's town hall. She's already missing this place, even though she doesn't leave until tomorrow. The space has been transformed for tonight's special town hall. What's usually a utilitarian boxy room now glows with warmth. String lights drape from the rafters, casting everything in a soft golden light, and the folding tables along the walls groan under the weight of the town's potluck offerings. The smell is truly terrible: that of Mrs. Chen's famous dumplings mingling with Mr. Rosati's spinach lasagna and Mrs. Pearl's apple pies. But yet it is on its way to be her favorite scent.

She can't believe she ever considered this place beneath her. Looking around at the familiar faces—Mr. Henderson adjusting his hearing aid, the teenage Murphy twins sneaking cookies before dinner, Mrs. Petrov knitting while she waits for the meeting to start—Megan feels a wave of affection so strong it surprises her. She's so glad that her mother gets to call this quirky town her home. And she dreads she has to return to Boston. She pictures her tiny office at the community college. It's a beige, fluorescent-lit box where she's slowly withering. She's not just troubled by trying to make ends meet, she simply doesn't enjoy her life there. Here, though. Here she feels alive.

"Megan!" A delighted shriek pierces the comfortable chatter.

She turns just in time to see Birdie racing down the center aisle, her pink trench coat billowing behind her like a cape. The little girl launches herself with absolute confidence that Megan will catch her. She does and Birdie lands in Megan's lap with a giggle that's pure joy.

"I brought you something special!" Birdie announces, proudly presenting two fists. What emerges from her grip might have started life as cupcakes. Purple frosting oozes between her fingers, and sprinkles cascade onto Megan's jeans like edible confetti. "This one's just for you because it has a cherry and this one's for me."

Megan accepts the demolished pastry with all the ceremony it deserves. It might just be the best gift she's ever been given.

"This is perfect. Absolutely perfect."

Birdie beams, adjusting her pipe cleaner tiara as she makes herself comfortable. Her outfit today is spectacular—the hot pink trench coat over what appears to be a tutu, paired with shiny black patent leather Mary Janes that kick happily against Megan's shins.

"Guess what?" Birdie says, taking an enormous bite of her own cupcake and getting frosting on both cheeks. "When I grow up, I'm going to join the Pooka Women's Club just like you and Mommy and solve all the mysteries!"

"Oh really?"

"Well," Birdie says seriously, "Mommy says I can't do

murders until I'm twelve, but I think ten is probably old enough. There'll still be murders then, don't you think?"

"Yes," Megan says, squeezing her hard. "I'm sure there will be."

The chair beside them creaks cheerfully as Amelia sits down with the rest of the kids, bringing with her a cloud of mashed sweet potato perfume and warmth.

She reaches over and squeezes Megan's leg affectionately. "When are you heading back to Boston?"

The question that's been dancing around Megan's mind suddenly has a clear, simple answer. It bubbles up from somewhere deep inside, surprising her with its certainty.

"I'm not."

The words feel like setting down a heavy suitcase she didn't realize she'd been carrying. "I'm staying right here."

Amelia's face breaks into a delighted grin, but before she can respond, Arthur Dillon approaches the podium at the front of the room. He taps the microphone with all the confidence of someone who's finally figured out how it works, producing only a minor squeal this time.

"Character development," someone calls out, and the room ripples with good-natured laughter.

There's a commotion at the end of their row as Ruby and Biddy shuffle sideways into it, apologizing cheerfully to everyone they bump into. Between them, is Charles the goat, munching on something that looks like the floral centerpiece from the buffet table.

"Scoot over, dear!" Ruby says, her eyes sparkling with mischief as they squeeze into the remaining seats.

Birdie abandons her cupcake to throw her arms around the goat's neck. "Charles! You're the very best. I love you so much!"

"That's sweet of you to say," Megan says.

Biddy leans over. "You know she means the goat, not your father?"

"I do," Megan smiles. "But it's close enough."

Megan heard her mother last night and accepts that Biddy has moved on from her marriage. But she also knows something her mother has yet to realize. Her mother can say what she wants, but Biddy loved her father. After all, who names a goat after her husband if she doesn't miss him a little bit?

Arthur clears his throat into the microphone, beaming at the assembled crowd. Ruby nudges Megan with her elbow.

"I think he's starting." She passes Megan some popcorn to go with her cupcake mash.

"Friends, neighbors," Arthur begins, his voice carrying surprising warmth for a man who's just been fired, "thank you all for coming tonight. As you know, it's been quite a journey these past few months. But despite the absolutely overwhelming"—he pauses for effect—"avalanche of love and support you've all shown me, I've decided it is time to pass the torch."

The cheer that goes up is enthusiastic but affectionate. Someone yells, "We love you, Arthur!" and he actually tears up a little.

Megan is grateful that this was handled in a way that left him his dignity.

"Yes, well. Try not to celebrate too hard," he says, dabbing at his eyes. "I'm delighted to announce the candidates for our next mayoral election. Up first, we have a...unique candidate to present for your consideration. In fact, she is our only female candidate. On behalf of the Pooka Women's Club, please welcome Sheila Ryan!"

Megan is proud to watch her mother cheering loudly for their friend.

Sheila glides to the podium with the confidence of someone who knows exactly what she's doing. She's wearing a pantsuit that somehow is both mayoral and alluring—a skill that defies physics. Several men in the audience sit up straighter, and Megan catches a few dreamy sighs.

"Why is Mr. Baker making that face?" Birdie asks in what she clearly thinks is a whisper but which could be heard in the next county.

"Questions for when you're older," Amelia says quickly.

"Good evening, everyone! I'm Sheila Ryan," Sheila begins, her smile radiant. "Though I think most of you know me here. Perhaps some, better than others."

The blushes that bloom across several faces are spectacular. God, Megan loves town halls.

"The reason that I stand her this evening is that I love Pooka," Sheila continues, her voice ringing with sincerity. "This is the place that welcomed me when I needed a fresh start. The place that believed in me and my business. The place that opened its arms and hearts. This town taught me what community really means. It is why I decided to be president of the Pooka Women's Club—to give back to the place that gave me everything."

Megan glances at her mother and sees pride shining in Biddy's eyes. There's something else there too—a grace in watching someone else succeed in a role she might have wanted. But Biddy's smile is genuine, full of real happiness for her friend.

"This town has had some challenges lately," Sheila continues, "and I think we need to acknowledge that this has not brought out the best in us. We've turned to blame, finger-pointing, hopelessness. That's not who we are. We're the town that rallies around each other. We're the place where success grows from community. I'm proof of that. Maude and her farm are proof of that. And I know we can build even more success together."

She pauses, letting her words sink in. "That's why I'm campaigning for a change. This town needs leadership that reminds us daily of who we are and what we're capable of. Someone who won't let us settle for less than our best."

The room leans forward collectively.

"And I know exactly the right person to do this. I'm pleased to announce that I'm retiring from my business to take on a new role."

Megan looks over and sees a smile fixed on her mother's face, her eyes a little watery above it. She reaches across Ruby to squeeze her mother's leg. What a gift to be selfless to someone who needs and deserves it.

Sheila clears her throat. "And that is the role of campaign manager. I am absolutely thrilled to nominate Biddy Bramley as our next mayor. You could not ask for a better leader."

There is silence and then every male in the room explodes with joy. It takes a few seconds to register, but then Biddy's face lights up like Christmas morning, her mouth forming a perfect 'O' of surprise. Charles, sensing the excitement, shrieks.

"Biddy loves this town with every fiber of her being," Sheila continues, raising her voice over the celebration. "She's a natural leader, and I can tell you from personal experience—

there's no better guide for Pooka's future. Plus," she adds with a wink, "on her brilliant advice, I'm opening a marketing company. Already landed my first client—someone from LA who could really use my help with a promising tech startup! Anyway, come on up, Biddy!"

Biddy finally unfreezes. She shoves Charles's leash into Megan's hands with surprising strength. "Hold this, dear. History is calling!"

She practically floats to the stage, her face glowing with joy. Sheila meets her with a stack of papers.

"You'll need to fill these out," she whispers while standing too close to the microphone. "I had to guess your birthdate—1912 is pretty close, right?"

Even this doesn't dim Biddy's happiness. Nor does she seem to mind that Sheila is wearing an identical pantsuit, just cut rather differently.

"So," Sheila announces with a flourish, "as campaign manager and CEO of Sheila Ryan Marketing Services, I present your next mayor—because she will win—Biddy Bramley!"

The applause is deafening. Men stamp their feet, whistle, and Arthur Dillon starts a chant of "BID-DY! BID-DY!" that catches on immediately.

"How are this many people thrilled?" Megan asks Amelia. "I thought they all hated her."

The baby Amelia is holding burps goo all over Amelia's sweater and she mindlessly shifts him to her clean shoulder. "I heard Shelia ran a going out of business sale and demanded their support to get her special rate."

Megan laughs with pure delight as Charles tries to eat her bracelet. Birdie snuggles against her stomach, getting frosting everywhere.

"Isn't this just the best?" Birdie says.

Megan looks around the room—at Ruby clapping with tears of joy in her eyes, at Amelia whistling with two fingers in her mouth, at Biddy approaching the microphone with the energy of someone a fraction of her age, at Sheila organizing papers with entrepreneurial glee, at their neighbors and friends celebrating together. She's sure her mom will have some stiff competition winning the campaign, but that's a problem for another day.

"It is," Megan says, squeezing the little girl tight. "Today is the best."

"You know what?" Birdie says. "If you want, you can live in our basement."

Well, hopefully it won't come to that, Megan thinks. But whatever comes next, Megan knows it will be better than Boston. Possibly even amazing. In Pooka, with these people, how could it be anything else?

The End.

THE STORY CONTINUES: A wine heist. A missing diamond. A dead vineyard owner. And a husband who may be too guilty to save.

Don't miss Book 3: The Thief of Traminette. Turn the page to read the sample chapter and make your purchase here.

https://www.amazon.com/dp/B0H63TWC7D

BONUS MATERIAL: Want to read about Sheila's reunion with her father? Get the exclusive short story for free here. This is my way to thank you for being a loyal reader.

https://dl.bookfunnel.com/etu335k11p

38

Preview of Book 3: THE THIEF OF TRAMINETTE

Only five minutes in, and I already know this is the worst heist in the history of mankind. To start, let's look at what we're stealing. Is it priceless works of art created by some French and Italian people with unpronounceable names? Nope. Jewels so rare and gigantic that they make movies about their provenance? Also no. Exotic cars in striking colors that zing down roads at a speed capable of making a buzzing noise like an insect? Not us. We didn't go after any of that. We decided to steal wine. I don't even drink wine.

Then there's the forgery aspect. Danny, Pete, and I watched every single episode of *White Collar* to prepare for this day. The one thing that is abundantly clear on that show is that a strong forgery is a must. It makes it nearly impossible for the police to determine when the item was stolen, which in turn makes it equally impossible to identify suspects who were in the vicinity at the time of the crime. So, not being completely stupid, we tried to hire a forger to recreate the labels on the wine we are stealing. He wanted $2,500 to do the work. Can you imagine? If we had $2,500, we wouldn't need to steal the wine.

Instead, Pete's eleven-year-old daughter, Jenny, who is rather artistic, taught him how to use a program called Canva, and we printed his creations on blank name tags from Best Buy. They aren't half bad, and Pete is very proud of them. That said, I'm pretty sure they are not at all identical to the real things.

Next is the equipment needed to tunnel our way under the stone wall surrounding the property and through the limestone foundation of the estate's wine cellar. We rented ours from Home Depot. We cannot figure out how to operate it.

I squint through the darkness at Chateau Belle Foret, the massive Indiana limestone estate on the other side of the stone wall. The night is moonless and absolutely frigid. I can see my breath. I can also see Pete's breath, and Danny's breath, and the clouds of breath are the only things moving towards the estate on this stretch of road at eleven at night in February. That includes our boring machine.

"The directions say to turn the head clockwise to increase the diameter and counter-clockwise to decrease the diameter, and this will eliminate backlash," Pete reads off his phone.

Danny looks up from the boring machine. "What's backlash? That doesn't sound good."

Pete shrugs. "Let's just twist the head so we don't have to find out."

"But which way? Clockwise or counter-clockwise?"

Pete looks back at his phone to decipher the answer.

"You know," I say, "maybe this isn't such a good idea."

Danny frowns. "Seriously? Now you get cold feet? Look,

this plan is absolutely foolproof. The estate is vacant until the summer and has so much land that you can't see the neighbors. And we're stealing bottles of wine people haven't bothered to drink for the last forty years. They might not even notice it's gone for another forty years when they get around to opening it. They might never know. No harm, no foul."

Pete glances up from his phone. Like me, Pete isn't fully convinced by the argument. He was never the brightest at school and has often learned the hard way that no plan is foolproof. However, when his eyes find mine in the dark, they are pleading.

"I need the money to save my farm, John. I've got to try."

His words are visible in puffs of condensation that hang in the cold air after he has uttered them like an exclamation point. I hesitate. Then I nod. The truth is, I need the money to save my farm too, and not just from the bank. I owe $42,000 to a man named Dino "the Shark" Ferretti. His name alone pretty much says everything you need to know about his family business.

Pete, Danny, and I have been friends since the fourth grade at Sacred Heart of the Woods. We have been through a lot together, including weddings, work, and kids. That said, I don't think any of us saw a moment like this coming. Sure, we knew there'd be tough times when crops were weak or the weather was destructive. But skyrocketing production costs and low margins due to wars and trade agreements with places we can't pronounce? This is out of our league. It is also out of our control.

I take a deep breath and think of my farm. Of my wife and kids who call it home. I pull out my phone and stare at the picture on the lock screen, the one taken at the Pooka

Founders Day picnic last summer, where the five of them are arranged on a blanket like a stair-step of escalating chaos. I owe them this. I need to try. Then I type a search into YouTube and hold the phone out to the others.

"This video on how to operate a boring machine should be easier to follow than the directions."

We have to watch it three times, but we finally get the hang of it. I step back as Danny maneuvers the head to a spot in the ground, and Pete starts the machine. It's a good thing there are no neighbors nearby, because it is loud. It rumbles the ground like an earthquake.

Pete and Danny get to work, and I look back at the estate. Most people think of Indiana as nothing but farms. However, a little-known fact is that it has a region famous for a specific white grape called the Traminette. This area is called the Indiana Uplands, or more commonly, the wine trail. The wine, I'm told, is decent. I'm more of a Miller Light kinda guy, so I wouldn't know.

That said, even we proud Hoosiers know our wine isn't worth hundreds of thousands of dollars. So why are we robbing this particular estate? Because the Uplands itself is pretty enough, convenient enough, and bucolic enough that it attracted a rich guy from Chicago named Elliott Faber, looking to buy a vacation house on a winery, given his passion for wine. And Elliott has a wine collection from Italy and France that IS worth hundreds of thousands of dollars. We know this complements of the Indiana Wine Enthusiast, which featured Chateau Belle Foret on the cover, along with a thorough description of the collection, including the value of each bottle, and multiple full-color photos of the cellar. This is the wine we are stealing. According to the article, the wine is already over forty years old, and no one has drunk it. Our theory is that we may be dead before they realize it is missing.

I look back at the machine and see that progress has been made. The head is now fully buried in the ground. Danny angles it to do the horizontal stretch under the wall and toward the house. The hole is narrow, but if we lie on our stomachs and use our arms as levers, we should be able to get through.

I look back at the chateau and wish it were closer to the road. Who needs a driveway that long? Somebody who isn't here in the winter to plow it all, I realize. Anyway, I estimate it will take about four hours to reach the estate. Four hours spent standing on a road with our pickup trucks parked beside us, clearly doing something we are not supposed to do. We are going to be arrested.

The house is still. It and its grounds are so large and ornate that they resemble one of those impressive stone college buildings on the cover of a recruiting pamphlet more than a house. Albeit a cold, vacant one, with its dark windows and its frost-covered panes. Then I see a flash of light through one of the second-floor windows. I blink. It's gone.

"Guys," I shout over the noise of the machine while still staring at the window, "are we sure the house is empty?"

"Why?" Pete snaps off the machine and stares at me.

Danny, his patience clearly wearing thin, slams his hand against the now quiet drilling mechanism. "I am positive it is vacant. It is ten degrees on a February weeknight. If you owned this house in Indiana, a house in Palm Beach, and a penthouse condo in Chicago, which would be your last choice to spend the night?"

Pete ignores him. "Did you see something?"

"I thought I saw a flash of light." I'm still staring at the window, but I haven't seen anything since.

"You thought you saw a flash of light," Danny mimics my voice, rather unkindly, I must say. "As in past tense. Have you seen it since?"

I hesitate and then shake my head.

"Then it was most likely the moon peeking out from all the clouds for a second and reflecting on a pane. I'm getting sick of this. Are you in or are you out? I'm not stopping what we're doing every five minutes to give you a hug and tell you everything is going to be okay."

I look at the estate. The wind blows. A stick from a nearby tree scrapes against a window. Other than that, there is nothing.

Danny is right. It was probably just a shadow created by changing light. I think of my wife.

"I'm in."

We take turns operating the machine over the next four hours. I keep my eyes on the estate, and I never see light again. This should reassure me, but I still have a knot in my stomach the size of a softball. By the time the machine reaches the limestone foundation of the wine cellar, yowling a screech of metal against stone, I just want to move fast and get this over. We are in too far to back out now.

Danny pulls the machine out and puts it back on the trailer bed attached to his pickup truck. The three of us look down at the narrow hole, which a rabbit could have burrowed better. Even Danny looks a little unsure of its structural stability. But I realized this was a bad idea four hours ago. I'm past that now.

"Let's go," I say.

I pick up a crate of counterfeit wine bottles filled with water and food coloring. I drop the crate in the hole, jump down after it, and begin pushing it forward as I crawl after it. It is not long before I hear the thuds of the other two and their counterfeit cargo falling in behind me.

Thankfully, we make progress through the tunnel an awful lot faster than the boring machine did. The mud is damp, smells of rotten organic matter, and presses in on me on all sides. One cave-in and I will be buried alive. I crawl faster. The others must have the same thoughts, because they do the same. By the time we reach the far end of the tunnel and see the exposed limestone foundation and the cellar beyond, I am ready to recommend this experience to nobody.

I am so grateful to breathe fresh air and escape the claustrophobia of the narrow tunnel that I throw myself through the opening. Danny and Pete land beside me, clutching their wine crates.

"We did it," Pete says. His voice is filled with awe.

He's right. We did. Somehow, most likely through sheer luck, we managed to hit the intended wall of the wine cellar.

"Of course we did," Danny says. "I told you. This plan is foolproof."

His words are confident, but I can tell he is equally surprised by our success.

"Now, let's find the expensive stuff."

Thanks to the *Indiana Wine Enthusiast* article, we know roughly where to look for the expensive bottles. We point our flashlights in the right direction and start reading the labels. It is not long before Pete announces he has found one.

"Alright," Danny says. "Here's what we're going to do. John, you take all the counterfeits out of the crates and pass them one by one to Pete when he calls the name he needs. That way, we make sure they all go into the right slots. I'll take the real thing from Pete and repackage it in the crates to take with us."

Pete points his flashlight at the label of the wine in his hands.

"Hey, our counterfeits aren't half bad. Should we take a picture side-by-side?"

"And what? Post it on Instagram?" Danny swats Pete's phone down.

"No." Pete sounds wounded. "I was going to show it to Jenny. She helped make the labels after all."

"Jesus," Danny rubs his head. "We just take the wine, sell it to the distributor we found, and then never think or speak of this again. And we do not turn our children into crooks."

Oh god. I love my friends. They are like brothers. But can I trust Pete to keep his mouth shut about this? Can I trust that this moment will just stay safely in the past for the rest of my life?

Pete nods and does as he is told. This does nothing to alleviate my fears. I uncrate the counterfeit wine and pass the correct bottle to Pete when he asks for it. Danny takes the real ones and carefully sets them in the now-empty crates. I am starting to believe Danny is somehow right. This just might work.

That is when I see the light again.

It is at the top of the spiral cellar stairs, faint and yellowish, the kind of light a phone screen makes when somebody is holding the phone cupped in their hand to keep the glow from spilling out. It's moving, but not on the staircase. It is crossing the hallway above us. I watch it pass the top of the stairs, and I watch it continue along the hall, and I watch it disappear.

"Guys," I whisper.

But Pete is reading off another label, and Danny is fitting another bottle into another crate, and neither of them looks up.

"Guys."

"What?" Danny snaps.

"I just saw the light again. Upstairs. Somebody is in this house with us."

Danny goes very still. Pete goes very still. The three of us listen to the silence of the Faber estate as if it might suddenly start telling us things.

"You're sure?" Danny asks.

"I'm sure."

"Hand to God, sure?"

"Hand to God."

Pete looks at the spiral staircase that winds up out of the cellar. Then he looks at the hole we drilled in the wall. Then he looks at the half-empty crate on the floor between us.

"We can't leave the counterfeits half-stocked," he says. "If we leave the counterfeits half-stocked, they'll see the difference between the labels and know somebody was here. They're going to figure out which bottles we took, and then we can't sell them."

"Pete," Danny hisses, "if there is a person upstairs, the bottles don't matter."

"But we won't have enough money to cover our foreclosures. All this would be for nothing."

I don't know which of us is right. I do not, in this moment, trust any of us to know what the smart choice is. All I know is that there is somebody in this house with us. If they find us, we're done.

"We take what we've got," I say. "You two start packing up. I'm going to go look."

"Are you out of your mind?" Danny asks.

"Two minutes," I say. "I'll be quiet. If somebody is here, we need to know if they've called the cops. If they have, we don't have time for the tunnel. We run up the stairs and use the front gate. If they haven't, we go out through the tunnel."

"This is a terrible idea," Danny says.

I do not disagree with him, but I think it's the best option we have right now. I start up the spiral stairs.

The kitchen at the top of the stairs is dim but not dark. There is a light on over the sink. This seems odd for a house that is supposed to be vacant until June. I move down the long hallway toward the front of the house. The marble floor is colder through the soles of my work boots than I would have guessed marble could be, and the air has a smell to it that I cannot at first place, something metallic, something warm.

To my left is a dining room with a table long enough to seat sixteen people and a wall of windows looking out onto a backyard that, if I had to guess, cost more to landscape than my entire farm. To my right, three doors farther on, is a room with the door open the smallest amount.

I push the door open with the tip of my finger.

Elliott Faber is in the leather chair behind his desk. I have never met the man in person, but I have seen him in the *Pooka Gazette*, shaking the mayor's hand at the ribbon-cutting for the new clinic, and on the cover of the *Indiana Wine Enthusiast*, holding a glass of Bordeaux. He is clearly the man in front of me. Actually, I should say was. Because he is dead.

His head is at an angle a head should not be at. There is blood on the desk, on the carpet under the desk, and on the front of his sweater. Still, I touch a finger to his carotid artery to make sure there is nothing I can do to save him. I feel no pulse. He is well and truly dead.

I look at the stains around me and notice that the blood has not gone brown yet. I have killed enough chickens in my time to know this means that whatever happened in this room happened recently, within the last hour, possibly within the last twenty minutes. The small light I saw at the top of the stairs, the one I watched move past in the hallway, was likely the person who did it making their getaway.

I take a step backward, away from the body. I trip and fall. I look to see what tripped me. It is a heavy piece of metal, the base of one of those small bronze horse statues that Faber has on every shelf in the room. I close my fingers around the metal. The metal is wet on the heavy end. I drop it. I think it's the murder weapon.

The clatter of the bronze hitting the hardwood floor is loud, snapping me out of my shock. I realize that I am now in Elliott Faber's study with his wet blood on the palm of my hand, the cuff of my sleeve, and on the fibers of his thousand-dollar carpet under the tread of my left work boot.

That is when I hear the sirens.

They are not far away and are coming from the direction of town. I pull myself off the floor and run.

I run back through the long hallway and down the spiral stairs into the cellar. Pete and Danny are both staring at me with white faces.

"Cops," I gasp. "There's a body, and the cops are coming. Get in the tunnel now."

I dive headfirst into the burrow, hear Danny dive in behind me, and Pete dive in behind Danny. I crawl faster than I have ever crawled in my life. The mud and stink press in, but this time I barely notice.

We are halfway through the tunnel when I hear the front door of the house slam open behind us, the heavy thud of footsteps, and the muffled shouting of police officers.

"How are they here already?" Pete pants behind Danny. "How is this possible?"

I don't know how to answer him. Did the same person who killed Elliott Faber walk out the side door and call the police on their way to wherever they were going? It seems unlikely. But that thought is going to have to wait until I am no longer crawling for my life through the cold mud of southern Indiana in the dark.

I burst out of the tunnel onto the gravel of the access road and gulp the cold night air. Then I see a second set of headlights.

Danny erupts out of the tunnel behind me, and Pete behind him. The three of us look at the headlights coming at us from both directions. My heart sinks. There is nowhere to go.

"Freeze!" The voice comes through an open window of the unmarked SUV that has just skidded to a stop ten feet from us. "Police! Get down and put your hands on your head!"

I do as I'm told. The officer lifts me to my feet by the back of my jacket. The sky above Chateau Belle Foret is the color of old pewter, just starting to go pink at the eastern edge. It is nearly morning. Which means that across town, in a small farmhouse with a leaking gutter on the south side that I have been meaning to fix since last April, my wife is asleep in our bed with her hand under her pillow the way she has slept every night since I married her. Her phone is on the nightstand, on silent, because the kids are asleep and she doesn't want any of them woken up before six. It also means she won't be able to hear the call that will tell her that her husband has been arrested.

Chief Halloran will probably be the one to knock on our door to wake her. Halloran has known us since high school. He will be gentle. He will tell her there is something she needs to come down to the station for, and he will not tell her what it is in front of the children. And then her life will be ruined.

The officer shoves me into the back of a police car and I close my eyes, resting my head against the cold of the passenger side window. I think only of her. Amelia Reagan. My Amelia. My wife.

PURCHASE THE THIEF OF TRAMINETTE (Book 3)
here on Amazon
https://www.amazon.com/dp/B0H63TWC7D

About the Author

Virginia Ann is an IPPY Gold Medal-winning author of cozy mysteries including The Pooka Women's Club Mystery series set in a small town in the Midwest. She is a former consumer industry analyst whose decade of experience following financial mysteries now fuels her passion for crafting intricate whodunits. Her insights have been featured in *The Wall Street Journal, Forbes,* and *Reuters*, and she has appeared on CNBC's Squawk Box, BNN, and Bloomberg. A lifelong fan of small-town mysteries, she blends intrigue, humor, and strong female friendships in her writing. She lives in Wisconsin with her cocker spaniel, Millie.

Also by Virginia Ann

The Pooka Women's Club Mysteries

The Potter's Final Piece (Book 1)
Biddy Bramley never expected to return to Pooka. But after her husband's death, she's back in her hometown—grieving, restless, and drawn into a decades-old mystery involving her estranged sister and claims to a stolen pottery fortune. Buy on Amazon.

A Cryptic Death (Book 2)
For a year, Dymphna has tried to remember who she was before she arrived at the convent of Sacred Heart of the Woods: a woman with an unexplained fortune in her pockets, no memory of her past, and not one answer the doctors could give her. She's finally made peace with her unknown past. She's ready to take her vows and become a nun. But someone won't let her. Buy on Amazon.

The Thief of Traminette (Book 3)
Amelia Reagan has spent years holding her family together through hard times. But when her husband is arrested for murdering a wealthy vineyard owner, her world shatters overnight. Buy on Amazon.